DUSK WALKER

DUSK WALKER

AN ORIGINAL NOVEL FROM THE BLACK BALLAD

CRYSTAL WOOD

Storytellers Forge, LLC.
5001 Prospect Ave, Unit 1B
Downers Grove IL 60515
https://www.storytellersforge.com/
info@storytellersforge.com

4 Horsemen
Publications, Inc.

4 Horsemen Publications, Inc.
1497 Main St. Suite 169
Dunedin, FL 34698
4horsemenpublications.com
info@4horsemenpublications.com

Cover & typesetting by Niki Tantillo
Edited by Laura Mita

Library of Congress Control Number: 2023948418

Paperback ISBN-13: 979-8-8232-0375-3
Hardcover ISBN-13: 979-8-8232-0376-0
Ebook ISBN-13: 979-8-8232-0377-7
Audiobook ISBN-13: 979-8-8232-0374-6

DEDICATION

To my husband, Chris, for seeing my dark
side and continuing to love me when I didn't
know how to love myself.

TABLE OF CONTENTS

PROLOGUE

In the grand halls of the Onyx Requiem, where power and secrecy intertwined, Professor Surrak Dradon, a diligent servant of the Godless Monarchy, immersed himself in arcane research, surrounded by a dedicated team of assistants. Together, they delved into the classified knowledge, uncovering ancient secrets that lay veiled to the world.

Driven by a singular purpose, Dradon toiled relentlessly, his sights set on ascending the ranks. He dreamt of the day when the monarchy would grant him the ultimate boon—an opportunity for resurrection. It was whispered among the corridors that such a privilege was bestowed only upon those who had dedicated their lives in unwavering service.

As the years passed, Dradon's pursuit of knowledge and power grew more fervent. His research reached new depths as he pushed the boundaries of forbidden magic, eager to prove his worthiness to the Godless Monarchy and secure his coveted resurrection.

Yet, just as Dradon stood on the precipice of achieving his long-awaited goal, tragedy struck. Within the confines of his labyrinthine laboratory, an unforeseen catastrophe unraveled, shattering the walls of his existence. An explosion, violent and consuming, tore the laboratory asunder, leaving no trace of the alchemist behind.

In the wake of the cataclysmic event, Dradon vanished without a trace. His fate became an enigma, an unsolved puzzle that lingered in the minds of those who'd known him. The Godless Monarchy, perplexed by the sudden disappearance of their devoted servant, launched an investigation.

The ripples of Dradon's absence reverberated throughout Nox Valar, casting a shadow over the Sunless Crossing. The loss of such a talented and ambitious alchemist left a void in the order and set in motion a chain of events that would reshape destinies and challenge the very foundations of the Godless Monarchy.

CHAPTER 1

ODE TO MORTALITY

In the vast expanse of life's domain,
A dance with fate, we all sustain.
Uncertainty weaves its delicate thread,
As time ebbs and flows, our mortality spread.

We wander through the light and shade,
In search of truths, that forever evade.
The whispers of time, a haunting refrain,
Remind us of life's transient reign.

Like fleeting embers in fragile fire,
We strive to unravel our deepest desire.
Yet in the grand design we see,
The fragility of life, a poignant decree.

Oh, mortality, enigma and dread,
Within your embrace, we often tread.
Each breath a reminder of our finite plight,
A flicker of hope, a borrowed respite.

Through trials and triumphs, we forge our way,
In the face of uncertainty, we find strength to stay.
For in the embrace of mortality's song,
We learn to cherish short moments, or long.

With every heartbeat, a precious refrain,
We navigate life's labyrinth, through joy and pain.
In the face of the unknown, we stand tall,
Embracing the mystery, embracing it all.

For it is in the shadow of mortality's gaze,
That we find the courage to live out our days.
To make our mark, however small,
And leave a legacy for all.

-Alaric Swiftwind, The Arcane Wanderer

 HALE

The twisted, withered form slouched toward me, standing out starkly against the golden expanse of the Ashen Fields. The sickly gray hue of her skin blended seamlessly with the shadows that clung to her, and warty growths protruded from her flesh like gnarled knots on an ancient tree. Nocking an arrow, I kept my breath steady as I took aim.

With a flicker of awareness in her malevolent eyes, the Night Hag grinned, vanishing like a wisp of smoke before my arrow could find its mark. Gnashing my teeth, I whirled around, draping my bow over my shoulder and across my chest. In a fluid motion, I drew my daggers.

Blades at the ready, my senses sharpened as she materialized behind me. Her hunched and twisted form contorted as she jerked her head with a disjointed tilt, lashing out, with elongated fingers. Her jagged claws slashed my cheek, and I could smell the rot and residue on her hands.

I returned the favor with a flurry of rapid strikes. Normally, hags are resistant to piercing weapons, but her withered flesh yielded to the bite of my silver blades. Her putrid, yellow blood tainted the air with a foul stench, but she remained resilient, her gnarled claws leaving deep gouges in my leather armor.

Two more hags appeared, their cackling laughter echoing through the Ashen Fields as their twisted bodies swayed and contorted, closing in around me. The one on my right smiled, her long black robe billowing as she held her hands out. Her lips parted, and a spell tumbled forth, the air trembling with the dark incantation.

The raspy sound was a twisted symphony of malice that echoed through the Ashen Fields, sending shivers down my spine. Shadows erupted, coalescing into a swirling vortex around me, the tendrils of darkness seeking to restrain and limit my movement. Tucking into a roll, I navigated the labyrinth of shadows, doing a somersault and narrowly evading their suffocating grasp.

The darkness clawed hungrily, its tendrils coiling and lashing out with a palpable hunger. A chill wind whispered through the air, carrying the faint scent of decay from the shadows' touch. Launching myself over a sweeping wave of darkness, I contorted mid-air, narrowly avoiding a cluster of thrashing tendrils. The rush of wind brushed against my skin, its cool touch mingling with the adrenaline coursing through my veins. As I landed with lithe grace, the ground beneath me quivered, a soft tremor caused by the despairing thrashings of the shadows.

Anticipating the hags' moves, I ducked and swerved, eluding their wicked grip. The acrid scent of diseased flesh permeated the air, a bitter taste that settled on my tongue and turned my stomach. My body flowed seamlessly, a silhouette amidst the whirlwind of blurred forms. The world became a vortex of motion, the flickering play of shadows assaulting my senses.

With a final burst of speed and a gravity-defying leap, I propelled myself out of the shadows, landing resolutely on solid ground. I stood, chest heaving, gasping air that carried a lingering chill of the encroaching darkness. Surveying my surroundings, the faint sound of frustrated hisses filled the air, their chilling echoes intertwining with the rustle of wheat.

The tallest of the hags dropped to all fours, crawling toward me with long, knobby limbs. The warty growths covering her flesh seemed to writhe and shift like it was animated by dark magic.

"How about a kiss?" Her matted hair hung like oily strands, entangled and swaying as if imbued with a life of its own.

Oh no you don't... I locked eyes with her, taking three steps back as I tucked my knives into my belt. The depths of her sunken sockets held a glimmer of wicked intelligence, a glimpse into the darkest recesses of the Abyss. I drew my bow and nocked an arrow. Her jaws opened unnaturally wide, revealing a row of brown, serrated teeth as her slimy tongue slithered over her bottom lip.

"Sorry, gorgeous." I fired three shots in rapid succession. "I hope we can still be friends."

Each arrow made a squelching sound as it struck the left side of her chest. She stopped, her hands falling abruptly to her sides. Then her scream echoed through the fields as she pulled the arrows from between her ribs.

The hags, recognizing the shifting tides of battle, cast a desperate spell, vanishing into another plane. I stood amidst the Ashen Fields, blades and arrows stained with syrupy yellow blood, remnants of the encounter.

Goodberries... I cast the spell, closing my fist as several yellow berries materialized in my palm. Looking down at the small, supple fruits, I tossed them into my mouth, waiting for the minor healing magic to ease the sting on my cheek.

My breath trembled as I closed my eyes and rocked my head back. The Ashen Fields, seemingly endless under an eternally swirling vortex of varying hues of purple, undertones of blue seeping in from the electric coloration of the magical lightning that often rippled through. It held a haunting beauty, I had to admit. I stood in the field, a silent witness as the sky rained soft, feathery particles upon the land, each delicate flake of ash descending with a weightless grace.

As it settled upon my skin, its gentle touch stirred a sense of surreal wonder within me. The stillness in the air was broken only by the hushed patter against the ground. It created a muted ambiance, veiling the surroundings in a ghostly serenity. The tepid breeze greeted me and I took a deep breath, reborn once again.

I couldn't possibly know how long it had been... if a concept as abstract as *time* even exists in this place. The Keepers of the Eternal Sands maintain countless sand dials and calendars around the city, but even when I'm there, I pay them no mind.

Nothing begins or ends. Every hour, day, week, season looks the same, and I've grown accustomed to it. Since I first arrived, I came with a passive awareness that I'd lost something. Unlike the other souls here, I'd had no mortal life. I was born fully mature in the Ashen Fields with no memory. It troubled me ... at first.

Pulling on my fingerless gloves, I packed up my campsite, gathering various herbs and mushrooms I'd collected into a bag and slinging it over my shoulder. *A man still has to make a living, even in the afterlife.*

The violet cloud cover rippled and swirled overhead like the waves of the sea, mirroring the movement of the golden wheat fields below that stretched out endlessly into the distance. Sweat beaded on my palms as I felt something stir... a tugging at the center of my chest. It's going to happen again.

Over the next few cycles, the sensation would build to a crescendo, and I would slip out of this dimension and into another—a hell where my tormentors slice, pierce and eviscerate me over and over until I die, choking on my own blood. Nightmares about that place haunted me often, and some part of me wondered if it was real.

I need not worry about that for now. Today, all I care about is the client waiting for me in Nox Valar.

He wasn't a likable man, but he paid well as long as I set firm boundaries. He was an alchemist who required various components from far outside the walls of the city. They were things I gathered near the turbulent storms that surrounded the realm. Most things can be manifested, but not *these* ingredients. Things that grow naturally here aren't found in any mortal realm; therefore, they cannot be manifested from the memories of mortal souls.

The empty path wound over the rolling hills and back to the city. Even with no sun to rise or set in this land, I'd learned to navigate the fields as if they were my childhood home. No aching hunger plagued me, and there was no war to fight.

As I crested the hill, Nox Valar, the great city of the dead, perched in the distance, high on its mesa in this world beyond the world. The strange nature of existence was tedious but tolerable. Despite the hell waiting in my nightmares, I always woke healthy and unbroken. The thing I found most curious was that my skin and hair had gone gray.

Is this how the dead age? Odd... I'd never heard of such a thing. That type of change is typically reserved for the living if I'm not mistaken.

Even at a distance, I could see the guards straighten up at the sight of me. One stood on either side of the hefty iron portcullis, each one loosely clutching a spear. The one on the left was tall with broad shoulders and a full gut hanging over his belt. The one on the right was short, lean, and clean-shaven.

The tall guard held up one hand before letting it rest on the leather belt at his waist. The fine chainmail and silver armor that encased their bodies glinted under the purple sky. I wondered what qualifies one to be a guard.

"Hail, traveler." He offered a polite nod. "Anything to report from the fields?"

I chuckled at first. Then, upon gauging the somber expression of the two men, I glanced over my shoulder.

"What would there be to report?"

The first guard exchanged a weighted glance with his comrade, and the long, chainmail skirt girding his waist swayed.

"It's just a standard question we're asking all who come and go." He tugged at the leather buckle of his grieves. "Nothing unusual going on out there?"

"No, sir." I forced a thin smile. "Nothing to report."

"Aye, then." He stepped aside and nodded for me to enter. "Welcome back to Nox Valar. *Blessed be the Sovereign!*"

"*Blessed be the Sovereign.*" As was the custom, I touched my forehead with two fingers as a sign of respect.

For the first time since I could remember, I felt the winds of fate shift, and for the briefest moment, I thought... *Perhaps things can change.*

 ECHO

"I hate to break it to you, Echo." Finn peeked around the corner of a massive bookcase. "But I think your old friend might have finally made his journey to the other side."

"That was my first thought too." Dust swirled and danced in the light from my lantern as I set it on the table. "But I have it on good authority that wherever he is, he hasn't left the Sunless Crossing."

"*Right.*" The halfling twisted her wavy purple hair up into a knot, sticking a silver dart through it to hold it in place. "Because your *mysterious* contact inside the Godless Monarchy is *surely* trustworthy."

"They are, I assure you." My shoulders sagged.

I don't know what I was expecting to find in the lab, but staring at the darkened hearth, a chill soaked into my bones. This place had once been my safe haven. I dare even say it was my home. Emaciated twigs stuck up from the four clay pots sitting on the table.

Despite the rumors that he's simply laying low after the explosion in his lab at the Onyx Requiem, if there was one thing I knew, it was that he never would have willingly allowed his beloved carnivorous plants to die. Finn stood on her tiptoes, swiping a pocket watch off the edge of the professor's desk, and the trinket disappeared between the folds of her shirt.

"Put it back, Finn," I said flatly.

"Put what back?" She ran her finger over the wood surface, tracing a crude phallus in the dust.

I gave her a pointed look.

"Ugh, fine." She rolled her violet eyes, begrudgingly tossing the watch back onto the desk. "I don't know why you care so much. You were perfectly content not speaking to the man until you heard he was missing."

My stomach clenched as a wave of guilt washed over me.

"We had our differences." I nodded. "But he was my mentor... and at one time, a friend."

"He was a *prick*, is what he was." Finn grumbled.

"You're not wrong," I sighed with a smile, closing an open book on the table to read the cover. *Risky Remedies; A Dark Alchemist's Memoir.*

Prickly as he was, the man was the closest thing to a father that I'd ever known, and the last words I'd spoken to him were said in anger. It was frustrating to try and learn from someone who always kept me in the dark about one thing or another, and it was worse when that person expected me to follow instructions without question.

"You don't owe him a damn thing." Finn chuffed as though reading my mind. "I say you take a few minutes to say goodbye and *move on.*"

I took a deep breath, holding it as I considered her words. It wasn't the worst advice. After all, Professor Dradon had been in Nox Valar longer than anyone I'd ever met. No one stayed in the Sunless Crossing forever. This was merely a waystation, and perhaps the Keepers of the Eternal Sands were simply wrong about the missing souls.

As I flipped through the pages of the book, a darkness lingered at the edge of my thoughts, the rumors about a soul-eating monster emerging from the Ashen Fields. Near the center, a frayed edge appeared where a page had been ripped out. *Something's not right.*

"Ew." Finn grimaced at her hand, shaking something off onto the floor.

"What is it?" I moved the lantern toward her.

"I don't know." She shuddered. "I thought it was a piece of paper, but it was sort of scaly."

The small patch of tattered material was grayish-yellow. I picked it up and held it in the light, noting the scaly pattern as I turned it one way and then the other. The citizens of Nox Valar had little to fear up until now. But if the whispers were true, the one person who had the knowledge and skill to stop the killer was Dradon.

If I knew him, he was already lying low and trying to figure out how to stop it. I lifted a glass vial from the table and popped the cork out with my thumbnail. Placing the mystery scales into the bottle, I re-corked it and dropped it into my satchel. In my heart, the decision had already been made.

"I have to find him, Finn. No matter what it takes."

"Gods..." Finn hung her head, resting her hands on her hips. She looked up at me and smiled. "You really are a pain in my arse, you know that? If we're going to hunt the old bastard down, we'll need *professional* help."

A grin tugged at the edges of my lips. As rough as she seemed, Finn always had my back, no matter what storm loomed on the horizon. I wished I'd known her in my mortal life.

Maybe things would have turned out differently...

CHAPTER 2

❧ FINN ❧

My stomach had been persistently growling for the past hour. After spending my afternoon combing the seedier parts of Nox Valar for adventurers who might be looking for work, I needed a rest, and there was at least one place I knew of where I could get a quick bite and simultaneously continue my search.

The Rancid Skull overlooked a sewage canal flowing out of the lower west side of the city, the foul smell affording the staff and patrons a little distance from *upstanding* society. One might even say that it added to the ambiance. Clumsy lute music overlapped drunk conversations that poured out of every window as I sauntered up the cobblestone path.

I may not be dead in the technical sense, but Nox Valar was my home, and these were my people. Golden light emanated from the windows, promising a warm fire and strong drinks. Approaching the door, I steeled my nerves. The last time I'd been there, a brawl between a handsy dwarf and a pissed-off centaur almost brought the whole damn building down.

Never a dull moment in the land of the dead. I pulled the pin from my hair, letting it fall around my shoulders. A little extra charm couldn't hurt since I was there on business. As I pushed the heavy oak door open, a familiar blend of odors hit me like a wall: pipe smoke, stale beer, and orc sweat.

I cleared my throat. We needed hired muscle—at minimum, a fighter and a spell slinger of some kind—just in case we actually found Dradon. He was a grouchy, old bastard, and he'd made a thinly veiled threat toward Echo when she'd left his service.

What he meant when he said she wouldn't be met with a warm welcome should she return, I could only speculate, but I wasn't taking any chances.

Crossing the room, I climbed up onto the barstool. *Why is it that, even in this world, everything is made for larger races?*

"What'll it be?" The half-orc bartender flared his nostrils.

"Ale and bread." I winked at him, dropping eight copper pieces onto the bar. "Keep the change, handsome."

The orc narrowed his eyes at me, and I apologized, switching out the copper for the appropriate Crossway Coins.

"One of those who hold onto the traditions of the living, eh?"

"Old habits…" I tried not to stare at his grimy fingernails. The half-orc growled, turning to the brass ale barrel to twist the spigot and fill a wooden mug. The smell of vinegar singed the tiny hairs in my nose.

"I made this batch myself." He slammed the tankard down in front of me.

Of course, he did. My eyes watered at the fumes wafting up from the cup, but this was part of the Rancid Skull's charm. I'd been blending with the locals for this long, and the last thing I needed was to lose credibility by offending the barkeep.

Bottom's up. I lifted the cup to my lips and took two long gulps. The bitter liquid sloshed over my tongue, and I nodded enthusiastically, hiding my grimace with a smile.

"That's good... Strong."

"I'll get your bread, lil' boss." He grinned, flopping a dingy dish towel over his shoulder as he headed back into the kitchen.

I shrugged, having had worse nicknames. Turning to face the lute player on stage, I leaned back against the bar and kicked my foot in time with the music. A table of six, red-eyed adventurers sat in the center of the room, a half-elf druid crying on the shoulder of her human companion. I'd seen it a dozen times, an entire party being wiped out by a dragon or a troll with no one left behind to resurrect them.

There was still hope for this lot though. It might not be today, might not be tomorrow, but it never fails to surprise me how many people have at least one person who was willing to go to great lengths to bring them home. At any rate, I doubted any of those chaps would be interested in working for a while. My gaze drifted to the far end of the room.

A group of dwarves occupied the other large table nearest to the fire, laughing, belching, and singing together. Dwarves were sturdy enough, but I didn't see a caster among them, and magical knowledge would be a must for this mission. I wondered briefly if the one who owned the massive hammer might be willing to break off from his group for a solo gig.

Of the other patrons scattered amongst the smaller tables, no one had the look of someone I'd trust for this particular job.

"Enjoy." The half-orc placed a wooden plate with sliced bread on the bar.

"I always do." I turned back around and held up my ale in a toast, noticing the cat woman seated against the wall at the end of the bar.

A native of one of the jungle kingdoms, perhaps? Short sleek fur covered her face and body in pale gold, dotted with black leopard spots.

Silver-forged scales and dark-tanned leather encased her muscular limbs, and the armor bore the scuffs and dents that only came from battle. This was a woman who'd seen combat, and often. Her black claws tapped the cup in her hands as she switched her long tail back and forth. Her long, black hair was woven up into dozens of tiny braids that fell down past her shoulders and her deep amber eyes darted up from her mulled wine to meet my gaze. I sensed pain there.

"What are you looking at?" She narrowed her eyes, crinkling her nose with the final word to show her gleaming fangs.

"A fighter, from the looks of you." I touched my forehead with two fingers. "Next round is on me."

"Everything is free here," she grumbled, shifting in her seat. "And I'm not interested. No offense."

"I'm not flirting with you." I rolled my eyes, biting off a small piece of bread. "I just noticed your armor, and it made me wonder if you're looking for work in the city."

"I don't plan on staying here long." She huffed. "I shouldn't be here in the first place."

"Don't know how you died?" I studied her stoic expression. "Or someone was supposed to bring you back and hasn't yet?"

She glared at me, and I knew I'd struck a nerve.

"Who left you high and dry?" I asked. "Friend, business associate?"

She sniffed and turned her head, looking away.

"Ahhh." I nodded. "A lover."

"That's none of your business," she snarled.

"*Lovers* are the ones who send half of us here most of the time." A tiefling with a long, lean frame took a seat about halfway between the cat and me and lit a cigarette. His accent was almost as smooth as the silky cloud he exhaled. "My first two times here, I was sent by a lover."

"How many times have you uh..." I clicked my tongue.

"This is my third time." He shrugged. "This last time was ... unrelated. It was a poorly negotiated business deal. Never trust a cultist."

"Damn." I grimaced. "You have anyone to bring you back?"

He took a long drag off his cigarette. "It might take some strategizing, but I'll figure something out. I always do."

"Let me know if you need to communicate with the living." I raised my glass. "I'll be making a trip topside after this mission."

"Truly?" The tiefling signaled to the barkeep and ordered a cup of tea. "I've heard there are living souls that work in both realms. I've never met one."

"The travel fare is expensive." I shrugged and took a sip. "And some would say it's not worth the risk, but it pays well, and I like having a retirement plan."

"We all end up here eventually, I suppose." The tiefling exhaled a long column of smoke toward the ceiling.

"Wait." The cat woman's ears perked up. "You're... not dead?"

"Not yet." I winked. "But I guess it depends on who you ask."

You're interested now, ain'tcha? I suppressed a smug grin as her whiskers twitched and the proverbial wheels started turning.

"Unfortunately, it looks like I'll be stuck here for a while." I frowned into my beer. "I'm normally great at finding people, but I bit off more than I can chew with this one. Damn slippery sorcerers." The tiefling laughed, and I reached a hand toward him. "I'm Finn, by the way."

He wrapped his long, slender fingers around my hand to shake it. "Hyperion Fiorello."

"Warlock?" My brows drew together as I gestured to him, my eyes wandering over his smartly tailored suit.

"How could you tell?"

"Reading people is a talent of mine." I nodded to the cat woman. "My offer still stands if you'd like me to buy you that drink now."

She took a deep breath, and the floorboards creaked under her boots as she came closer to sit between us. I smiled, scooting the plate of bread to rest between us.

"Lieutenant Rivka Stonewell..." She glanced over at me. "...at your service."

"I'm very pleased to meet you." I raised my tankard, and she clinked her wooden cup against it.

Over the next few minutes, I told them about Surrak Dradon and how the Nyxian Guard had launched an investigation regarding several souls that the Keepers of the Eternal Sands had claimed vanished from the realm entirely. Obviously, if they weren't called to their afterlives and they weren't resurrected, they had to be here. Perhaps they were hidden, but souls don't just dissolve into nothing.

The names of the missing hadn't been announced, but the word on the street was that there was a creature on the loose consuming souls of the dead. After finding Dradon's herbarium in the shape it was, we could only assume that he was either lying low or he'd been taken with the others. And whether he wanted it or not, we were going to help him.

"So, you want us to find this elf sorcerer." Hyperion rubbed his chin. "And you want us to capture him without injuring him? It doesn't sound that complicated."

"More or less." I made a vague gesture. "I highly doubt you'll be able to bring him in without bruising him up a little. He's a bit of an asshole. Just don't kill him. He's already had a couple of accidents. He would just reappear out in the ashen fields somewhere, and we don't want his brain getting all gooped up."

"What do you mean?" Rivka blinked.

"If you die in the Sunless Crossing, your soul reforms out in the fields." Hyperion leaned on the bar, crinkling his nose, having difficulty articulating what he wanted to say. "But if it happens more than a few times... people start becoming a little... *off.*"

"Dying in purgatory..." Rivka shook her head. "How is it that we know so little about this place?"

"The dead forget and the living are sworn to secrecy." I swirled the ale in the bottom of my mug around. "If you were to get resurrected tomorrow, you'd forget everything that happened here. That's one of many reasons why the Nyxian Guard that aren't gargoyles are made up of the living despite the obvious risks."

"What risks?" Rivka's slitted pupils darted to Hyperion and back to me.

"We die here, we cease to exist." I twinkled my fingers, miming dust blowing away on a breeze.

"Heavy stuff." Hyperion raised an eyebrow. "But beyond that, the Nyxian Guard need to recruit living souls so they don't get either called to their afterlife or resurrected in the middle of their shift."

"It's hard to find dependable help these days." I clicked my tongue and drank down the last of my ale. "Speaking of which, are you guys out or in?"

"Will you take me back to the land of the living, if I help you?" Rivka asked.

"Woah, slow down now." I held up a hand. "I can't bring you back from the dead. Even if I could, it would cost more than I could ever make in one lifetime."

"Then why did you bother?" She growled.

"I can take a message back to someone for you." I set two silver pieces on the bar and gestured to the bartender who rolled his eyes. *I must be the only rogue in the realm that feels wrong about not paying for things.* "Maybe they can find a living cleric to rez you."

"And we're just supposed to trust you?" Rivka dug her fingernails into her cup.

I leveled my gaze at her as the bartender filled each cup with our respective beverages.

"If I had a habit of ripping people off, I wouldn't have lasted this long." I pulled my full mug to the edge of the bar. "But you're welcome to walk away if it doesn't sit right. With the Guard sniffing around, the last thing I need is someone who gets cold feet when the pressure is on."

"My feet are fine," Hyperion interjected. "I assume that any messages you ferry back and forth will be kept private?"

"Of course." I furrowed my brow. "I'm a professional."

"And may I also assume that these will be delivered *promptly* after we find this Professor Dradon?" He stirred his tea, clinking the spoon delicately against the rim before setting it on the saucer.

"Right again." I flinched as a fight broke out on the other side of the room.

The barkeep leaped over the bar, shoving a great bulging arm between the dwarf who held the lute over his head and the scrawny human bard who was now swinging his bony fists wildly.

"Then I'm in." Hyperion picked up his jacket, slipping into it and smoothing down the lapels. "I'll start immediately, and I think I know just who to ask."

"Fine." Rivka huffed. "I'm in too, but if I find out at any point that either of you are double-crossing me—"

"Cheating my associates would be bad for business." I flashed a wide smile as I scooted off the barstool, passing each of them a card with the address of my flat. "We regroup in one cycle, that's twenty-four hours."

"Understood." Hyperion glided past the growing commotion, opened the door, and stood aside. "After you, ladies."

I offered an appreciative nod and exited. Rivka hung back, insisting that Hyperion go first, allowing her to close the door behind them.

"Happy Hunting," I said under my breath as I put my hood up. *These two should make for an interesting partnership.*

 **HYPERION**

My black, polished shoes clicked against the cobblestones as we left the Rancid Skull behind and made our way into the heart of the city. It was a strange feeling to be back after all this time. Though after my resurrection, I'd forgotten my time in the Sunless Crossing, every moment that passed brought with it more memories of people I'd done business with. Even the layout of the city was becoming familiar again.

The warm air carried the scent of ripe fruit and fresh bread and despite the dark sky, the city felt more alive than ever. Laughter and chatter rang through the streets and Rivka, my new companion, kept pace as we turned a corner to enter the marketplace. Her yellow eyes and their slitted pupils flashed to one side and then the other, continuously scanning the faces of people in the crowd.

She was a lovely creature, graceful and poised. And much like me, it didn't come naturally for her to blend into a crowd. Though if the halfling rogue had trouble tracking down this *Professor Dradon*, perhaps subtlety wasn't an angle that would have worked anyway.

On the left, a group of adventurers huddled around a map, whispering in discussion, and I smiled to myself, wondering what a ragtag group of humans would be looking for in a place like this. Up ahead, roaring torches cast dancing shadows on the walls of surrounding buildings and lanterns illuminated colorful cloth awnings. The everlasting night meant the market was always in full swing with vendors hawking all manner of wares—everything from enchanted trinkets to exotic spices.

"Hail, gentle travelers." A hook-nosed gnome with wild, bushy white eyebrows manned a stall, lining up various bottles of colorful swirling potions and elixirs. "Could I interest you in a potion of clairvoyance?"

He smiled at me, revealing crooked teeth as he lifted a glass jar containing yellow liquid with a gray eyeball floating around inside. Not the slightest bit unnerved, I flashed a wide grin back at him.

"I'm actually looking for an old friend who's been laying low." I leaned on the counter, lowering my voice. "Maybe you've seen him. An elf sorcerer with gray hair that's always in the market for rare alchemical supplies?"

"Sorry." The gnome's smile dissolved. "Doesn't sound familiar."

I shrugged, giving a subtle nod. "Well, if you happen to bump into him, please let him know that Hyperion Fiorello has some lucrative work on the horizon that I think would interest him."

His eyes glinted at the prospect of money as I turned to leave.

"If your friend is laying low..." He raised a hand, and I stopped to listen. "...he'd likely be doing business with my brother. It may be wise to check with him."

"And where might I find your brother?" I slanted my head, reaching into my coin purse for a Crossway Coin.

The gnome licked his lips, picking up a stick of charcoal and a scrap of parchment to sketch out a crude map as I placed the coin on the counter.

"He doesn't stay in one place for long." Extending the paper to me, he glanced at Rivka. "Dealing in rare ingredients can be dangerous." Scratching his chin, he added, "Are you sure you wouldn't like to stock up on a few potions?"

"You know what..." I reconsidered. In the past, my willingness to throw money around had proven useful in shaking people loose from their hiding spots, and it wasn't as if I couldn't afford it. "I'll take an assortment."

After purchasing a few random potions, I took a last look at the map and tucked it into a pocket on the inside of my lapel. Nodding for Rivka to follow me, I headed through an alleyway toward the northern wall of the city. The cat woman glanced over her shoulder, her long blue cape swaying with every step.

"You seem on edge," I said over my shoulder.

"You would be too if you woke up dead with no idea how it happened."

"That's fair." I shrugged. "Do you want to talk about it?"

"No," she said flatly.

"Suit yourself." A grin tugged at the corner of my lips. "Death can be a touchy subject for some."

She remained silent as we traversed the dark alleyways, turning toward the outer wall of the city. It was darker here, and the street looked all but abandoned.

"That must be it." She nodded toward a single, lit window and strode across the street, stepping over jagged holes in the unmaintained cobbles. Something about this place made the tiny hairs on the back of my neck stand up.

"Wait!" I grabbed her cloak at the shoulder, and she spun to face me with a snarl on her lips.

"Don't *ever* touch me." Her amber eyes glinted and I put my hands up in surrender. The muffled sound of raised voices pricked my ears.

"Just wait..." I leveled my gaze and her stare softened as I tapped on my ear. "Listen..."

Her ears perked up and we both backed into the shadows, and the voices became clearer as we flattened our bodies against the building.

"The Nyxian Guard aren't the only ones looking for you..." The gnome's nasally voice was ragged with age. "A living halfling that keeps company with a human cleric has been quietly asking around about you."

"Not quietly enough, apparently." A gravelly male voice was followed by the soft footsteps of leather-soled boots crossing the rotten floorboards. "Did you tell her anything?"

"What would I tell her?" The gnome snorted. "It's not like I'd know where to look for you."

"True," the man responded, coming toward the door, "and I aim to keep it that way."

Too easy... I grinned. I'd always had fairly good luck in the land of the dead. The door of the shop opened and out strode a cloaked elf that practically glided as he walked. I locked eyes with Rivka. *This has to be Dradon.*

Placing a finger to my lips, I signaled for her to move quietly as we darted into another alley. I kept a keen eye on the hooded elf, my enhanced senses attuned to his movements. His figure weaved through the decaying surroundings with a sense of purpose and agility. Then under his breath, he spoke a single word.

"Biscuits." He stepped into a discolored patch on the wall. Rivka and I exchanged determined glances, a silent understanding passing between us.

This must be the entrance to *Anywhere*. Hidden within the depths of Nox Valar, the city's criminal underbelly converges to trade in forbidden goods. It exists as a pocket dimension, forever remaining elusive to most law-abiding folk.

The entrance to Anywhere constantly shifts, making it nearly impossible to find unless one possesses the ever-changing password. Thanks to our target, we knew exactly what it was for the time being. This professor was cunning and resourceful, so we'd need to be wary as we entered behind him. A wave of energy rippled through the bricks as we came near.

Smiling at Rivka, I reached out a tentative hand, and the wall trembled beneath my touch, acknowledging my presence. I stepped forward and crossed the threshold into the portal, and instantly, a surreal sensation enveloped me. It was as if I had entered a space suspended between worlds, caught in a transient state of existence. I felt weightless, disconnected from the Sunless Crossing.

Moving deeper into the portal, a flurry of color swirled around me in a breathtaking display. Reality blurred, replaced by an ethereal dreamscape that defied the laws of nature. I moved my feet like they were still on the ground and the atmosphere shifted subtly.

A mixture of ancient herbs, lingering enchantments, and whispers of forgotten spells teased my senses. Finally, emerging from the portal, I found myself in the heart of Anywhere.

Market stalls lined narrow, dimly lit alleyways, creating an intricate labyrinth of hidden commerce.

The air was thick with incense and the whispers of illicit transactions. Shadows danced along the cobblestones, obscuring the identities of those who trod these forbidden grounds. The wares of Anywhere ranged from cursed trinkets to ancient artifacts steeped in dark magic.

Arcane tomes with forbidden knowledge beckoned to those daring enough to peruse their pages, promising power at a terrible price. The stalls were a mismatched collection of tents, carts, and makeshift shops, each showcasing their dubious merchandise in a haphazard display. There, the vilest of contraband awaited those willing to pay the steep price.

My senses heightened as I caught a glimpse of the pale, gray-haired elf slipping into a warehouse. Adrenaline surged through my veins as I quickened my pace, Rivka right by my side. We entered the dilapidated structure, the air heavy with dust.

Inside the warehouse, darkness embraced us, broken only by the faint beams of light that pierced through cracks in the decaying walls. We navigated between the carcasses of aged crates, our eyes scanning the vast space for any sign of the elf's presence.

I'd hoped if we moved quickly, we might be able to nab him before he exited Anywhere and re-entered a more populated part of the city. At first, I thought I'd lost him, but part of me sensed the quiet alley wasn't as empty as it appeared.

I jerked my head back when something gusted past my cheek. An arrow hit the wall, inches from my face, and I turned toward the shadows. Two beads of light glinted in the darkness as the elf stepped forward, and I took a step back.

He drew a dagger and swung as Rivka lunged, teeth bared as she deflected the dagger with the shining silver grieves on her forearm. Her sword sang as she pulled it from its scabbard, and the elf ducked the blow.

"We're supposed to bring him alive," I said from the corner of my mouth.

His eyes... They looked like the night sky, completely black with shifting particles of light glowing within. Rivka's gaze flitted toward me, barely acknowledging my words as the elf's dagger came slashing through the air.

Finn said that Dradon was more likely to try and kill us than allow us to introduce ourselves. Apparently, she was right, and our only chance at bringing him in would be to render him unconscious.

Frostbite... The cantrip began as a whisper in my mind, forming a numbing chill in my chest that crept down my arms. A misty glow emanated from my hands crystalizing as white residue on the elf's feet.

He scowled in a fierce grimace, ripping one boot from the ice as Rivka swiped her claws across his chest. Stumbling backward with one foot still stuck in the ice, he took another swing, slowing as the ice magic spread through his body. *He's resisting.*

Rivka struck him across the face with the pummel of her sword, her claws moving with lightning speed as she slapped the dagger from his hand. The elf roared, hurling a powerful punch to her throat. She doubled over, grasping her windpipe and wheezing.

Reaching for his bow, the elf shook off the effects of my spell as he loosed one arrow after another. Rivka weaved to one side, her feline reflexes affording her an otherworldly grace and speed that moved within the flash of a second. The elf lifted his aim toward me, continuing his rapid-fire movements.

Shit! A sharp sting bit into my shoulder, I fell back, taking a deep breath, and cast another spell. *Chill Touch.*

A dark pulse tingled at the base of my skull as I slowly exhaled, fixing my eyes on the elf. He nocked an arrow aiming at Rivka. She dodged, but it sliced a long gash in her cheek. A transparent, skeletal hand materialized in front of the elf's face, closing its fingers around his lower jaw. His black eyes widened, turning pale and milky as his hood fell back.

Rivka lunged, taking him to the ground as the necrotic magic soaked in, saturating his flesh. Her fist made a packing sound when it connected with his jaw, once, twice ... three times before he caught her fist in one hand, reaching for his dagger with the other.

"Sleep," I said with a wave of my hand.

His arms went limp, and she punched him one last time.

"Why didn't you just do that in the first place?" She glared at me.

I shrugged. "I didn't think of it until just now."

Her sinuous muscles bulged and flexed with every movement as she wiped the blood running from the open cut on her face. She shook the red liquid off her hand with a splatter, hissing at the motionless figure at her feet.

"Did your magic make him look like that?" She picked up her sword and sheathed it, nodding toward the elf.

"I'm not sure," I grunted, sitting up to take in the elf's unusual appearance. His face and hair were the same shade of milky gray. "The halfling didn't say anything about him being undead, but the spell wouldn't have hit him this hard if he wasn't."

"We're all dead, yes?" She pulled a bandage out of her satchel and pressed it to my shoulder.

"Technically... *Mnn*." I winced. "But in the Sunless Crossing, our bodies should function just like they would on the material plane."

"Not our problem." Her nose twitched as she plucked the arrow from my shoulder.

"*Aaahg!*" Pain tore through my body and dark blood pumped from the wound. "What in all hells, woman? Are you trying to kill me?"

"Shut up." She rolled her eyes popping the cork off a small potion bottle and handed it to me.

I swallowed the bitter liquid and immediately felt the tissue in my shoulder knitting back together. She took out another potion and drank it herself.

"Didn't expect to need healing potions in the afterlife." She used her thumb to hold the cleaved flesh on her cheek together, allowing it to grow closed.

"Well," I grunted, getting back to my feet. "If we play our cards right, we'll be walking amongst the living again in no time."

"*If* the halfling delivers." She kicked the unconscious elf in the ribs one more time before pulling a rope out of her bag and binding his wrists with skillful precision.

"One last thing." I cracked my knuckles and made a sweeping gesture over the sleeping elf. A foul cloud of stench rose from him and I chuckled.

"Uhg," Rivka gagged, covering her nose. "What the hell kind of spell is that?"

"Stinking cloud." I grinned, holding my head high. "The halfling was right about him being an asshole. I figured he should also smell like one."

She slugged me in my sore shoulder, knocking the wind from my chest.

"*You're* the asshole." She doubled up her fist, possibly wanting to hit me again, but stopped herself. "I still have to carry the son of a bitch."

"Oh..." I frowned down at the heap of stinking elf. She had every right to be upset because he truly smelled like shit. "Apologies, my lady..."

Rivka muttered curses as she pulled a bandana up from her neck to cover her nose and mouth. In one mighty heave, she slung his limp body over her shoulder like a sack of flour.

Such a stunning creature...

CHAPTER 3

Baptized in the heat of battle as little more than a child, I've seen many warriors breathe their last. I accepted that one day I would do the same, but what I didn't expect was to fall asleep and never wake again... The shame was more than I could bear.

When I'd drifted off that night I actually believed that my life would finally begin. I dared to hope that my legacy would be about something other than honor, terror, and blood. *He* made me believe I could be more than a killer. *I should have known better.*

Waking in a golden wheat field, I remember blinking a stinging sensation from my eyes, staring up into a swirling vortex of clouds. The wind hissed through the swishing stalks and it sounded like the ocean. At first, I thought I'd wandered into a dream. Time passed, and I didn't wake, so I started walking, calling out for Nev, who was nowhere to be found. It felt like an eternity, wandering in the misty fields as feathery ashes drifted down like snow.

An ominous purple glow emanated from beyond the ever-churning vapor above, and in the distance, a massive city jutted against the skyline, beckoning me like a lighthouse in the darkness. By the time an Ashen Shepherd found me, I already suspected the horrible truth. This was *not* the world of the living.

Now here I am, lugging an unconscious, gray-skinned elf through a city. It's not something that can be done with much subtlety. Especially since he smelled like the backside of a sibriex. I suggested that we wrap him in a blanket, but Hyperion insisted that would look even more suspicious. Acknowledging that the tiefling probably knew more about kidnapping, I bowed to his judgement.

"Hurry up," I whispered.

"Easy, gorgeous." Hyperion grinned over his shoulder. "If you don't stop looking so damned nervous, people might assume that we're up to no good."

"Now why would they think *that*?" My tone dripped with sarcasm.

"We're just taking our drunk friend up to a room to sleep off his bender in peace." The lock clicked, and he opened the door, bowing as he gestured for me to enter. "Milady."

His chivalry was shallow, the yellow light behind his eyes, cold and calculating, and I knew I could only trust him as long as our interests aligned. It was a dangerous position to be in, but what choice did I have? I entered the room and tossed the pale, stinking elf onto the floor.

When I first arrived, I'd spent days wandering the city, trying to make sense of it all. I maintained the belief that something unforeseen must have happened to Nev. *Just because he's not here, doesn't mean he hasn't been captured. Whatever the truth of the matter may be, I have to find him. Even if it means clawing my way out of the grave.*

"The hells is this?" Hyperion picked up a note from the windowsill. His eyes danced over the scrawled ink. "Apparently, Finn wants us to bring our new friend here *all the way across the city* to some herbarium."

I rolled my shoulder, speaking through clenched teeth, as I pulled down my face mask. "Then why didn't she tell us to do that in the first place?"

"Who's to say?" He huffed, stuffing the paper into his lapel. "I wouldn't blame you at all if you need a rest for a bit. Son of a hag looks heavy."

My eyes wandered over the neatly tailored suit hugging Hyperion's long spidery limbs. Of course, he wouldn't offer to carry him part of the way. The man was a total weakling.

"Thanks." I stared flatly. "But I'll manage."

Picking up the elf, I heaved him back over my shoulder, and we set out to cross the city *again*. Nox Valar wasn't as bad as one might expect a purgatorial realm to be. My senses danced amongst the flickering of the eternally lit streetlamps, and the air was thick with the scents of roasting pork, baked goods, and pungent spices.

I could feel the elf taking shallow breaths against my back as I carried his limp body, and I wondered if the halfling would be upset at the state he was in. More concerning was the thought of whether or not she would hold up her end of the deal if he died in transit.

"You have the look of a seasoned officer." The tiefling's eyes glinted as he smiled at me, his long tail twitching with every step. "Which nation did you fight for, Lieutenant?"

"I'm..." The sting of my own betrayal tugged at me. I no longer had any right to claim my rank and title. *I never should have introduced myself as Lieutenant.* "I *was* under the fifth division serving the Sangsha Dominion."

"Sangsha." He nodded. "I've never had the pleasure. What's it like there?"

"It's..." I thought of my homeland and tried to offer an honest answer. "...hot," I said.

The tiefling pressed his lips together and nodded thoughtfully. I could have told him how the first thing that hits you is the dense humid air, the intoxicating scent of wet earth, and the perfume of dozens of colorful flowers mingling with decaying leaves and rain. But I detested small talk. In my opinion, it was a waste of focus and energy that could be better spent elsewhere.

Conversation should be meaningful. It should have purpose. There was no reason to ruin perfectly good silence if you didn't actually care about what was being exchanged. Perhaps I was wrong, and he would have wanted to hear how the lush canopy cast dappled light onto the forest floor. How the crystalline rivers sparkled in the sunlight and the towering trees stood with their thick trunks covered in vines and clinging ferns.

In my memory, the throng of birds and insects was deafening and the ground under my feet was soft and spongy, carpeted in moss and fallen leaves. But even if he was earnestly interested, it wouldn't have mattered.

"I'd be an outcast if I ever get the chance to see it again." The thought of being ostracized broke something inside of me, creating a throbbing ache at the center of my chest. "So, I'd rather not talk about home if it's all the same to you." My attention was drawn back to the weight I was carrying. The elf groaned.

"We'll need to dose him with a sleeping potion or give him another knock on the head if we plan on keeping him compliant." Hyperion sighed.

I readjusted the elf's weight as we turned a corner, bumping into a group of rowdy dwarves.

"Oh, devils!" One dwarf pinched his nose and another fanned the air in front of his face. "I think yer' friend might've shat himself."

Their friends shouted and sang as they stumbled out of a nearby tavern.

"He's... had a bad day." I tensed, throwing an irritated glance at the tiefling.

Hyperion's white ruffled silk shirt was still speckled with blood from the arrow that had struck his shoulder. He shook his head, telling me not to react as the dwarves slapped each other on the back and shambled past us. The crowds thinned as we entered Whetstone Bluff and another light shower of ash began to fall.

"How does one know when to sleep when the night in this cursed place never ends?" I muttered.

"You're dead." Hyperion gestured to the large hourglass that sat atop the temple for the Keepers of the Eternal Sands. "You sleep whenever you want."

The entire city was filled with various timepieces and calendars that marked the passage of each hour, but without day or night, they simply referred to a twenty-four-hour period as one cycle. I supposed there was a certain freedom in being dead. Things couldn't get much worse, after all. But even the bleakness of that thought brought me no comfort.

The buildings loomed on either side of the darkened street, like judges waiting to witness an execution. Gnarled chimneys belched thick clouds of acrid smoke and the smell of burning coal tainted the air. A few small, barred windows shed a faint glow from lamps inside and the low hum of forges vibrated underfoot.

To the left, just past the elegant marble buildings, stood a black marble structure with red veins that sparkled like spiderwebs. On top, a steeply sloped roof covered in dark purple tiles and dry tangled vines, and the heavy wooden door hung on wrought-iron hinges. I sniffed the air, catching a whiff of the sour beer the halfling had been drinking.

This must be the place. I turned my back to the door to watch for anyone who might have been following us. Hyperion tugged a small metal chain and somewhere inside a bell jingled. Her feet didn't make a sound, but a few moments later the door opened and the halfling's large violet eyes stared up at us, quickly followed by a grimace as she covered her nose and mouth.

"Gods alive..."

"Special delivery." Hyperion grinned as he lifted the elf's head to show off our prize.

The halfling's flat expression made me shrink inside myself. *I should have known it wouldn't be this easy.*

"Who the hell is *this*?" Her eyelids fluttered as she pointed to the elf. "And why does he smell like—"

"This... isn't your missing professor?" Hyperion frowned.

"Are you—" Finn pinched the bridge of her nose before frantically ushering us inside. "Get in here before someone sees you. We should probably open a window, though."

She opened the door wider, leaning out to scan the dark street outside. The smells of mildew and dust were a welcome distraction as the floorboards bowed under my feet beneath the tattered red carpet. A delicate-looking woman with creamy skin and large green eyes glided into the room, her white dress swishing as she halted, facing me.

"Who's that?" She eyed the elf hanging over my shoulder like a deer carcass. She jerked her head back as she caught a whiff. "Oh..."

"This is going to be a long night." Letting out a long frustrated sigh, I flopped the unconscious elf into an armchair and reached into my bag for some more rope.

Long night... What an understatement in a realm with no sun.

 HALE

I can't remember the last time I slept this well. Eyelids heavy, as if weighed down by iron chains, fluttered when I feebly attempted to open them, and the dimly lit study materialized around me. Shadows danced on the walls as the stale scent of dust and mold woke my senses fully. My skull throbbed, pulsing with the beat of my heart as memories of the fight came flooding back.

The cat woman. The tiefling. The overwhelming rush of adrenaline as her claws sliced the flesh on my chest, ripping through my leather armor like it was silk. Then ... darkness. Panic bubbled up in my chest as I tried to shift in my seat.

Why can't I move? As I tried to stand up, a thin leather cord bit into my wrists and ankles. My breathing grew fast and shallow, intensifying the ache in my bruised ribs as I pulled against my restraints. *What is that gods-awful stench?*

Where the hell am I? The air in the room grew heavier as my thoughts raced, and I tried to imagine who those people were and what they could possibly want with me. Warm coppery blood stung my eyes as I recalled the vicious blows to my skull. My clothes were soaked in a combination of blood and sweat and I wasn't sure which was more concerning.

If I could remember who I was before this, maybe it would all make sense. Had I done something to deserve this, or was it just some kind of mistake? Fear of all the unknown variables of my predicament dissolved into a cold, murderous rage as I realized I didn't care.

It didn't matter who did this to me or why... I was getting out. Hushed voices from the other room pricked my ears, and I strained to listen.

"We overheard the gnome say that the Nyxian Guard were looking for him along with a living halfling and a human cleric." A woman with a stern voice sounded like she was speaking around a mouthful of fangs. *Could this be the cat woman from the alley?* "It wasn't a stretch to assume he meant you. If he's not Dradon, I say we turn him over to the authorities."

"Are you serious?" A higher-pitched voice responded. "You just said the Nyxian Guard were looking for *us*. We don't want to go anywhere near them, definitely not to hand over someone who can point us out as having abducted him."

"It would be simpler to kill him and be done with it." *That was a voice I recognized.*

It was the tiefling that had been following me outside the herbalist's shop. I glanced around, looking for any sharp objects that might be lying out in the open. My eyes settled on a quill pen protruding up from an inkwell. *That'll do...*

"Killing him would be pointless." The high-pitched voice must have belonged to a gnome or halfling. "He'd just reappear in the ashen fields and come looking for us."

"Not if we toss him into the storm outside the city." The tiefling lowered his voice.

He wasn't wrong. If the rumors were to be believed, there was no coming back from that. Twisting my wrists one way and then the other, I hoped to stretch the cords binding me, but the rough braided rope sawed into my raw skin, and the more I struggled, the deeper they cut into me.

"We're not killing anyone." A third woman piped in. This one spoke with some authority.

"Then what do you suggest?" The stern woman asked. "Now that he's seen us, we can't just let him go."

"Not to mention, he looks like a damned corpse." The smaller voice grumbled. Shame burned in my cheeks. Surely I was above something as shallow as vanity, but her words called out a fear that had been squatting in the back of my mind. "What if it's a *disease*? Maybe Dradon found out about an epidemic and the Sovereign set out to have him silenced to avoid inciting a panic."

"That's ridiculous." The third woman's voice was thoughtful, and the sound of footsteps paced to the opposite end of whatever room my captors had gathered in.

I used the sound of those footsteps to mask the sounds of my own movements as I scooted my chair toward the desk. But the wooden leg caught on a wrinkle in the carpet, and the chair teetered precariously to one side. I held my breath, tensing every muscle in my body as I tried to lean in the opposite direction, but it was too late to counter the imbalance.

No point in playing it quiet now. I tumbled clumsily to the floor with a loud, clamorous thud. A split second of silence was followed by a stampede of footsteps rushing up the hall. Contorting my body, I thrashed, applying as much strength and leverage as possible to try and break the chair.

The first to enter the room was a female halfling with purple hair. The cat woman was close on her heels, followed by the tiefling and a human woman in a flowing dress. Her hair cascaded around her shoulders in loose waves and her silky garment swayed with every step, clinging delicately to her curves.

The chair they'd tied me to was solid as a brick and all my undignified flailing got me nowhere. My head snapped back as the heel of the cat woman's boot connected with my forehead.

"Stop!" The human woman shoved the cat woman to one side. "It's bad enough that you abducted the wrong person, and I already said, we're *not* killing anyone."

"Yeah." I spat blood on the carpet and glared at the cat woman. "As you probably figured, I'm not your guy. The sooner you cut me loose, the sooner you can get back out there and try to find whoever you're actually looking for."

"Not happening." The halfling crossed her arms. "You'll squeal to the guards the first chance you get, and that's if you don't decide to try and take us out yourself."

"The Nyxian Guard are looking for us both." I locked eyes with the halfling. "And in case you haven't noticed, I'm a bit outnumbered. Let me walk out of here, and we'll say all's well that ends well."

"Get him off the floor." The woman in the white dress stepped forward, trying in vain to pick the chair up.

Rolling her eyes, the cat woman snorted and tipped my chair upright with her foot.

The woman in the white dress shot the feline a sideways glance before leaning forward to look me in the eye. "What's your name, Sir, and... what race are you?"

"Hale." I tilted my neck, cracking the bones. "As for *what* I am, your guess is as good as mine."

"Are there others like you?" She blinked. "Where did you come from in your mortal life?"

"Don't remember." I shrugged.

"I can make him remember." The cat woman snarled, stepping forward and grabbing me by the tattered remnants of my shirt.

"My life in the Sunless Crossing is the only one I've ever known." I glared at her. "Torturing me won't change that. If I was something else before... *this*..." I gestured to myself by flexing my fingers. "I don't remember any of it."

The cat woman's wrinkled nose relaxed and she let go of me as the human woman placed a delicate hand on her shoulder, signaling for her to back off.

"You really don't remember *anything* before the Sunless Crossing?" The woman's large green eyes searched mine. "No childhood home or parents or—"

"Nothing." I raised an eyebrow. "I told you, I'm a blank slate."

She stood up, rubbing her chin as she paced toward the dark fireplace.

"What is it?" The halfling followed her. "What are you thinking?"

"Maybe this does explain what happened to Professor Dradon." The woman spun to face me and her eyes lit up. "If he woke up one day with no memory of who he was, he'd be confused. Maybe he'd even go into hiding until he could try and figure it out."

"That's a big if, Echo." The halfling frowned, putting her hands up like she was talking to a wild horse. "Even if that's the case, we have no way to help him."

The human woman smirked at me. "I have *him* to help me figure it out."

"Woah, now." I furrowed my brow. "I don't want any part of this."

"With all due respect, Mr. Hale." A feeling of darkness came over the woman's expression. "I'm not giving you a choice. If there's a chance that my friend is suffering from the same memory loss affecting you, I need to run a few experiments to figure out how to reverse it."

A chill sank into my bones as I clenched my teeth, imagining being sliced, bled, and injected with previously untested potions and elixirs. She came closer, smiling wickedly with a sway of her hips. *So pleased with herself.*

Well... I'll not be letting this witch conduct any experiments. I'd been beaten into submission and dragged here against my will, now this cleric speaks of me as if I'm diseased. *Better to face the wrath of the storm than whatever torment she has in store.*

The holy symbol hung glinting around her neck, a hand pointing upward, with jagged flames carved around its edge. *I need to be quick... And it needs to be now.* A cold, calculating calm washed over me, and with a single burst of willpower, I jerked my right hand upward, snapping my restraints.

Her green eyes widened and she didn't even manage to let out a scream before I yanked the charm free from her neck. In one smooth motion, I used its serrated edge to slice through the bonds holding my other wrist. The flesh of my palm cleaved open, collateral damage. Blood spattered across the cat woman's face as she rushed me.

As she landed on me, I jabbed the tiny metal hand into the cat woman's ribs. The chair came with us, still bound to my ankles, and the cat woman screamed, looking more animal than before as she hissed, bearing her pearly, dagger-like fangs at me. The tiefling swept his hands through the air, muttering an incantation

"*Silence,*" I held a hand toward him and cast the spell.

His voice ceased and a wave of serenity came over me. I looked toward the human to find her whispering a spell of her own. She was a vision of serenity and hope, a beacon of light in the midst of darkness. And as I beheld her, I couldn't help but feel a sense of awe and reverence, for she was more than a mere mortal. She was a living embodiment of all that was beautiful and pure in this world.

Then I felt the halfling's blade against my eye socket and the illusion dissipated.

"We may not want to kill you just yet, but I'm fairly certain you'll be *almost* as useful without the use of your eyes."

I wanted so badly to call her bluff. I could have flipped her over my shoulder and smashed her skull against the cat's before anyone had a chance to react. Or at least that was what every instinct in my body was screaming for. But no matter how hard I tried, my limbs wouldn't move.

The tiefling had shaken off my silence spell and his whispers seeped into my flesh, caressing every corner of my mind like the sticky silk of a spider's web. The cat woman shoved herself up off of me, pulling out the charm I'd left stuck between her ribs, and letting it clatter to the floor.

The cleric raised her hand, whispering something as a healing aura emanated from the cat woman's wound. The trail of blood slowed as she took a couple of deep breaths. Then the cat woman ran her fingers over the healing cut before glaring at me and reeling back a punch that landed against my cheekbone like a cinder brick.

"Son of a whore." The cat woman snarled. "You won't get another chance like that again."

I gritted my teeth, feeling the warlock's spell beginning to fade, but not before I was returned to the chair. This time, they used enough rope to ensure I wouldn't be moving anytime soon.

"Do you think the library has everything you'll need to start working on your experiments?" The halfling grunted as she pulled a hobble knot tight around my right wrist.

"Most of it should be in the herbarium." The cleric rubbed the back of her neck where the necklace had broken. "The one thing that might be somewhat difficult to track down is a philosopher's stone."

"Any friends that deal with black market enchantments?" The tiefling leaned against one of the bookshelves as the women worked to restrain me. "I could comb through my old list of contacts."

"I know someone I can ask." The halfling shot him a sideways glance. "You and Rivka should try and dig up some new leads on Dradon."

"What about *him*?" The cat woman jerked her head toward me. "We can't just leave him here."

"I can watch him." The cleric—Echo, the halfling had called her—picked up the bloody amulet from the floor.

"You're the reason he almost escaped!" The cat snapped. "He could have killed any one of us if we hadn't worked together to subdue him."

"She can handle herself." The halfling cut her off. "Echo never makes the same mistake twice. Right?"

"That's right." Echo glared daggers at me. "He won't get the jump on me again."

CHAPTER 4

ECHO

Using a holy symbol as a shiv… That was something I never thought I'd see. Dipping my medallion into a basin of water, I rinsed off the thick blood and bits of tissue left behind from Rivka's wound. Upon seeing Rivka and Hyperion injured, I didn't hesitate to heal them both.

Now, I felt the magic well within me running dry. When I channeled my healing spells, I became a conduit of light and vitality. I focused my intention, and a warm, soothing sensation spread through my hands, resonating with the essence of life. It was a gentle hum, a subtle vibration that connected me to the healing energies of the universe.

The once vibrant flow of energy became fainter, more strained as if I was stretching a taut thread to its breaking point. As pitiful as the elf looked—battered, bloody, and strapped to the chair—I needed to be careful and use my magic sparingly. He had to settle for good, old-fashioned, first aid, and honestly, he was lucky I was giving him that after the stunt he'd pulled.

His pale face and hair were spattered with red from when he'd stabbed Rivka. Blood dripped from the deep cut on his left palm that he'd inflicted on himself when he slashed through his restraints. *Odd that the dead can still bleed.*

What was the purpose of all this waiting, anyway? It made sense that there were some people that the gods weren't sure yet what should be done with them. But I'd lived my life according to all the rules. My god had to have known where I belonged, and yet here I was ... *waiting* with everyone else. I imagined that maybe I was like a cluster of fresh vegetables being dipped in a cool river to stay fresh until Azuth was ready to take me home.

Although, maybe I wasn't as kind and good as I believed I'd been if I was willing to let a complete stranger suffer for the sake of finding my friend. Guilt twisted at my stomach as the elf's dark nebulous eyes rose from the floor to meet my gaze.

"I'm going to try to treat your wounds." I tried not to let my hands shake as I came closer, kneeling to inspect the gash on his hand. "It would be in your best interest not to do anything stupid."

"I'm sure you have my best interests at heart." He arched a pointed eyebrow, clenching his fist as more blood gushed between his knuckles.

"I have nothing to gain by harming you." I crossed my arms. "If you prefer for me to let you bleed until you're unconscious, I will, but I'd rather see you walk away from all this in better shape than you walked in."

The elf seemed to study my expression, the thin flat line of his lips not so much as twitching as he narrowed his eyes. Finally, he opened his fingers, exposing the cleaved flesh splayed open from between his thumb and forefinger down to the heel of his hand.

"Damn." I frowned, gently tilting his hand one way and then the other to assess the depth of the laceration. "You almost hit the bone. I'll need to go grab some water and gauze. Don't go anywhere, I'll be right back."

"Wouldn't dream of it," he muttered.

"I can't fault you for trying to escape before." I picked up a lantern and stepped out into the hall, hoping that if I could keep him talking he wouldn't make another foolish escape attempt. "Since you don't know us, I'm sure you felt as though you were fighting for your life. I want you to rest assured, we're not bad people, and I won't let anything ill befall you while you're under my care."

"Your *care*?" He chuckled. "You're delusional. I'm not your patient… I'm a prisoner here."

He was technically correct, but only because he didn't know better.

"Regardless of the semantics," I opened the cupboard, and took some bandages from the bottom of the stack, hoping to avoid dust contamination, "I am going to help you get your memories back."

"I don't need my memories back." His voice was choppy. "I didn't ask for any of this."

"What if you have a family out there waiting for you to come home?" I said, "Maybe you have a wife … or a pet turtle or something."

Opening a drawer, I collected a set of sterile needles and thread for stitching wounds.

He didn't respond, and I wondered if he'd even thought about that possibility before now. I hurried, picking up a few bottles of astringent and minor healing potions. Walking down the long arched corridor always reminded me of being swallowed by a dragon with its baroque wooden beams lining the hall like ribs carved with ornate filigree that prompted the shadows to swirl and shift as I walked past.

"It must be sad to have no memory at all." I rounded the corner, half-surprised to find him still sitting there. "You must sense on some level that there's a void in your life where the people you cared about used to be."

"No." He clenched his jaw. "There's no wife. No damned turtle either."

"Everyone has someone who misses them." I pulled a small round table up and spread out the bandages and a small silver tray for the needles.

"You can't possibly be that naïve." His gravelly voice trailed off.

My heart sank. The truth was, I wasn't that naïve. Before I'd come to the Sunless Crossing, the only people in my life were there because of what I had to offer them.

"I'm not." My voice cracked.

He furrowed his brow and looked at me with a question in his eyes.

"I grew up in a monastery." Uncorking one of the bottles, I poured some antiseptic onto a clean piece of cloth. "I was left there when I was pretty young. Sometimes I think I remember my mother, but I can't be sure if what I'm picturing is real or just something I made up."

He relaxed his hand, turning it over to present the wound. "That why you're a cleric?"

I shrugged.

"This might sting a little." As I pressed the wet cloth to the cut, he didn't wince. Every muscle in his body seemed relaxed as I wiped the blood, disconnected tissue, and debris from the wound. "Becoming a cleric was the only thing that made sense to me. I was curious about Azuth and wanted to learn everything there was to know. The wizards I served were very studious, and I wasn't always the easiest student to teach."

"Didn't like to pay attention?" He smirked, and I felt a flutter against the inside of my ribcage.

"I asked a lot of questions." I smiled as warmth rushed to my face. "I was more interested in discovering things that were obscured from view rather than memorizing bits of information."

"Those sound like the qualities of a great student." He stretched his neck, leaning his head forward to examine his hand. "Maybe you just didn't have good teachers."

I wasn't sure if he'd meant the statement as a compliment, but it warmed my heart nonetheless.

"When I got old enough to go out on my own, I discovered that clerics were in high demand for groups adventuring into dungeons and questing for treasure and glory."

"You joined an adventurer's guild?" He grimaced.

"I did." I wrinkled my nose, pressing my lips together. "I mean, it's not that surprising, is it? What was I supposed to do, follow the Bishop around like a puppy and hope that I'd one day be promoted into the clergy? No thanks. Maybe it's cliché, but I wanted to see the world."

"If it's cliché, there's a reason." He got a far-off look in his black eyes, and for the first time, I got the chance to look deeply into the sparkling lights floating around within. "Why take someone else's word for what's out beyond the horizon when you can go see it for yourself?"

"Exactly." I caressed the edge of his thumb, and his eyes locked back on mine.

His high cheekbones and square jaw looked like they'd been chiseled out of marble. His flowing silver hair fell around his face, and I found myself wondering how soft it might be. I cleared my throat.

"Hale, I'm going to use one of my healing spells on you." I let go of his hand. "But you'd better not make me regret it."

"You don't have to." His brows knitted together.

"I could never expect you to trust or forgive us when we captured you and held you against your will." I rested a hand on his forearm. "But we're not bad people. I promise."

His lips parted slightly as he tilted his head, eyes darting around as he gauged my intentions. Taking a deep breath, I closed my eyes, reaching out for the power gifted to me by Azuth, the god of knowledge and arcane.

Cure Wounds... In the depths of my mind, a pearl of light unfolded like a budding flower greeting the spring. As my lids drifted open, the world around me faded and my focus sharpened, homing in on Hale's injured hand.

The sting of the cut burned into my awareness as I opened a channel between us, allowing a rush of warmth to move from my body into his. Relief radiated and pulsed in gentle waves of light as the ripped flesh knitted back together. Just before the connection severed, I felt a swell of gratitude, despite his reluctance to trust me, and the smile on my lips deepened.

He flexed his fingers, opening his eyes wide and taking a deep breath. Even though he didn't say anything, I sensed that he didn't take this kindness for granted. I may have done this man a terrible disservice by pulling him into all this, but I was determined to give him more than I would take away.

Hopefully, if there was still some kind of karmic scale out there weighing deeds, both good and evil, I could tip the scale in my own favor just a little. And what was more, if I managed to help him, maybe there was still hope for Professor Dradon.

 HYPERION

Admittedly, I should have known when the pale elf started shooting his bow that we were dealing with a ranger, not a sorcerer. *Curses...* Even after the cleric worked her magic, my nerves echoed with the memory of my injuries. It was nothing a nice massage wouldn't fix, but I doubted that was on the menu for the evening.

Trailing along behind Rivka, I watched the graceful sway of her hips until my eyes inevitably found their way to the purple bloodstains on her blue tunic showing through from under her armor.

"Odd, don't you think?" I broke the silence.

"What?" Rivka said flatly.

I walked faster, lowering my voice as I leaned in to speak. "What kind of adventurer knows how to find such a small chink in a soldier's armor? Eve a skilled ranger would have a hard time making a shot like that. And do you really buy his story that he doesn't have any memory of his existence before?"

"I don't buy anything from anyone." She shot me a pointed glance. "Least of all any of *you*. We should have turned him over to the Nyxian Guard."

"Do you still think yourself above all this?" I chuckled. "You do realize that whatever powers you were beholden to in life cannot reach you here."

"I'm beholden only to myself." She glanced behind us. "What's right is still right, even if no one is watching."

"It must be exhausting." I shoved my hands deeper into the pockets of my coat. "Confining yourself to such rigid standards of morality. Is it a family trait or perhaps cultural—"

"It's who I've always been!" She spun to face me. "Soldiers must adhere to a code, or else... or else..."

"Or else, they're just murderers?" I looked up at her. "The law values order and structure. It's easier for those in power to keep control if their murderers follow a set of established rules. But make no mistake, the nobles who held the leash at your throat in life were no more honorable than any common crime lord or street urchin."

"Shut up." She grumbled, turning back to enter the city square.

The glinting obsidian hourglass overlooking the courtyard at the center of the city cast a prism of purple lights across the crowd as the swirling clouds churned overhead. In this part of the city, gnarled spires reached up toward the heavens. The informant that Finn told us to question would be found down an alley past the north side of a seedy pawn broker's shop.

The weather-worn storefront was dingy and decaying with cracked walls and dirty windows displaying a haphazard array of goods that were in the same state of disrepair as the building. A lute missing two strings leaned against a dented breastplate, and a rolled-up carpet, propped diagonally, sat on an overturned bushel.

A faded banner sagged over it all that read, "BUY SELL TRADE," and in tiny letters underneath, "all transactions are final." Entering the alleyway, we found a doorway leading into a rickety spiral staircase. The rusted iron creaked and swayed as we made our way up to the second floor.

"Slow down." I put a hand on Rivka's arm. "Could you at least try to walk quietly?"

"I want to get this over with so I can get out of here." She jerked her arm away but froze as another set of footsteps turned down the alley we'd just come in from.

I mouthed a curse as Rivka leaped silently up into the rafters. Far from agile enough to pull off such a move, I backed as far as I could into the corner, hoping the shadows would conceal me. My heart raced as a soldier with wide shoulders and a bone-white tunic scaled the stairs two at a time, racing past me to reach the door at the top of the stairs.

Glancing up, I could see Rivka's dark silhouette hiding up amongst the rafters as he pounded on the door. Her reflective eyes seemed to glow in the shadows.

"Open up, in the name of the Sovereign!" The guard pounded on the door with his leather-gloved fist.

His uniform was simple and utilitarian, more suited for speed and easy movement than heavy battle. The long sleeves looked soft and breathable, but the high collar was stiff and likely reinforced with some kind of material that would resist stabbing. The edges of his cape were accented with a dark purple and an ornately embroidered emblem of the city was emblazoned in the center.

"Fine." A grunt from inside the office was followed by labored footsteps limping toward the door. "Just keep your breeches on, eh?"

A pot-bellied man with a receding hairline answered the door wearing a robe that hung open revealing his dingy undershorts.

"What the hell have you been doing?" The guard curled his upper lip back. "You said you'd utilize your network to root out the killer, and yet I hear of you spending the Sovereign's goodwill gambling and drinking and whoring... Do you know what's at stake here?"

"I was under the impression that I could spend the Sovereign's goodwill any way I damn well please." The balding man hiccupped, scratching his rump as he yawned.

"Gods..." The guard fanned away the man's breath.

"Besides, I'm the secretary of the Chantry of Endless Acquisition." The man grinned, bouncing on the balls of his feet. "Or in the language of you living overseers in the Nyxian Guard, looking down from your perches upon us poor dead souls ... thieves guild. If you want me to gather intel, I'll need to do so by carrying on with business as usual. Gamblin', drinkin', and whorin' is what I do. If you want someone gathering intel in the temple pews, you should've hired a priest."

"There was another death reported." The guard grabbed the lapel of the secretary's robe. "It's bad enough that so many rumors are circulating in the city. How long do you think we can keep this quiet before we have a full-blown panic on our hands?"

"That's above my pay grade, inspector." The secretary plucked the guard's hand off his collar and patted him on the chest. "But I promise I'll clue you in as soon as I know something."

"What about the halfling and the human cleric?" The guard rested his thumbs on his belt. "Has your network been able to figure out where they're hiding out?"

"Not yet." The secretary dug in his ear and flicked something on the floor. "But it won't be long before we track 'em down. Word is, they figured out they were being watched and hired a couple new arrivals to do their dirty work."

"Great." The guard pinched the bridge of his nose. "So you're saying you blew your cover, and they're in the wind. Remind me again, what in all hells we pay you for?"

"Relax." The secretary clapped a hand on the guard's shoulder. "All we need is to find out who else is trying to track down Dradon, and all roads will lead back to the cleric. Where she goes, the halfling goes. No sweat."

"You'd better get me results." The guard held up a pointer finger. "My patience is running out."

With that the guard tugged up his white leather breeches and stormed down the rusted metal staircase, his cape swirling behind him as he went. The secretary exhaled a sigh along with a curse under his breath, closing the door and locking it behind him. Rivka lowered herself from the rafters and started to head back up the stairs.

"Don't." I grabbed her wrist, and she hissed, scrunching up her lips and showing her teeth. With an apology in my eyes, I let go and explained, "We obviously can't trust that informant not to turn us over to the Nyxian Guard. We need to figure out something else ... and *fast*."

Rivka glanced up toward the door, snorted, and went back down the stairs. As verbal as she was about not trusting any of us, I couldn't help but wonder, with all these double agents lurking about, was *she* really someone who could be trusted? We headed back toward the herbarium in silence.

My wariness of the Nyxian Guard ran deep, and with good reason. They were a force like no other, comprised not only of living individuals but also of gargoyles. What set them apart, however, was their connection to oblivion, a state devoid of any afterlife. Once they died, their existence simply ceased.

This made them incredibly dedicated and, frankly, fierce as shit. Thinking about it—if the guard was made up of souls, resurrecting or animating them became a double-edged sword. You would lose your main force. But not the Nyxian Guard. They remained intact, unyielding, and unwavering in their loyalty.

They were a force to be reckoned with, unafraid of death because it was something they accepted as an eventual certainty. Facing them meant going up against adversaries who knew no fear, who fought with everything they had because they had no afterlife to look forward to. It was a chilling thought but one that I had come to understand all too well in my encounters with them.

CHAPTER 5

The pain in my hand had faded instantly, and despite the fact that I was still caked with dried blood and sweat, I felt better than I had in a long time. It had been ages since anyone had used potent healing magic on me, and the intimacy of the channel opening between us had caught me off guard.

Who was Echo really, and why was it so important for her to help this Dradon character? My mind raced with unanswered questions as I watched her curled up in a cozy sofa chair at the other end of the study. Her knees delicately folded to one side, she held a large tome in her lap, turning the pages gently with her graceful fingertips.

I couldn't tear my eyes away as she settled into the chair. She moved with fluid grace, like a dancer finding her perfect pose. The soft curves of her body seemed to mold perfectly to the contours of the seat, and her long, wavy brown hair cascaded over her shoulder, each strand catching the warmth of the lantern light. As she opened the book, her fingers delicately traced the edge of the first pages.

My gaze traveled, drawn to the contours of her high cheekbones. A small, pointed nose added a touch of playfulness to her otherwise composed demeanor. But it was her lips that caught my attention, their fullness beckoning me with an unspoken invitation. They held a natural allure, shaped in a perfect heart that hinted at a tender warmth beneath.

Her green eyes flickered with intelligence as she lost herself in the words on each page. There was obviously more to her than just some orphan raised by Azuth's Order. Part of her seemed so jaded by what she'd been through, and yet there was another part of her—a seemingly more dominant part—that believed in helping others, even if it meant risking her own freedom to figure out how to do so.

Tiny strands of chestnut brown hair hung across her face as she read. As her eyes danced to and fro across the page, I found myself wishing that I could keep her attention in that way. But I was about to realize what a foolish thought that was. Her lips softly curved up at the edges, and a spark ignited behind her eyes.

"Okay…" She stood up and crossed the room, laying the book open on the desk. "I found a recipe for Elixer of Amnesia. In theory, if I reverse engineer it using ingredients that counter all these memory-altering components, it might undo whatever was done to you."

I chuckled.

"What?" She frowned.

"Look at me." I gestured with the limited mobility of my bound hands. "You think a simple potion did this?"

"We can't be sure that what's going on with your memory is what's causing you to look so… different." She stood a little taller, radiating with a newfound optimism. "This might bring your whole life into focus."

"No, wait!" I called after her as she dashed down the hall toward the herbarium room. "Shit..."

I didn't need my life to come into focus, all I wanted was to be left alone. I tugged at the wrist restraints and started rocking back and forth, thrusting and scooting the chair across the carpet toward the desk. If I could knock over one of the candles, there was a chance I might be able to—

"You horse's ass!" Echo ran back in with an armload of jars and bottles. "I seriously can't turn my back for one second with you, can I?"

"Listen, lady, I don't want your cure, alright?" I rotated my clenched fists, attempting to stretch the rope and loosen it. "My life is fine the way it is."

"Our memories and life experiences make us who we are." She tipped my chair back and it hit the floor with a thud. "You lost something precious, and I'm going to return it to you."

"Enough!" I jerked violently against my restraints. "Let me go!"

Ignoring my screams, she opened several jars, mixing petals and mushroom caps with dried berries, grinding them with a pestle and mortar.

"There's nothing precious about this!" I shook my head. "You have to realize how insane this is."

She curled the tip of her tongue up over her top lip in concentration as she transferred the dry ingredients into a dull gray glass bottle containing a clear liquid. Covering the top with her thumb, she shook it vigorously until the liquid glowed a bright pink.

"There we go." She waved the bottle under her nose and winced. "Oof. It would probably be nicer for you to drink this, but I'm guessing you're just going to spit it out."

"Please, don't do this." My chest heaved with every breath, heart pounding with desperation. "Just let me go."

Taking out a wicked-looking syringe, she dipped the hollow needle into the bottle and drew most of the pink liquid up into the glass cylinder.

"Don't be nervous." She seemed to be telling herself as much as me as she held it up, thumping the air bubbles clinging to the inside of the glass. She pressed her thumb against the plunger, squeezing out a thin stream of glowing pink elixir from the tip of the needle. "This will only sting for a second and then you're going to feel so much..." She crouched next to me, and a sharp pain bit into my neck. "...better."

I stared into her eyes as the muscles in my neck bunched around the cold metal sticking out of my neck. "Don't try to pretend this was about helping me." I swallowed hard. "I'm just a rat in a cage to you."

Her eyes clouded with tears, but her expression remained stoic. The dull ache at the injection site throbbed, burning hotter and hotter, as it spread like fire up the side of my neck. Searing pain surged through my skull, and I screamed. My skin crawled, and my limbs contorted as if they had a mind of their own.

My vision blurred as the room spun around me. Echo just looked on with wide expectant eyes. Was this what she wanted? Did she get some kind of sick entertainment from watching me writhe helplessly against my restraints?

"Make it stop!" Sweat beaded up on my forehead, and on the palms of my hands as my whole body trembled uncontrollably. My jaw clenched shut as foam and bile forced their way up my throat.

This is it... I thought as the room went dark. *This is how I fade from existence.*

"No, no, no... Don't you die on me." A blurred figure loomed over me, untying me and letting my body slide onto the floor. She smelled lovely... like flowers. I felt her turning me onto my side, her cold hand caressing my cheek. "You'll be okay, Hale. Just breathe."

"I can't." The words didn't make a sound and the vision of beauty over me faded into a dark, endless void.

I suppose it had to end sometime, right? The monotony of existing forever with no goal or purpose would have grown tiresome eventually. My body sank limply to the floor as the cords at my wrists and ankles were cut, and something darker than death settled over me like a warm owlbear-skin blanket.

Just as my consciousness began to dissolve, I felt something calling to me. The healing light, far in the distance. She'd opened up the channel between us once more, and I was drawn to it like a moth to a flame. The warmth of her presence was like a string of musical notes, so familiar even though I'd never heard her song before.

When the world finally solidified around me, my lungs forced themselves open, pulling in a rough, ragged breath as my eyes popped open and I sat straight up. Echo screamed, her concentration broken as she fell backward. *This might be my only chance at getting out of here!*

Leaping to my feet, I charged for the nearest window, picking up a stool and swinging it into the glass. It cracked but didn't break.

"Stop!" She ran after me as I stumbled into the hall. "What are you doing?"

"Getting the hell away from you!" I doubled over and vomited something that looked like black tar all over the rug.

I was weak, disoriented... but I couldn't give up. Once the others came back, I'd have no chance of escaping. Finding a staircase leading down, I leaned against the wall, dragging one foot in front of the other, tripping and rolling down the last half of the stairs.

The taste of blood filled my mouth, and I realized my nose was broken. But it didn't matter. I could see the heavy oak door with wrought iron hinges. *That has to lead outside.* Blood sprayed from my mouth and nose when I let out a sharp exhale. I pushed myself up to my hands and knees. My right arm was completely numb, probably dislocated.

Here I was, literally crawling to freedom, nonetheless. I was too close to give up now. Suddenly, I felt a sickening tug deep in the pit of my stomach. *No... This can't happen. Not here! Not now!*

My hellish half-life called to me. It would take me and for hours or days, my sadistic tormentors would inflict searing, mind-shredding pain beyond any man's comprehension. I tried to fight it... Just like I had so many times before. But I already knew it was no use.

My body and mind were consumed by a falling sensation. I had no choice but to submit to my fate. My chance at escape had slipped through my fingers...

FINN

The narrow streets twisted and wound downhill as I followed the inner-city wall toward the old sewage entrance. The alleys were somehow even darker than the streets, for which I was grateful because the last thing I wanted was to be noticed. My good friend and associate, who also worked in the *import and export business,* had gotten wind of a client that stashed a very specific artifact in the catacombs under the city.

I'd navigated the sewers before, along with the vast expanse of the coastal cliffs. That was where I kept my ship harbored, safe and sound. This was all going to pay off eventually. By the time I become a permanent resident here, I'd have a whole retirement plan before getting sorted into my afterlife, whatever that ended up being.

Smuggling is an ugly word, but it boiled down to the fact that we carried items safely between the land of the living and the land of the dead. It was rare that I ventured outside of my profession, but I wasn't inexperienced when it came to retrieving items that weren't exactly *mine* in the strictest sense of the word. Besides, it was unlikely that the one who placed the philosopher's stone down there had procured it by honest means in the first place.

No, this wasn't the time for a moral dilemma. Echo wasn't going to quit until she found out what happened to Dradon and, if it was possible, helped him out of whatever pickle he'd gotten himself into. I only hoped I'd get the chance to tell the grouchy old bastard that I would have preferred to let him figure it out on his own.

Despite his insistence that he only ever did anything for the pure reward of research itself, the man enjoyed the prestige that came with working for the Godless Monarchy. He liked the privileges that it afforded him and the chance to pick his own assistants and apprentices, of whom Echo had been one.

Slipping through the shadows, I'd pause every time it got darker to allow my eyes to adjust. Sometimes I wished I'd been half dwarf for the night-vision alone. *Left, left, right, straight... right, right, left, straight... left, right, left, straight, straight.*

I repeated the directions in my head like a mantra because if there was a map of the catacombs under Nox Valar, I'd never heard of it. *A good cartographer would make a killing if they cornered that market though.*

The wind carried the smell of stagnant water and algae, so I knew I was close. Turning sideways, I slid down the steep concrete to the bottom of the canal. Tepid water pooled around my ankles, and I followed it to where a dark tunnel gaped like the maw of some horrible beast. My pulse rushed in my ears, and I took a few seconds to steady my breathing.

It would be way too easy to get lost down there and even easier to get spooked. I could lose myself to panic if I wasn't careful. If I was going to make it all the way in... and more importantly, *out*... I would need to keep a clear head.

Taking out my flint and steel, I lit my small hand torch and raised it over my head. The rusted tunnel gave way to brick walls as I marched into the depths of what had likely been a watery grave for many of my fellow mortals. My boots squelched, sinking into the muck on the bottom of the tunnel as I waded further in.

I smiled to myself. The other halflings back home would have teased me for wearing boots, but they wouldn't dare walk through this disgusting stuff with their bare feet. Or at least, I would hope they wouldn't. The end of an adventurer is just as likely to be a poisonous berry, a rusty nail, or a broken bottle as a dragon or an ogre.

I reached the first junction where two tunnels crossed over each other. *Left...* I reminded myself and repeated the rest of my mantra.

The air thickened, growing heavier with the scent of mold and decay and the distant sound of dripping water echoed off the walls in a steady rhythm. I couldn't decide if its relentless tapping was soothing or unsettling. A cloud of insects swarmed toward the light of my torch, and dozens of tiny sticky gnats rushed up my nostrils.

Their tiny corpses burned up in the flame of my torch, and I swatted at them, blowing my nose, hoping and praying I didn't swallow too many. The light of my torch illuminated brightly colored words and images that had been painted all over the inside of the tunnel. Some were actually not that bad... most were bordering on the obscene, and many of the words were misspelled.

The cold stone walls seemed to press in, sapping the heat from my bones with every step.

"Echo..." I said to the darkness. "You're going to owe me big time after this one."

The sound of my own voice took away a small bit of the fear creeping up my spine. There was something about being down here all alone that made the tiny hairs on the back of my neck stand up. I rubbed the goosebumps on my arm, trying to stave off the urge to shiver as the air and water got colder, as the incline went deeper into the earth.

The corridors almost felt alive ... breathing and contracting, ready to clench down around me at any moment. The tunnel hissed, rumbling and raspy as the air pressure changed. I pressed my back against the wall, closing my eyes to try and keep my courage. Cold sweat formed on my palms, and I reminded myself that the key was to stay calm.

The shadows of another junction crept in at the edges of the tunnel up ahead. *Another left*, I told myself and pressed on. *Then right, and then straight.*

I'd made it about a third of the way in when I spotted a pressure plate on the ledge I'd been walking on.

Ha... Seriously? I gingerly stepped over it.

"Amateurs," I muttered. "I'd have expected more from—"

A deep rumble shook dust from the ceiling, and the walls on either side of the tunnel started to shift inward. I was trying to convince myself it was my imagination when the flame on my torch wavered. *Nope... This is actually happening.*

I dashed forward at full sprint, my screams echoing as I pushed my legs to pump faster. The murky water sloshed back and forth like a toddler's bathwater as I ran. The walls closed in, moving faster with every passing second. I tripped over the broken stones at my feet, faltering but not falling. I could feel the rush of air as they came together. Throwing myself forward, I dove through the narrow gap, barely clearing the trap as I flopped face-first into the brown water.

The stone walls slammed together with a grinding sound, pausing before slowly sliding apart again, sucking the water back into the shaft. I got to my feet, frantically wiping at my face before realizing I'd dropped my torch.

"Shiiiit." I groaned. *Now I'll have to feel my way through this place.*

The suffocating darkness pressed in as I dragged my fingertips along the rough, slime-covered walls. *Right, right, left...*

It felt like an eternity before I reached the junction where the straight path inclined upward out of the water. I was so grateful that I practically danced my way out of the mud.

Thank gods! I chuckled, spotting a light up ahead. I'd been worried that I'd somehow miscounted the number of junctions or misremembered the directions, but this was as sure a sign as any that I was on the right track.

My smile quickly faded when the hall opened up into a large chamber with a complicated network of pressure plates. I wiped the loose strands of my hair out of my face and let out a heavy sigh. *Of course...*

Eyeing the pressure plates, I followed the tiny spokes, cogs, and gears to where they attached to their mechanisms. They were laid out in a pattern, and if I could just figure out which order to step on them in, each one would disable the previous one's trap before it could go off.

I sat down, rubbing my chin as I went over it and over it in my head. That was when I spotted a lightly etched inscription on the wall amongst the phalluses and curse words.

I reflect on what's right in front of me, but ne'er my own identity. What am I?

"A mirror…" I said out loud. My eyes wandered back over the pressure plates, and I realized the first sequence was… *Right, right, left, middle…*

It was an exact inversion of the directions to the stash chamber. Getting back onto my feet, I took a deep breath and rubbed my hands together. "Just like a game of hopscotch."

I ran through the directions again, but this time exactly opposite, hopping on each corresponding plate. Gears and cogs whirred as the little mechanisms triggered each other, and by some blessed miracle, I made it all the way to the other side. Turning on my heel, I took a bow to the empty room behind me, imagining a crowd of spectators cheering me on.

By this time, my eyes had grown accustomed to the darkness, and I made my way through the last quarter mile of tunnels without incident. As much as I would have liked to think I'd made it through the worst parts of the pirate captain's booby traps, I'd been around long enough to know that there are never less than three.

Well, what's it going to be this time? I cracked my knuckles. *More pressure plates or…*

An ethereal green glow filled the final chamber and a dark, vaguely human-shaped form appeared before me. Drawing my dagger, I took a step back, bending my knees. My nerves prickled as its breath hissed through me, cold and rotten. Remembering that rumbling rasp that had been sending chills up my spine since I'd entered the tunnel, I told myself to trust my instincts in the future.

Its jaw snapped open as it let out an ear-piercing shriek that almost made me drop my knife. The creature lunged forward, swiping its unnaturally long fingers toward my face. I slashed my dagger in wide arcs, carving bits out of its ethereal form.

"Damn wraith!" My dagger was silver, so it was doing some amount of damage, but at this rate, it would take too long, and

I was running out of energy a lot faster than it was. "Why'd it have to be a wraith?"

Tucking and rolling to the right, I thought about how much easier it would be if I knew I could run out into the sunlight. But the Sunless Crossing is, and always has been, notably *sunless*. The wraith screeched, swooping down with claws extended as I leaped over it, swiping my blade through it as I flipped end over end, landing on my backside and then springing back up.

It spun and grasped as I rolled to the left, thrusting my dagger into its incorporeal chest repeatedly. It burst upward then dove back down, clawing blindly like a feral cat. Two claws grazed my cheek, leaving a trail of blackened flesh, so cold that it sizzled. I exhaled a frostbitten breath, pressing my hand against my cheek.

Echo would be able to take care of that for me when I got back... *if* I got back. It had been a bad move to try and go down there alone, and I knew it. I should have brought Rivka and Hyperion. I should have waited until Echo could have come along to watch my back.

I couldn't afford to be careless like that again. Another hit like that, and I'd never get the chance to see daylight again. The thought occurred to me that while I always figured I'd be happy to lay my life down for a friend... this wasn't how I pictured myself dying—cold, wet, and alone, who knows how far under the city where no one would ever know what happened to me.

"Nope... This isn't how I go." I locked eyes with the wraith and it charged in, howling with its dark eye sockets gaping at me.

Blades and claws danced in the shadows. No matter how quick it was, I knew I had to be faster. It raised a lanky arm over its head, and I took the opening. Rushing forward, I dropped to one knee, ducking its grasp as I slid into its bosom. I thrust my blade under its exposed ribcage and into the glowing orb at the center of its chest.

It didn't move at first, then it jerked, trembling with broken disjointed movements as it wailed. Tendrils of green light waved like wild tentacles as the darkness swallowed itself like a collapsing star, sending a shockwave of energy out in every direction. My back hit the hard stone floor, knocking the breath from my lungs.

The silence that followed was deafening. Bruised and exhausted, my entire body ached and sagged under the weight of my wet clothes. Still, I couldn't rest. My ears rang as I sat up and crawled to the walnut-sized stone that had fallen to the floor when the monster disappeared. It had been bound to a sinew necklace for easy transport.

All that for this little thing? I held up the stone to admire my prize. The scarlet-colored gem emanated a flickering glow, like a warm ember in a kitchen stove. In theory, the right person could use this to attain immortality.

That was likely why it was considered one of the rarest and most powerful items in existence.

"Nice…" Tucking it unceremoniously into my pants, I turned to make my way back toward the entrance.

CHAPTER 6

HALE

The scent of pine mingled with wildflowers, and the smoke from my campfire still clung to my cloak. Sunlight filtered through the emerald leaves, dancing on the mossy path before me. I held out my hand, marveling at the rich olive tone of my skin. *Is this a dream?*

The warmth of the dappled sunlight on my hand brought tears to my eyes, and my throat tightened at the memory. The snap of a twig made me whirl around to find a beautiful spotted doe stepping out from a thicket. A spindly fawn came out behind her and they both twitched their ears.

Not knowing how to process the swell of emotions within me, I laughed. It was a childish sound that I wasn't used to hearing in my own voice. The two deer bounded off in the opposite direction. The wind rustled through the leafy canopy overhead, and I put my head back to breathe it all in. The sound of birdsong mingled with a babbling brook in the distance and several squirrels chittered as they leaped from branch to branch.

The world around me was a vivid tapestry of greens and browns, overflowing with a life and vibrance that was alien to me. As I walked, the crunch of twigs and fallen leaves delighted my senses, and I knew I had to hold onto this. I'd been here before.

I knew this place... Somehow, I *remembered*. Thoughts rolled over me like the gentle foaming tide on a sandy beach.

The witch was right.

I had a mortal life.

Maybe ... I even had a family.

My heart sank as the falling sensation took hold and a seeping mental anguish tore the vision of paradise from around me. The forest slowly pulled apart like ripping flesh in the fabric of my mind as darkness clouded my vision and a familiar nightmare took shape. A stagnant, bloody stench filled my nostrils as the world tilted, and I found myself restrained, naked on a cold, grimy surface.

The back of my head ached, and iron shackles dug into my wrist bones as I blinked something gritty from my eyes. My arms being stretched so far over my head made it hard to take a full breath as I craned my neck to try and take in the room around me, but I barely had the strength to lift my head. My parched lips cracked, stinging as I sucked in my first breath.

Flies buzzed, and I realized the crawling of my skin was more than a phantom sensation. The metallic rattle of chains swaying overhead drew my gaze upward to an array of rusted blades caked with dried blood. *Is it mine?* Something told me it was. The moisture in the air gave the darkness a corporeal weight along with the stench of blood, shit, and rotting flesh that saturated my every pore.

"It's getting harder and harder to bring you back, Carcass." A gravelly voice breathed as a haggard face bowed over me. "And expensive... But don't worry, I can afford it."

My torturer grinned, displaying black, decaying teeth. His putrid breath singed my nostrils as I resisted the urge to vomit, rolling my head back and forth. The anticipation was almost as excruciating as the pain ... *almost*.

"Try not to kill him so quickly this time." A familiar male voice said from somewhere behind me. "I need as much blood as possible if I'm going to replicate the loophole."

"Sure, sure, Professor..." Humming a jovial tune, the necromancer thumbed through the selection of knives hanging over me.

He wasn't the scrawny scholarly type. The hulk of a man practically trembled with excitement as he rolled his broad imposing shoulders, gracefully dancing to the sound of his own voice. Veins bulged under his weathered skin, and his muscles flexed and rippled with every motion. His crooked nose bore a long, jagged scar that one would have expected that a man of wealth would have been able to have magically removed, but somehow, I knew he had other priorities.

To this man, I was the center of the universe, and his only joy was found in my misery. *Why is this happening? What did I do that he hates me so much?*

My analytical thoughts shattered in an explosion of panic as he selected a thin blade with a twisted hook on the end. My heart raced, every hair on my body prickling as he brought the knife down, slowly waving it through the air like a magic wand as he began to sing.

"Once she was lovely, that Daisy of mine, once she could dance like the spring." The blade sang as he dragged it over my ribs, too softly to break skin. His baritone voice rumbled with every note. "Clappin' and tappin' her toe in time, ode to the joy she would bring."

"Why?" The word fell from my lips before I realized I'd said it.

"What was that, Carcass?" Saliva glistened on his bottom lip as he pressed the tip of the blade against my side.

I wasn't sure why I'd never bothered to speak to him before. Was it because I knew this was all some hellish nightmare? Or maybe I felt like speaking would give him some kind of victory over me that I'd managed to withhold until now. Regardless, my desperation outweighed my pride, and I had to know.

"Why are you doing this?" My voice crackled up through the bone-dry passage of my throat. "Why me?"

"Because I will it." He curled his lip back. "I. Will. It."

The despair that had sent tremors through my limbs mere moments earlier dissolved into a defiant rage that spread through my belly like flames. Suddenly, the why no longer mattered, and all I wanted was to get it over with.

"If you're going to gut me, then do it." I spat. "At least it'll be less painful than listening to you sing."

A flash of rage flickered behind his eyes before his lips twitched into a grotesque smile.

"We'll get to that, Carcass..."

The sounds of my own screams were deafening as he shoved a dull instrument up under the front of my ribcage.

"Once she was lively, that Daisy of mine. For her, my heart always burns..." The sickening squelch of tearing flesh and the smell of viscera erupted from my torso.

"Missin' a kissin' her lips o' red wine, now Daisy sleeps with the worms."

A small boy holding a tray of smelling salts and minor healing potions approached, periodically administering his aid to make sure I stayed alive and conscious as the torturer worked. There was no bound to the cruelty, no limit to the pain this man wanted to inflict. He'd practiced his craft with passion and skill, forging himself into an artist... and my mutilated body was the canvas for his sadistic masterpiece.

I don't know if it was hours or days. I prayed for death to anyone who would listen. My heart contracted with every agonizing beat as bile rose up in my throat. The boy would run out of potions eventually... Only then would the nightmare be over so that I could return to the *real world*.

 ECHO

My eyes stung as I poured another bottle of cleaning solution onto the black, ink-like substance on the carpet. Scrubbing the pig-bristle brush back and forth, I tried not to inhale the noxious fumes. My mana was depleted completely, and even if it wasn't, I couldn't think of a single cleansing spell that would have worked on this.

Whether I'd meant to or not, I'd killed that man. As a cleric, I'd never used my power to do harm. I'd been out of practice at alchemy and potion making, but in a million years, I never thought it could have gone so wrong. Every time I closed my eyes, I saw Hale choking, vomiting this black watery venom as he fought to reach the door. That was an image that would haunt me for the rest of my days.

Then when his body blinked out of existence... Tears rushed to my eyes at the thought. How can a soul be erased completely? We're taught that energy never truly dies, that it only changes form. I'd always accepted that as a fact, so I'd taken the rumors about soul-eating monsters with a grain of salt.

When our mortal lives end, we come here, and here is where we wait until our souls can be judged and sent to whatever afterlife we belong to. There are some who avoid this, knowing that their destination isn't pleasant, but everyone in existence can normally take solace in the thought that they will always exist *somewhere* ... in one form or another.

Even when the Sovereign surrender themselves to the storm outside the city, their life force becomes part of the Sunless Crossing. But what happens to a soul when it's consumed by another creature? What happened to Hale when I injected him with my experimental antidote and he blinked out of existence?

No corpse crumbling to ash, no flickering lights ... nothing.

It didn't make any sense. None of it. Tears rushed to my eyes, and a knot formed in my throat as I imagined what a horrible way to die that must have been. *I forced him to take that potion... All that suffering was because I thought I could counteract the memory spell on him.*

The sound of the door creaking open downstairs forced me to compose myself. I cleared my throat. Sniffling as I wiped my eyes on the sleeve of my dress, wet footsteps padded up the stairs, and Finn's smiling face appeared from the dark hall.

"Has anyone told you lately that you have the most incredible best friend in the world?" She held up a glowing ruby, and I forced a smile. *Of course, Finn came through. Didn't she always? But now how am I supposed to tell her what I've done?*

"Uh..." She frowned, glancing around the room. "Where's the corpsy-looking elf?"

Time to come clean.

"I... I—" Guilt burst forth as a torrent of tears poured down my face, and I sobbed uncontrollably into my hands.

"Woah, hey..." Finn rushed up, putting her arms around my shoulders. "It'll be okay. What happened? Did he hurt you?"

The shame dug it's claws in, twisting my guts into knots. Of course, Finn's first thought would be for my safety. She'd never have believed that I was the one who'd done something so cruel and reckless.

"I've done something horrible, Finn." My chest jumped with every sob as I cried into her shoulder. "I... I think—"

"Forgive me if I'm interrupting." Hale's voice came from out in the hall as the pale-skinned elf-ranger stepped into the light.

Relief crashed over me like a tidal wave, and before I realized it, I'd rushed halfway across the room, throwing my arms around him like an old friend. His clothes were clean like he'd been reborn into the ashen fields all over again. Letting go of him, I smoothed his shirt down and took a step back, clearing my throat.

Hale looked even more surprised than I was.

"I... I thought I'd killed you." I grasped for words as I blinked back tears. "I guess maybe I did. What happened to you exactly?"

He offered a half-smile that made my heart flutter. "You didn't kill me."

"Your memory is restored then?" I cocked my head, trying to contain the hope in my voice.

His expression fell somber, and he walked over to the chair where he'd been tied up only hours before. Tipping it upright, he brushed away the shreds of rope and sat down.

"I think I got a glimpse of *one* memory." He leaned on the armrest. "Just a glimpse, mind you ... of a forest. I think my afterlife is also trying to pull me in, but I can't go. Not yet."

"I don't think that's how it works." Finn, now visibly more tense than before, shifted her body so that he couldn't see her hand resting on her dagger's handle. "No one gets to decide when or where they go after this."

"You said earlier that our life experiences make us who we are." He arched an eyebrow at Echo. "Maybe my lack of memory is causing me to get pulled into the wrong place."

"Is that even possible?" Finn's brows pinched together as she looked to me for an answer.

"I don't know." I put a trembling hand to my cheek, still overwhelmed. *I didn't kill him... I'm not a murderer.*

"Whether it is, or not," Hale continued, "I'm willing to participate in more of your experiments. But only if it's on my terms. No secrets, no lies... and *no* restraints. Deal?"

Finn and I looked at each other. How could I say no? I was just happy he was alive, let alone that he'd come back and was willing to let me try again.

"It's a deal." I smiled.

"Good." He cracked his neck and stood up. "Shall we get started?"

"You mean *now*?" My eyes widened, and I took a step back. "Hale, you just went through an intensely traumatic experience. You need to get some rest."

"I *need* to figure out who I really am." He crossed the room and stood to face me. "Please, Echo. For the first time that I can remember, I get the sense that maybe I belong somewhere."

Looking up into those deep, soulful eyes, my heart ached for him. When I opened the channel of healing between us, I sensed a hidden sadness, and all I wanted was to take it away. I wasn't exactly eager to repeat my mistake after seeing him die in front of me, but judging from his present demeanor, it seemed that I was more traumatized by the whole thing than he was.

What kind of life had this man led if he was able to shake off something so gruesome like it was nothing?

Hale knew what it was to suffer ... to endure the unimaginable loss of one's sense of self. Now that I'd started down this path with him, I had a responsibility to help make him whole again.

"Alright." I nodded, taking a deep breath to steel my nerves. "There is *one* thing we could try..."

After cleaning up a work area in the lab, I pulled on a pair of gloves and looked through the shelves for the powdered herbs and potions I needed. Hale sat expectantly on the examination table while Finn squinted at a jar that contained a preserved lizard brain that had been smuggled over from the material plain.

"Do lizards have souls?" She tapped on the glass.

"Of course they do." I sprinkled some powdered mica into my miniature cauldron with the ground unicorn horn and basilisk blood. "At least, I think they do."

"Then how come there are no animals here?" She sighed. "Everyone says it's because animals don't have souls."

"I never believed that." I shook my head mixing the ingredients into a paste. "Anyone who's ever had a dog should be able to tell they have souls."

"Maybe animals go straight to whatever heaven is to them," Hale said. "It would hardly be fair for a cow to get killed and eaten in the mortal realm, then wake up in the Sunless Crossing only to be slaughtered and eaten again."

"Gods, that's a grim thought." Finn frowned.

"Exactly." Hale shrugged. "Why should they have to endure our kind more than once? I imagine the gods consider the animals as having paid their dues."

"Straight to the front of the line, then?" Finn smiled. "I actually like that a lot more than the notion that they have no souls."

"Me too." I took a wand and began stirring the mixture. As the tip of the wand illuminated, the heat from it melted the paste into a thinner liquid. I looked up at Hale as I approached the table. "Are you ready for this?"

"Ready as I'll ever be." He smiled, and I felt a swell of butterflies in my stomach. I wasn't sure if I was nervous from being so close to him or if I was just afraid of accidentally killing him again.

"You'll uh … need to take off your shirt." My cheeks grew hot as I glanced away.

Finn made a subdued groaning sound as Hale's eyes danced over my expression. He gave a curt nod and stripped his shirt off over his head. His light gray skin was hairless and completely smooth except for his scars... and there were a lot of them.

I'd always found it interesting how some people came to the afterlife bearing such marks, wounds that had been so deep that they'd somehow become a part of a person's identity. As he lay down on the table, I took the tip of the wand and began etching out the alchemical symbols from the book onto his skin.

"That's cold." Hale stared up at the ceiling.

"Sorry." I met his eyes only for a moment, focusing on keeping my lines as clean as possible.

The energy in the wand built slowly, and I felt the staticky charge in the palm of my hand as the dark brown liquid began to pulse with a golden light. It was time for me to begin the incantation. Whispering the words of binding, I summoned the powers of the universe to find what was lost.

The spirits responded in a gentle throng that hummed in my ears. Closing my eyes, I visualized Hale standing in a dark room, his skin pulsing with that golden glow. His memories would be drawn like a ship to a lighthouse. But it still wasn't strong enough. Wherever his memories had gone, they were too far to be reached from here.

Unless... I could lend him some of my own light.

I imagined Professor Dradon scolding me for opening up my own life force to such a complicated spell when I'd never attempted it before. Still, what choice did I have? Hale was depending on me, and I didn't want to fail him. Not again. Opening the channel between us, I allowed my magic to flow out.

The glow intensified as I concentrated.

"Echo, stop!" Finn's screams broke my concentration, and I opened my eyes. The entire study was shaking, and every lamp and candle was a burning inferno. Finn was holding down Hale's body as it convulsed violently on the table.

"Shit!" I raked my fingers over the crown of my head, grabbing two handfuls of hair. *What do I do?* Black liquid poured from his gaping mouth and from his eyes, nose, and ears. Placing my hands on either side of his face, I tried to cast the only spell I could think of. "Purify... *Purify!*"

His eyes locked onto mine, and he grabbed me by the shoulders. There was a flash of light, and suddenly ... everything went dark.

CHAPTER 7

ECHO

I was supposed to help someone… I couldn't remember why or who, but I knew there was someone counting on me, and I'd failed. Confusion and fear surged through my veins as my eyes strained to perceive anything in the darkness. The cold, hard stones were rough against my naked skin, and I tried to think back on how I got there.

But… there was nothing. My teeth chattered as I shivered uncontrollably trying to piece together my fractured thoughts. My pulse raced in my ears, and the seed of a scream trembled in my throat. *Where are my clothes? Where am I? Who am I?*

Taking a deep breath, I focused on slowing my pounding heart. The damp, musty air stank of blood and filth, and something that I could only assume was a rat squeaked and scurried along the floor.

"Uffh." Someone exhaled a pained breath somewhere in the darkness and my pulse quickened again.

Who else is in here? I cowered against the wall, chest heaving and palms sweating as I clenched my eyes shut. One thought that kept needling me over and over, a powerful compulsion that I was here to help someone… He needed me, and I couldn't simply abandon him to his fate, no matter what horrors lurked in the dark.

Standing up, I felt my way along the wall until I emerged from behind a stack of wooden crates. As my eyes adjusted, I took in the barely perceivable torchlight flooding in through a small, barred window on the cell door, and a man's pale body stretched out on a torture rack in the center of the room.

Hugging myself to cover my exposed breasts, I tiptoed closer, leaning in to see if I recognized him. His handsome face was smeared with dried blood, but I couldn't see any injuries. He groaned again, opening his eyes, and I shrank back.

"Who are you?" he whispered.

There was something familiar about his voice, and the shadow of a memory danced just beyond my reach. Slowly, some fragments of my memory came into focus.

"Echo." My voice shook as I flexed my fingers, trying to force my blood to start circulating. "My name is Echo, but … I can't remember how I got here. Who are you?"

He blinked, staring up at the torture devices hanging over him. "I'm … not sure." He swallowed hard, shaking his head slowly. "I can't remember anything."

"Well, I don't need a memory to know we need to get the hell out of here." I peered tentatively through the barred window on the door to see if there was anyone standing guard out in the hall, but it was empty.

I eyed the various metal utensils hanging over my cellmate. Finding one with a wiry angle that resembled a large fishing hook, I took care unfastening it from its chain. I don't know why our captors had left me unchained, but I hoped to live long enough to make sure they regretted it.

Starting with the shackles at his hands, I jiggled the pointed tool into the keyhole. The chunky iron manacles had practically fused to his flesh, and I wondered how long he'd been trapped in this place. If his complexion was any indication, it had to have been months since he'd seen the sun.

He winced as I removed the manacle from his right wrist.

"Check all the walls." His dark eyes darted around the room as he held out his free hand for the tool I'd used.

I nodded, handing it to him so that he could finish freeing himself while I searched for any cracks or ventilation shafts that might lead to the outside. My fingers were raw by the time I'd worked my way around to the other side. The entire room seemed to be carved out of a single stone block.

Cursing under my breath, I turned back to the elf who was kicking the ankle restraints aside. "There's no way out."

"There's *always* a way out." Mischief glinted in his black eyes, and I felt a rush of excitement as he approached the door to the cell, scanning the hall before curling his fingers around the iron bars. "Can you fit your arm through there?"

"I can try." I reached through the bars, but I couldn't squeeze past my elbow.

Pressing my lips together, I shook my head. He nodded with a soft expression as if to say it was alright before spreading his hands out over the wooden door to examine the cracks at the edges and even the hinges.

"A hammer would be nice," he whispered, heading back toward the torture rack and picking up a bulky knife from the end of one of the chains. "But this'll do."

Turning the blade sideways, he jiggled it under the top edge of the nail holding the hinge in place. A muffled voice echoed from somewhere down the hall, and I stood on my tiptoes to look through the window. My eyes met the elf's, and we shared an unspoken agreement that I'd keep watch while he worked. He grunted, leaning all his weight on the handle as he slid the dowel upward and pulled it free.

"Daisy, my Daisy." The booming voice sang drunkenly, growing louder and louder as my cellmate worked quietly on dismantling the bottom hinge. A gigantic shadow appeared on the floor outside, and I frantically tapped the pail elf on the shoulder.

Metal keys jingled as the singing continued, "Once she was lovely, that Daisy of mine, when she did shine like the sun." The jailor belched. "I've missed you, Carcass! Our last session was too short, don't you think?"

I darted to the side, crouching in the shadows as the elf shoved the dowel halfway back into the top hinge. I glanced at the grimy blades hanging over the torture rack. I wanted a weapon, but I couldn't risk being seen. Holding the knife across his chest, the elf backed against the wall.

With a stoic expression, he waited. A moment later the lock's mechanism clicked, and the door swung inward. The hulking man stumbled inside, weaving as he squinted at the now-empty torture rack.

"What the—" His brow furrowed as he tilted his head.

The elf nodded toward the door, and I began to edge my way toward the exit. The man's eyes widened as he spotted me, roaring obscenities as he called for more guards. Swinging meaty fists like boulders, the man lumbered after me, and I ducked, crawling as fast as I could toward the door.

A massive bearpaw-sized hand closed around my ankle, pulling me backward and causing me to scrape my knee as I tried to roll away. I yelped as my ankle twisted, sending a surge of pain up through my hip. With my free leg, I threw a powerful kick to his groin. He winced, his face contorting in anger, but his grip only tightened.

The elf leaped out from his hiding spot, thrusting his knife into the crook of the man's neck, not one blow but three in quick succession. Warm blood spurted over me, and my stomach churned as I scrambled away. The thunderous roar of the man's screams gurgled as blood flowed from his mouth, and he fell forward.

"We need to go … NOW." The elf yanked the door open, darting out into the hallway, and I followed close behind, our bare feet padding against the cold stone floor as the sound of clanging swords and heavy boots echoed up the corridor.

"They're coming," I breathed.

"This way." He tugged at several locked doors before reaching one that opened to a narrow staircase. I glanced back at the trail of bloody footprints we were leaving. With my heart in my throat, we dashed up the stairs. As we reached the top, my eyes fell upon a small wooden door.

Its weathered surface bore the marks of time and use, hinting at the secrets it held within. Without hesitation, I turned the aged handle, revealing a sparsely furnished room beyond. The worn floorboards creaked under our weight, echoing through the quiet space, and a sense of faded memories lingered in the air. The humble surroundings spoke of humble inhabitants, perhaps servants who had once sought solace in this modest sanctuary.

The pale elf grabbed a chair, wedging it under the door handle and scouring the room for anything we might be able to use. The walls enclosed us in a fortress of hewn stone, their rough surfaces bearing the scars of countless years. A tangible weight settled upon us, an oppressive darkness that seemed to seep through the very stone.

No ray of light dared to penetrate this chamber, for there was no window to offer respite. The absence of natural illumination left us to navigate in the dim glow of a single candle. The poor souls who worked here were probably treated with little more respect than we were.

"What's the last thing you remember?" The elf opened a cupboard and started pulling out the few possessions the room's occupant owned.

"I was just in a battle." I scrubbed my hands down my face. "My party was getting picked off by a tribe of hill giants, and I was healing them. You look familiar, but I don't remember you being there."

In the corner of the room, a rickety, wooden bed stood, its frame worn and weathered from bearing the weight of countless restless nights. The mattress, once soft and inviting, had succumbed to the passage of time, its surface marred by stains and lumps. At the foot of the bed, a small trunk rested, its weathered exterior hinting at the stories it held within. Crossing the room, I knelt down and opened the lid.

Thank the gods... clothes!

Pulling on a tunic and a pair of trousers, I tossed a stack of garments to the elf. The clothing seemed a mismatched fit, clinging a bit too snugly to his lithe frame and hanging loosely on mine, but practicality outweighed style. Swiftly, the elf donned the attire, his nimble fingers adjusting the fit with a few deft tugs.

As he leaned into the hearth, his gaze wandered up the chimney's mysterious depths. His eyes narrowed, scanning the hidden recesses as if deciphering a hidden puzzle. I stood nearby, the anticipation tingling in the air between us.

"Are you strong enough to climb?" he asked.

"I think so?" I folded my arms as he nimbly disappeared up the chimney.

Great... I looked around briefly then went in after him.

Ash and soot fell in my eyes, and I blinked forcefully, bracing a foot on either side of the chimney, as I forced my way up. Tears streamed through the grime on my cheeks, and my eyes burned, every breath choking me as the muffled sound of splintering wood signaled that our pursuers were close behind.

I cringed, imagining that man's wet screams. His black rotten teeth and his bulging, bloodshot eyes.

It was self-defense... I told myself. *And someone could have given him a healing potion moments after we ran.* Still, I couldn't help but wonder, *Who are these people? What could we possibly have done to deserve this?*

The elf grunted overhead, banging against something until beams of moonlight cut through the darkness. He'd broken the chimney crown, and in seconds, his hand reached down to grasp mine. Suddenly, I was weightless as he pulled me up onto the roof. The star-filled sky smiled down on us as I sucked in that first breath of fresh air.

We're free ... for now.

Sprinting along the rooftop, we could hear the chaos unfolding in the courtyard. An arrow hissed past, inches in front of me, and I skidded to a halt, yelping as I dove for cover. The elf looked back, rushing toward me and grabbing me by the hand as he slid down a wide, sloped gable, pulling me with him.

The shingles disappeared out from under me, and suddenly, I was dangling in the open air. Lifting me by the wrist, the elf pulled me close and told me to hold on. Wrapping my arms and legs around him, I clung for dear life as he descended the rain gutter. We crept along the wall, turning back when we heard voices coming from around the corner.

My heart thrummed in my ears, and sweat poured from my forehead, but the elf remained calm and poised, confidently striding as if this castle was his own. His hand found mine again, and he led me into a side door, softly closing it behind us. Heat flushed through my cheeks as he put one arm around my waist.

He held a finger up to his lips, and I watched his expression relax as the soldiers' footsteps passed outside. His black eyes darted around the room at the horse tack and farrier supplies and for the first time, I realized the remarkable ocean of stars shifting within.

I *knew* this man, and while I couldn't be sure how or why, I wanted so badly to remember. Picking up a leather whip, he nodded.

"We must be close to the stables. Come on, we can't stay in one place for too long."

Making our way through a narrow passage, the smell of wet hay and horses filled the air, and the animals whinnied in their stalls. A dusty breeze swept through the open windows as the elf walked along, peering at each one of the horses, before spotting the one he wanted and nodding for me to follow suit.

Through a stone archway, I could see an open field and in the distance, a dark forest. We were so close... In moments we'd be free and beyond the reach of these horrible men. I placed my hand on the latch to open the first stall when the sound of a sword being pulled from its scabbard made me whirl around.

"Stop thief!" A guard pointed his broadsword in our direction as he called over his shoulder, "He's in here! And look, he's got a little friend with him."

Two more guards raced in, taking their places on either side as they drew their swords. The horses stirred, prancing in place, their coats gleaming in the moonlight as the pale elf stepped in front of me. He held up a hand, facing the guards that stood between us and our escape.

"The necromancer is dead." The elf lowered his chin and held out his whip. "We can all walk away. But if you choose to fight, I will think nothing of ending you all."

"Nah. That tattooed freak don't die so easily." The guard in the center scowled, spitting in the packed dirt at his feet. "Plus, even if you did manage to get the drop on him, we can't let a monstrosity like you walk out of here." He exchanged a glance with his comrades. "I think it's time we put him down for the last time. Eh, lads?"

The guards surged forward, their intentions clear. But the elf, a blur of agile grace, reacted with a speed that defied comprehension. With a swift flick of his whip, he ensnared one guard's leg, causing him to lose his balance and crash into the dirt, his face meeting the ground with a resounding thud.

In one seamless motion, the elf seized a pitchfork from a nearby haystack, twirling it skillfully in his hands. In a swift and fluid motion, he impaled another guard through the chest, the sharp prongs piercing through flesh and bone. Without missing a beat, he deftly snatched up the fallen guard's sword as it clattered to the ground.

The fallen guard kicked free of the whip and scrambled to his feet, determination gleaming in his eyes. In the hands of the pale elf, the blade became a mesmerizing blur, moving through the air with effortless grace. Each strike was a symphony of precision, leaving streaks of crimson upon the dusty earth. The two remaining men, their defenses crumbling under the onslaught, succumbed to the swift and deadly dance of the elf's blade. Their bodies joined the fallen guard's, scattered on the ground.

"Hurry." He wiped the blade off on the tunic of one of the fallen men, reaching for the dagger on his belt and tossing it to me. Then, acting like it was just another day at the market, he returned to placing a bridle on a black horse with long slender legs. "There will be more."

Opening all twelve stalls, we chased out all the horses except the two we rode out on. The pale elf hung onto his sword, ready for anyone that might ride out after us, but no one did. We urged our horses forward, their hooves thundering against the ground as we raced through the dense foliage.

Wind whipped through our hair, carrying the thrill of our speed as the horses strained against the exertion, their breaths ragged and labored. With each stride, my thighs screamed in protest, aching from the relentless gallop. Yet, we pushed on, the urgency of our escape propelling us through the forest, until finally, we allowed our horses a moment to catch their breath.

All the while, I watched my strange and ruthless companion. The blood on his gray skin and silver hair looked black against the sparkling moonlight filtering down through the leafy canopy. He hadn't even hesitated. I couldn't fault him for saving our lives, but when he killed all those men, it was like he felt nothing about it at all.

What had happened to my guildmates? A chill of apprehension crept into my mind at the realization that I'd broken this man out of a dungeon, and now I'd be alone with this man … out in the middle of a dark forest … where no one would hear my screams should he decide I was no longer of use.

CHAPTER 8

HALE

My lungs relished the sweet mountain air as we rode at a full gallop through the trees. I couldn't remember the last time I'd been out of those chains... Come to think of it, everything before the torture chamber was a complete blank. This strange woman who freed me seemed familiar though, and for some reason, I trusted her.

The full moon was high, illuminating a clearing as we crossed, slowing our horses to a trot. Riding down into a creek, we walked our horses along in the shallow water, knowing that if anyone was tracking us, they'd have a hell of a time figuring out how far upstream we'd gone. As we ventured deeper into the woods, I stole a glance over my shoulder at the girl.

Her wide eyes darted nervously from tree to tree, her face etched with growing fear. The dim light filtered through the dense foliage, casting eerie shadows that danced across her trembling form. The forest seemed to close in around us, its ancient trees standing tall like silent sentinels, whispering secrets only they could hear.

"Are you alright?" I asked. Her apprehension was palpable, reflected in the way her body tensed, and her breath came in shallow, uneven gasps. The weight of our journey weighed heavily upon her, and I couldn't help but feel a pang of concern for her.

She nodded. "I just keep expecting them to show up behind us."

"I doubt they will." I guided my horse's face to the right and veered off toward the mountains towering in the distance. "But if they do, I won't let anything happen to you."

A moment of silence passed before she continued. "Have you started to remember who you are yet? How you ended up in that place?"

"I remember being tortured..." I drew my brows together in concentration and did my best to conjure a memory. "...being healed, over and over again just to be sliced up and torn apart."

She shuddered but didn't push the line of questioning further.

 ECHO

My empty stomach churned with grief as we ventured further along the treacherous mountain path, a sense of anticipation mingled with the thinning air. *How did I go from fighting hill giants with my party to being in that dungeon?*

The memory of their faces twisted in pain as their bodies were ripped apart, cycled through my thoughts in an endless loop as the rugged landscape stretched before us. Towering peaks shrouded in mist loomed, jagged across the skyline. Suddenly, a piercing screech cut through the silence, languid cries echoing through the valleys and cliffs.

The elf and I exchanged a worried glance. I'd felt floaty ever since I appeared in the dungeon ... sort of disconnected from myself, and I wasn't sure if I could heal my new companion should the need arise. My gaze drifted up to find a shadowy figure perched in a tree. As my eyes adjusted, my breath hitched.

"Hells," the elf whispered, placing his hand on the hilt of his sword. "Mountain harpies."

Another and another seemed to materialize from the darkness. Their sharp, piercing eyes gleamed with cold intelligence. Framing their faces, long, tousled locks of feathers cascaded, mirroring the colors of the mountains.

The creatures were unlike anything I had encountered before—hybrids of women and avian, ethereal beauty coupled with an unmistakable promise of danger. The one nearest to me made a twittering sound in its chest. Its wings were folded at its sides, seemingly ready to take flight at a moment's notice.

Every muscle in my body tensed, but I tried not to show fear. Her chest moved with shallow, hungry breaths, her large sapphire eyes blinking in the starlight. She emanated an air of quiet strength and an aura of mystery, leaving me with a mix of curiosity and caution.

"Maybe if we don't provoke them, they'll let us pass." My words sounded more like a question than a statement. Aden, my party leader ... or my former party leader would have scolded me for being annoyingly optimistic.

"Maybe," the elf said under his breath.

With our senses heightened and weapons at the ready, we pressed forward. We'd only advanced a few steps when the creatures descended. With widened eyes, I beheld their wings, expansive and majestic, unfurling with a grace that defied their predatory nature. My heart raced, and the thought sliced through my denial like a razor. *I don't want to die again.*

*That **is** what happened to me, wasn't it?* My entire party and I died at the hands of those hill giants, and somehow, I was resurrected. It had been my first time dying. Maybe that was why I felt so … strange. Another screech pulled me back to the present moment.

The feathers, a blend of earthy browns, grays, and muted blues, created a mottled pattern that helped them blend seamlessly with the rocky terrain. They spanned wide, casting ominous shadows upon the rugged landscape.

Their massive wingspans cast an eerie shadow upon the rugged terrain around us. Each flap of their wings emitted a soft rustling sound as they moved through the air. Their shrill voices echoed through the valleys, and my horse bolted forward.

"Woah!" Wind whipping through my hair and dagger in hand, determination steeled my nerves. I screamed at the top of my lungs, "I'm going to be so pissed if we just survived all that nonsense to be eaten alive by bird-women!"

The ranger rode up beside me, his eyes focused on the incoming threat as he drew his sword.

"So much for slipping by peacefully," he said over the roar of wind and frenzied hoofbeats.

The harpies darted through the sky, their feathers glistening in the sunlight. I tightened my grip on the reins, my heart pounding in anticipation. As the first harpy swooped toward us, I urged my horse forward, meeting its attack head-on. With swift precision, I lunged with my dagger, aiming for its vulnerable flank.

A sharp sting bit into my flesh as razor-sharp talons grazed my shoulder. Beside me, the ranger swung his sword, slashing at the flurry of wings. His blade sliced through the air with a resolute grace, narrowly missing. The creatures circled us, their haunting cries filling the air as we maneuvered our horses along the rocky path.

With each pass, I struck with my dagger, aiming for their exposed feathers or the delicate joints of their wings. But the harpies were relentless, their talons slashing at my exposed limbs. We fought back with everything we had, our horses weaving and dodging amidst the tumultuous dance of battle. The wind whipped against my face, and the sound of flapping wings created a cacophony of chaos.

Courage... I tried to call upon Azuth, but the light of his presence was faint and distant in the recesses of my mind. My heart sank with a sense of loss as the light faded even further. *I guess I have to rely on my own courage today.*

With a surge of adrenaline, I sensed an opening. I guided my horse closer to the ranger, our movements falling in sync. As a harpy dove toward us, I positioned myself for a joint attack.

"Now!" The elf and I struck simultaneously, our weapons finding their mark in the meaty underside of the nearest monster.

One by one, the harpies faltered, their screeches turning into shrill cries of defeat. Our relentless assault had weakened their resolve. Our horses panted and were covered in sweat as we reigned them in.

The exhilaration of victory mingled with the relief of survival. As we took a moment to catch our breath as the adrenaline of battle faded, leaving us amidst the quiet serenity of the mountain landscape.

"W-We did it." I let out a nervous laugh.

 HALE

"I still can't call on my healing magic." Echo shuddered, touching the puncture mark on her shoulder. "Do you think that tattooed man imprisoned me to heal you because I'm a cleric?"

"I can't say." Spotting a cave in the side of a steep rockface, I dismounted my horse. "But I'm grateful for what you did."

"I didn't really do much." She turned to slide off her horse. "What good is a cleric who can't even cast Cure Wounds?"

"I'd still be strapped to that rack if it wasn't for you. I'm in your debt."

Tying up the horses to face opposite directions, I checked the inside of the cave for any scat or other indications that an animal would be returning by morning. When we were confident that our shelter was clear, we sat across from each other.

"Your eyes..." I tilted my head, homing in on the dark, nebulous orbs. "I've never seen anything like them."

"What do you mean?" She smiled, a slight blush warming her cheeks.

"Th..." I stammered at first, then pressed my lips together and composed myself. "They're like the night sky, completely black with tiny flickering lights like flecks of gold floating in oil."

She frowned. "Your eyes look like that too."

"Hmmm." I took a deep breath and rubbed my chin. "I haven't been near a mirror since... I'm not even sure."

She rubbed her arms, shaking her head as if unwilling to further explore the subject. Standing, she closed the space between us and sat next to me.

"A fire would lead them right to us, wouldn't it?" She shivered, breathing into her hands.

"I'm afraid so." I put my arm around her shoulders. "Don't worry, the sun will be up soon."

"Isn't that messed up?" She snuggled in closer, reaching across my chest as she smiled up at me. "Having to choose between freezing or leading that necromancer to us?"

It struck me as odd, how natural it felt to be close to her. Caressing her cheek, I whispered, "I won't let you freeze."

Despite the warmth she made me feel, the rest of the world seemed dull and gray. My senses were muted, and my fingertips, which normally would have been thrilled at the touch of her soft skin, just felt numb. The only thing that I could assume was that my time in the dungeon had altered my mind and body to such an extent that I was forever changed.

"You don't think the rest of my party is being held back there, do you?" She stared into the fire. "I never would have run off like that if—"

"I've been there for a long time," I said. "They've never brought in anyone else before, and I can't imagine what they wanted with you. But if we find out that they have your friends, I swear to you, we will go back for them. I owe that necro a thousand years of hell for what he did to me."

I'd lost count of how many times I'd woken up in that dungeon with that madman. This was the first time I wasn't alone. What did it mean that our eyes had changed? What was my torturer trying to accomplish? I didn't have the answers. But as the dawn broke and the bright blue sky ignited behind the tree line on the horizon, I dared to think that whomever I was might have a place beside *her*.

 HALE

There's nothing quite like waking up to the screams of a frantic halfling who just watched her best friend blink out of existence for nearly a week and then reappear. When I fully regained my senses, the laboratory faded into focus around me. The examination table lay on its side, and Echo and I had toppled to the floor.

"Her eyes..." The cat exchanged a wide-eyed glance with the tiefling. "Look at her eyes."

"You were gone!" Tears streamed down Finn's round cheeks. "You both disappeared and the three of us have been up to our eyeballs in Dradon's old notes trying to figure out how to bring you back. Say something Echo. Tell me you're okay."

"Should we be concerned that *he's* not tied up?" The tiefling pointed at me.

"No, you leave him alone!" Echo glared at the tiefling before returning her gaze to her friend. "I'm okay, Finn."

Echo put a hand up, signaling for Finn to step back and give her room to breathe. When Echo's eyes met mine, the recognition between us made my stomach drop.

"I think we ... traveled to the mortal plane," Echo said.

That was real? I felt the warmth drain from my face. *How is it possible?*

"You resurrected *yourself*?" Finn's eyes widened. "You didn't say anything about messing with death magic. Echo, this is seriously dangerous."

"That wasn't what I was trying to do." Echo stood up and paced back and forth. "I was trying to bind the missing pieces of Hale's soul to fix his memory, but I think someone in the mortal realm had possession of his earthly remains. I think they were ... resurrecting him ... over and over just to torture him."

"No..." I stood up and stumbled backward. "No, I've been getting sucked into that nightmare over and over ever since I got here. It's some kind of hell dimension or ... or—"

"It wasn't a nightmare." Echo put her hand on my arm. "That was the mortal realm. That would explain why neither of us remembered anything about our time in the Sunless Crossing when we were there. Something must have gone wrong with the necromancer's magic; that's why you can't remember who you are now."

"You mean like when people die too many times?" Finn's mouth fell open, and her brow furrowed. "Is that why you have eyes like him now?"

"I have eyes like..." Echo touched her cheekbone, and her lids fluttered. "I don't know... I have heard that after dying three times in the Sunless Crossing, people start losing one memory at a time. Eventually, they can become wights or specters. But this is something else altogether."

"How many times did they kill him?" Finn shot me a sideways glance.

"I don't know..." Echo frowned. "Hundreds?"

"Probably thousands," I said. "I'm sure as hells not an elf anymore. Not in mind or spirit. So what does that make us?"

The fear in her eyes crushed me, and I had to look away.

"I don't understand how you got pulled into his resurrection." The tiefling picked up the book from the desk and started scanning the page with his yellow eyes, his slitted pupils darting back and forth as he read. "You didn't even use the philosopher's stone.

"I was trying to reunite Hale with the missing pieces of himself." Echo fanned herself, trying to keep calm. "I guess our souls got entangled."

"Kinky..." The tiefling smirked.

Rage welled up in my chest.

"Glad this is all so amusing." I snatched up my shirt and put it on, stalking off up the stairs and out the back door into the greenhouse. I needed to be alone.

The arched ceiling, adorned with an array of vibrant crystals, emitted a gentle, ethereal glow, mimicking the warm embrace of sunlight. The beams of radiance cascaded down, casting an iridescent veil over the sprawling indoor garden that unfolded beneath. Lush foliage flourished in abundance, their verdant leaves reaching toward the shimmering light.

I'd been telling myself that I didn't need to know what or who I was before. I'd been fine living moment to moment, but some part of me wondered if that was just my way of hiding from the truth. What if all there was to remember was pain, death, and loneliness? What if no one mourned my passing?

Echo knocked softly on the open door as she entered, a somber expression on her face.

"Hale?"

"Funny how the Godless Monarchy think they have things all figured out." I chuffed. "Do you think this is what happened to your sorcerer friend?"

"I don't know." She stood beside me. "I don't know what any of this means for Dradon. All I know is that the rules of this realm are changing, and we're in the eye of the storm."

We looked around at the mesmerizing oasis of green, a vibrant sanctuary that offered respite from the somber hues of the outside world. A surge of wonder and appreciation washed over me. The remarkable beauty that thrived within the confines of this place was so unlike the world outside.

"Was it always this complicated?" I hung my head.

A deep gurgling sound drew my gaze down to a rusted metal grate that covered a drain in the floor.

"There are some who don't think resurrection magic should be allowed at all." She let out a weighted sigh. "Now that I've seen how it can be abused... What that necromancer did to you... I don't know. Maybe they're right."

"You know the worst thing about all this?" I shook my head, offering a melancholy smile. "The whole time we were there, I could feel in my body that I didn't belong. I watched the sunrise and breathed free air and none of it felt like it should have. I'm a part of this place now. I don't think I can ever feel like a part of that world again. I'm not even sure there *is* an afterlife for me anymore."

She put her hand on my arm. "We're going to figure this out, Hale. I promise I'll do everything I can—"

Echo jumped as a heavy fist pounded on the front door.

CHAPTER 9

⟨ HALE ⟩

"Open in the name of the Sovereign!" said a voice from outside. "Do not attempt to flee. You're completely surrounded."

All five of us entered the parlor at the same time.

"Maybe we should just surrender." The cat woman huffed. "They're looking for the soul eater, and if we cooperate, they'll see that we have nothing to do with it."

"This place is full of magical contraband." The tiefling shot a suspicious glare at the cat woman. "Did you tip them off and bring this unholy hell down on us?"

"I'm no traitor, you fucking snake!" She grabbed him by the front of his shirt, and he shoved her off.

"Enough!" Echo thrust herself between them. "We don't have time to fight among ourselves. We need to think."

"Are you sure you have the right house?" Finn shouted through the door in the voice of an elderly woman. "I'm fairly certain there's an unlicensed house of ill-repute three blocks down if that's what you're looking for."

"We've reason to believe that you've abducted someone against his will with the intent of illegal experimentation. We are authorized to search the premises."

"The princess?" Finn said in her granny voice. "No princess here I'm afraid. Come back after my nap."

"You have ten seconds to comply." The voice outside grew more insistent.

"They're not buying it, Finn," Echo whispered. "We have to get out of here."

"I'll handle this." I stepped up to the front door and opened it. "Officers, hello. I believe I probably match the description of whoever was supposedly abducted."

The female guard seemed taken aback by my appearance, leaning to one side to look around behind me. "I understand you're a ranger and spend considerable time outside the city."

"That I do." I leaned to the right, drawing her gaze back to my face. "I don't think there are any laws against that, are there?"

"We've been asked to bring you in for questioning regarding a related investigation." The woman snapped her fingers, and one of her associates stepped forward, presenting a scroll. She handed it to me. "You'll be coming with us, and we will still be searching these premises to confiscate any illegal materials."

"Very well." I nodded.

"Hale," Echo breathed, and I held up a hand behind the door.

"Give me a moment to assure my comrades that everything will be alright, and we'll cooperate fully."

"You have one minute." The guard narrowed her eyes.

I smiled.

"Your patience is appreciated." I bowed my head and closed the door as I turned to my companions. "Is there another way out of here?"

"Dradon liked to pretend he was all high and mighty, but this place is filled with priceless banned books!" Echo's eyes were as wide as dinner plates. "Not to mention the scores of ingredients we won't be able to replace."

"Fine." I nodded. "If this is where we make our stand, I'll take out as many—"

"No!" Echo snapped. "I don't want to kill anyone."

"Listen." I took her by the shoulders and looked deep into her eyes. "I realize this is hard, but if you don't want to fight, the best we can hope for is to run with what we can carry, but we need to get out now!"

The door bowed inward as the wood splintered.

We're out of time.

Just as the center plank of the door split open, Finn scooped up the philosopher's stone and the tiefling grabbed the book. Everyone ran in opposite directions.

There was enough evidence of forbidden alchemy in this place to put Echo away for gods only knew how long, and I wasn't about to let that happen. Rushing headlong between two rows of bookshelves I headed back into the herbarium and closed the door, sliding a bookshelf in front of it. Returning to the spot where I'd been standing earlier, I reached down and thrust my fingers into the metal grate covering the drain and lifted with all my might.

"Halt!" A voice came from the other side of the door. "Where do you think you're going?"

The muscles in my arms and neck bulged as I heaved the heavy grate off the drain. As soon as there was enough room, I set it aside and knelt down to look inside. Water rushed below but there was enough room to stand.

"What about Finn and the others?" Echo clapped a hand over her mouth. "What if—"

"We all stand a better chance by scattering." I held a hand out to her. "Finn can take care of herself."

Echo bit her lip and took my hand, allowing me to help her down into the hole. Once she was in, I lowered myself down and then got to work lifting the grate back into place. The sound of breaking glass and hurried boots rolled over the top of us, and I put my hand on Echo's lower back, pulling her just out of the reach of the light, but she planted her feet, looking back expectantly.

"How did we lose *all of them*?" The commanding officer roared.

As the relief registered on her face, Echo finally came along. Together we waded through the frigid, knee-deep water allowing the current to guide us toward the open canal.

Echo and I moved cautiously through the noxious darkness of the sewage tunnel, each step accompanied by a squelching sound and a putrid odor that assaulted our senses. Our footsteps reverberated off the damp, grimy walls, and every sound seemed amplified in the suffocating stillness, making my senses prickle with heightened awareness.

With each stride, my eyes adjusted, taking in the dilapidated brickwork and moss-covered stones. But beyond ten or fifteen paces, the darkness swallowed everything, rendering our surroundings into an abyss of uncertainty. Still, I scanned the shadows, peering into the murky depths for any signs of movement.

Echo curled her hands around the crook of my elbow, and I took solace in the closeness. The dim light played tricks on our vision, casting dancing shadows that seemed to morph into lurking threats at every turn. The slightest drip of water or faint squelching of small shambling mounds set our nerves on edge, as our imaginations conjured imagined dangers lurking just beyond our sight.

An unseen presence pressed down with a stifling force, adding a corporeal weight to the air. The pungent stench of decay and waste clung to our clothes, invading our nostrils with a nauseating intensity. Each breath felt like a struggle against the putrid atmosphere that filled the tunnel.

With every inhalation, the noxious fumes invaded our lungs, causing our eyes to water and our throats to constrict. It felt as though the tunnel seeped with a malevolent energy, as if it were alive, feeding on the decay and excrement that permeated its depths.

The acrid miasma clung to us like a second skin, but it did not extinguish the flame of our purpose. With every breath, we inhaled determination, exhaling resilience. One way or another, we would see the outside world again.

My ears strained, listening intently to the hushed whispers and the rumblings from above. The very silence seemed alive with anticipation, broken only by the soft splashes of our footsteps and the occasional distant drip of water. We came to a fork in the tunnel, both paths leading in the general direction of the city wall.

"I'm not sure which way to go from here."

Echo glanced one way and then the other and then pointed to the right. I wasn't sure if her divine connection granted her an intuition that served as our guiding compass, or if she just picked a direction at random. Her senses seemed attuned to the unseen, perceiving hidden dangers that eluded me.

"Finn genuinely cares about you." I smiled, leading the way.

"She's my best friend." Echo shivered. "We would do anything for each other."

"I ... don't know if I ever had anything like that." My heart sank at the realization. "She's lucky to have someone like you in her life."

"*I'm* the lucky one." Echo managed to smile despite our grim surroundings, and I couldn't help but smile back.

Something about her presence felt like warm sunshine on my skin. Her unwavering belief in the goodness of others was nothing short of awe-inspiring. I found myself drawn to her inner strength, yearning to be a source of support and solace in her life.

Every gesture, every word, every shared moment fueled the fire of affection within me. My heart had found an unexpected sanctuary, and I could only hope that one day I would have the courage to say what I felt. *Perhaps if we make it through this and find Dradon...*

I froze in my tracks. Unease settled in the pit of my stomach, a nagging intuition that we were not alone in the darkness. Suddenly, I noticed a subtle disturbance in the air, a shimmering ripple that caught my attention. My eyes narrowed as I focused on the ethereal threads hanging suspended, like gossamer strands, barely visible in the dim light. Echo's voice trembled as she confirmed what I feared—*Ethereal Weavers.*

RIVKA

The guards' shouts echoed in my ears as they closed in, their heavy footsteps clanking against the polished marble streets. I ascended a rain gutter, hoping to lose them as I leaped from rooftop to rooftop.

The ash-kissed wind caressed my fur with every bound, my muscles coiling and releasing with precision. Bolts from crossbows whizzed past me, and I looked over my shoulder. *Damn gargoyles... I forgot that in this city, many of the guards had wings. My agility was no match for an opponent that could literally fly.*

Their massive wings cast eerie shadows over me as I dropped into a narrow alleyway, where I hoped their wingspan would be rendered useless. I twisted and flipped through the air, kicking off walls and narrowly avoiding their claws as they scrambled after me. No matter how fast I was, the gargoyles matched my every move, their powerful wings propelling them with incredible speed.

A narrow bridge spanning a deep chasm lay ahead, and without hesitation, I sprinted toward it. Adrenaline surged through my veins, and I channeled every ounce of strength into a powerful jump, sailing over the gap yawning below me. Time seemed to stand still while I soared through the air, a mix of fear and exhilaration coursing through my veins.

I landed on the other side, skidding and changing direction as the guards swooped over me.

Lightning flashed overhead, and I ducked behind a brick wall, vanishing into the shadows of Nox Valar, leaving the guards and their winged companions in my wake. My heart still raced, but I took a deep breath. *I made it.*

As a sense of triumph and liberation washed over me, a sudden glint of light caught my attention, and before I could react, a net soared through the air, its silver mesh closing in around me. I thrashed and struggled, each tug and twist pulling out tufts of fur as the guards closed in, triumphant grins etched across their faces. My claws did nothing to free me, snagging on the tight metallic webbing.

My worst fear had been realized. *My gods... How did it come to this?*

I knew... Of course, I knew. I'd fallen in with common criminals, and now, I was about to be treated like one.

CHAPTER 10

ECHO

Hale's daggers sang as he pulled them from their sheaths, and I could tell by how he moved that something bad was about to happen. Heart pounding, I strained to see through the darkness, reading myself for the ambush that was sure to come. I could feel the tension in the air, the hairs on the back of my neck standing on end.

A spider the size of a rabbit descended with a terrifying grace, its form materializing from the inky darkness above. A shiver crawled up my spine as its spiny limbs manifested, a nightmarish vision etched in my mind. Its body, sleek and sinewy, glistened with a silvery-gray hue, reflecting the faint glow of latent light.

Eight spindly legs, covered in fine, prickly hairs, stretched out with uncanny dexterity, and time seemed to slow as it dangled inches from my face. I screamed, cupping a hand over my mouth as I took a step back.

"Stay behind me." Hale swept in with a rogue-like grace, and the spider's multifaceted eyes, like gleaming amethysts, shifted to meet his. The fangs snapped in a sinister display, and the heat of its breath, a pungent mixture of venom and decay, tingled against my skin. The acrid odor wafted into my nostrils, assaulting my senses with a sickening blend of decay and menace.

Hale slashed, missing narrowly as it swayed backward on the dangling web.

The creature gurgled, its fangs glistening with a toxic iridescence, poised to strike.

My heart raced, its rhythmic thrum drowning out all other sounds.

"Courage." My voice should have infused the battle with a slight flicker of renewed hope, but instead, a wave of unease swept over me. Azuth's light was distant, and calling for it in vain left me feeling drained and vulnerable.

The weaver's form blinked forward, wrapping its legs around my forearm. Its chitinous exoskeleton, smooth and yet somehow jagged, exuded an otherworldly coolness. Hale dodged but moved too slowly, and the Ethereal Weaver's fangs met their mark.

Hale screamed and I could hear the burn of the venom in his voice as he staggered.

"No!" I reached out and gripped the back of Hale's neck, digging deep within myself as I said a silent prayer. *Please, Azuth… Hear me, I beg you.* A small wave of healing magic rippled from my chest and out through my arm. Not enough to fully heal him, but better than nothing at all.

Shaking off the fatigue, Hale drew his dagger and bent his knees, coiling for another attack. It was a macabre ballet of danger and dread as the ranger contorted his body, evading another deadly strike. The brush of displaced air, the faint whisper of ethereal silk, and the malevolent glimmer in the spider's eyes lingered.

Hale parried its assault, his blades slashing through the air in a desperate bid to defend us. I called again and again for divine energy to intervene and help us, but the connection felt cold.

There was a loud cracking sound as Hale's blade punched through another bony thorax, and the Ethereal Weaver let out a piercing screech. Hale lunged forward, blades slicing through the air with a swift, calculated precision. His strikes cut deep into the spider's sleek exoskeleton, eliciting a retaliatory cry. In its wounded state, the Ethereal Weaver thrashed, its movements wild and unpredictable.

One of its sharp limbs thrashed and grazed my side along with Hale's, leaving a searing trail of pain in its wake. My breath caught in my throat as the agony surged through my body, momentarily paralyzing me. The impact threw me off balance, my grip on my weapons faltering. The world spun in disorienting chaos, and for a split second, it felt as if time had come to a standstill.

I gritted my teeth, pushing through the pain with a fierce determination. With a surge of willpower, I regained my footing and focused my attention on the injured Ethereal Weaver. I couldn't afford to succumb to weakness now.

As the spider writhed in pain, a newfound awareness whispered to me. The threads of space and time tying the spider to the realm of the Sunless Crossing became barely visible to me. I reached out a hand, conjuring a banishment spell to send it back to the other plane, but sadly, it felt as though Azuth was finished listening to my requests for the time being.

Hale stabbed it again, and its movements became sluggish, its once graceful strides faltering. A deep gash in its iridescent exoskeleton oozed a dark, viscous fluid. The creature's multi-faceted eyes glinted with a mixture of rage and desperation, its ethereal aura flickering with waning strength.

Hale screamed curses, channeling his rage, frustration and pain into precise strikes. Each blow landed with a satisfying impact, weakening the Ethereal Weaver further. It fought back with vicious tenacity until its injuries proved too much to bear.

The once formidable creature faded from the Material Plane, dissipating into the ethereal depths with an air of defeat. Its departure left behind a faint whisper of vanishing energy, and I breathed a sigh of relief.

"It's not over." Hale panted, pressing a hand to a slash on his ribs. "It can come back any second."

"Shit." I hugged myself, tucking my elbows close to my body. "What do we do?"

"Stay close." Moving forward, Hale's gaze oscillated, and I hoped that he could see better than I could.

More Ethereal Weavers flickered into our path, blinking in and out of existence with an ethereal shimmer. My muscles tensed, and I clenched my fists, knowing that I wouldn't be much help without magic, but I was unwilling to go down without a fight. Their strikes came from all directions as if their very existence defied the laws of reality.

With each onslaught, Hale's blades became a blur as he parried and countered, the metallic clash reverberating through the tunnel. The sharp edges of his weapons bit into the air, slicing through the space the Ethereal Weavers occupied for only a fleeting moment.

The spiders' conjured ethereal webs snared our limbs. The strands clung to my skin, but I clawed at the sticky membranes, pulling it free from my arms and then helping Hale so that he could keep fighting.

"We have to run!" I screamed, pulling against the tug and resistance of the ethereal webs. The stench of the spider guts and mildew, filled my nostrils, mingling with the putrid odors of the sewage-laden tunnel.

"I agree. Go!" Hale sliced and slashed at the air around us. The clatter of his blades echoed alongside the Ethereal Weavers' screeches, creating a discordant symphony that reverberated through the cramped space.

"Don't stop, Echo." Hale shoved me forward, and I could sense his footsteps growing weary. "Don't slow down."

"I'm not leaving you!" I spun, casting a flurry of dancing lights from my fingertips, and the spiders hissed, using their pedipalps to cover their faces.

Hale twisted and turned in a desperate bid to break free from the webs gumming up around his legs. Each step became a calculated maneuver, a dance with danger, as the tunnel's darkness seemed to close in around us, the shadows flickering with the unpredictable movements of the Ethereal Weavers.

Their ghostly forms shimmered with an otherworldly radiance. I lunged and dodged, my senses growing hyper-aware of the spiders' plane shifting. Their touch, when it landed, was a cold caress, a chilling invitation to follow them through the mysterious passage through space. Hale's daggers deflected their attacks and retaliated with fierce determination.

Blood spattered on my face as a spiny, serrated leg penetrated Hale's cheek. The grizzly sight gnawed at my focus, but Hale didn't stop carving through their ephemeral forms with a mix of skill and frenzied desperation. Every strike, every parry, became an act of defiance, proof of his indomitable spirit.

There has to be a way... There has to be. I dug deep into the memories of my old lessons. Azuth was a native deity of Realmspace. If I couldn't reach him through my usual tether, perhaps I could draw on the powers of these vermin.

Looking down at a limbless bleeding weaver, I reached down and picked it up by its oozing thorax. Though the life was rapidly fading from its eyes, I could feel its connection to the endless number of universes out there and the malleable space that connected all realms. I channeled my prayer through the spider's life essence.

Azuth... Father of Mages. God of spellcraft and arcane, I implore you to guide me as you've always done. Do not let our journey end here. Please. If your will is for your servants to seek knowledge, I beg you to give me and my companion that chance.

From across a sea of arcane and stars, I sensed the gaze of Azuth turn to me, and a massive wave of healing energy filled me with warmth. A deep booming voice vibrated through my bones from a place existing outside of space and time.

<Echo,> Azuth's protective embrace enveloped me. *<I would never forsake you. Walk in my light, child.>*

Hale's posture straightened as he was healed and reinvigorated. Gratitude filled my soul to the brim as I seamlessly transitioned from healer to warrior. My movements became a graceful dance of divine intervention, striking down the Ethereal Weavers with spells that disrupted their ethereal essence. Back to back, Hale and I fought in tandem, a symphony of coordinated efforts.

The clash of steel against the walls mingled with the sound of my prayers, creating a rhythm that reverberated through the tunnel. Azuth's divine energy shielded us from the spiders' venomous strikes, deflecting their fangs. The ethereal webs that ensnared me seemed to quiver in response to his presence.

With a flick of my wrist, I called upon the sacred power of the arcane, the threads recoiling as if repelled by an unseen force. This created precious moments of respite, allowing us both to maneuver more freely, Hale's blades finding their targets with newfound precision. The combined strength of our wills and abilities kept the Ethereal Weavers at bay.

Radiant beams of divine light seared through the spiders' ethereal forms, forcing them to retreat momentarily. It was in those precious gaps that we capitalized, striking with coordinated ferocity.

Throughout the fray, healing magic continued to mend our wounds, a lifeline that sustained our resilience. Azuth's presence became an anchor, grounding me amidst the chaos. His love gave me the reassurance that he did not abandon me as I'd feared, that our bond transcended the horrors I faced. Exhaustion crept through my limbs, wounds stinging with every movement, but I refused to give in.

Breathless and with hearts pounding, Hale and I knew this was our chance to retreat. The sounds of the spiders' legs clicked on the damp stone floor, and the air grew colder, the stench of decay mingling with the dank humidity. Shadows danced along the walls, distorting our perceptions and making us feel that unseen terrors lurked just beyond our sight. Every turn we took was a gamble.

Their skittering movements grew louder, closing in on us from behind. I could hear the disturbing whisper of their phasing in and out of existence, the very fabric of reality warping with their presence. Panic welled within me, urging me to run faster, to outrun the encroaching horror that threatened to consume us.

As we darted through the winding tunnels, the walls seemed to narrow, closing in on us like a vice. My outstretched fingertips grazed the stone walls as we felt our way through the dark, and claustrophobia clawed at the edges of my mind, threatening to unravel my sanity.

With each twist and turn, the tunnels seemed to stretch on endlessly. Desperation surged through me, urging me to find an escape, to break free from this nightmare. I stole a glance over my shoulder, catching a glimpse of the spiders' ethereal forms, fazing in and out of sight with an unsettling fluidity.

The sight of their grotesque forms, a twisted fusion of otherworldly grace and menace filled me with a primal terror. With every step, my muscles screamed in protest, my breath was ragged and shallow. But giving up was not an option. Finally, a narrow opening far ahead betrayed a faint light from the surface.

"There!" Hale's hand closed around mine, and we sprinted toward freedom, diving through the exit just in time. Innumerable legs writhed, reaching through the opening, but in the light of the stormy sky, they withdrew, retreating back inside their murky lair.

I laughed, collapsing on the flat of my back in utter relief. The purple glow from the cloud cover shrouded Hale in a moonless light, and, despite everything we'd been through, all I could think about was how no one but Finn had ever fought to protect me the way he did.

The Burning Pages

In the hallowed halls of wisdom's might,
A library stood, a beacon of light.
But dark clouds loomed, a storm drawing near,
The Nyxian Guard sought to instill fear.
The shelves, once adorned with knowledge and lore,
Now trembled under the weight of the oppressor's score.
For in their eyes, knowledge was a dangerous seed,
To be controlled, suppressed, and decreed.
With heavy steps, the authorities came,
Their eyes cold, their intentions untamed.
They scoured the aisles, shelves lay bare,
Seizing forbidden words, leaving nothing to spare.
The whispers of wisdom silenced, like a dying ember,
As books were torn asunder, each chapter surrendered.

The pages, once alive with stories and dreams,
Now burned to ash, lost in their schemes.
But within these walls, the spirit remained.
The yearning for knowledge, a flame unchained.
For words have power, no chains can subdue,
Ideas that linger, forever pursued.
From the ashes, a resistance will rise,
As hearts seek truth, with unyielding eyes.
The minds, unbroken, will not be confined,
For the thirst for knowledge can't be denied.
So let the monarchy raid and molest,
But the essence of knowledge can't be repressed.
In the hearts of seekers, the fire ignites,
For truth and wisdom, our people will fight.

-Unknown

Seeing the Nyxian Guard tear through the herbarium would have broken Professor Dradon's heart. So many years... *centuries* of knowledge compiled and curated in a library that would have turned any wizard green with envy—all gone in a single evening, raided because those in power will always feel compelled to prevent others from knowing too much.

Crossing the city was nerve-wracking. Even after procuring a hooded cloak for Hale, we knew now that there was a full-blown manhunt underway, and none of us were safe. Exora's Belfry stood on top of a bridge that spans one of the waterfalls cascading down the side of the mesa. At the tower's apex hung a great iron bell.

The interior of the tower is a place of study for magic users from every walk of life. Denizens of the tower are often the first to see the warning signs of any calamities looming over the Sunless Crossing. But the bell is only ever rung when the very existence of the realm is believed to be in jeopardy.

Thus, the top floor remains vacant most of the time. Perched on the stone floor, arched pillars shielded us from the falling ash, and the golden fields were visible just over the city wall. In the distance, the monolithic statue of Nyxia stood proudly with her back to the ever-raging storm of broken worlds. Beautiful and terrifying in equal measure, just like life, death, and all the uncertainty that comes with them.

"I found us some blankets." Hale put a soft shroud around my shoulders and handed me something wrapped in wax paper. "And food."

"Thank you." I crossed my legs and snuggled into the blanket. "I don't feel much like eating."

"Your friends are going to be alright." His brows knitted together. "Eat. You'll need your strength."

"You realize we technically don't even have to eat in the Sunless Crossing." I smirked, tearing open the paper and pulling out a piece of grilled chicken. "Food and water here is an illusion. Our bodies feel nourished because we believe they're being nourished."

"Well, regardless of how it works, it'll make me feel better to know you ate... even if it's just a little."

For a few minutes, we ate in silence, watching the storm.

"Do you think we left corpses behind?" I licked the wine reduction from my thumb. "When we fell asleep in that cave, did we freeze to death, or did the spell just run its course and send us back here?"

He pressed his lips together and shook his head softly. "I don't know."

Thunder rumbled overhead and light gray ash began to fall heavier.

"When we were there," he continued, "you were the only thing that seemed familiar. You were the only thing that made me feel anything good."

"What happened to you..." I reached out and put my hand on his. "It never should have happened. I couldn't have imagined someone would use resurrection magic for something so horrible. I'm sorry for everything you went through."

He squeezed my hand, a smile barely appearing at the edge of his lips. "It might have been the best moment of my life, falling asleep with you in that cave. It's the only time I could remember feeling ... like this. Up to that point at least."

Hale was a man who obviously had a lifetime of experiences. Men who have faces and bodies like his don't go through life without taking their share of lovers. I wondered if his body would remember such things in the same way he remembered how to fight. That was another matter.

Whomever he was before he was put in that dungeon, he'd been a trained killer, and I wasn't sure how to feel about that. Even knowing all this, sitting together, hand in hand, there was an innocence in the gesture, a vulnerability that I felt honored to behold.

Setting my food aside, I slowly crawled forward, the anticipation building with every inch. His eyes met mine, and a smile tugged at the corners of my lips. It was a silent invitation, a shared understanding that the connection between us meant something profound, and I couldn't bear to let this moment pass us by.

He turned his face, his breath mingling with mine as his nose brushed against my cheek. The soft caress sent a shiver down my spine, igniting a spark of desire within me. I reveled in the warmth radiating from his proximity, the sweet anticipation hanging in the air.

Closing the remaining distance, I brushed my lips against his, a gentle touch that spoke volumes of my longing. The hunger in his eyes mirrored my own, both of us seeking solace and passion in each other's embrace. The warmth of his mouth enveloped mine, a delicate dance of tender affection.

A surge of heat coursed through my body as his hands found my waist, drawing me closer. I melted into his lap, a perfect fit, as a sense of peace washed over me. Our hearts beat in sync, a rhythm that echoed the depth of our connection.

As our kiss deepened, time seemed to stand still. The world around us faded, replaced only by the intensity of our embrace. I reveled in the taste of his lips, the mingling of our breaths, as our passion ignited like wildfire. I pulled at his shirt, untucking it from the top of his trousers, and slid my hands up over the rippling muscles of his torso.

His arms enveloped me, creating a cocoon of desire and tenderness. Down the tender flesh of my neck, his warm caresses stirred a symphony of sensations, each touch sending ripples of pleasure through my body. My skin was ablaze with anticipation as his lips left a trail of feathery kisses along my jaw, igniting trails of fire that danced in their wake.

His hands moved under the silky fabric of my dress, cold palms sliding up my thighs sending a thrill through my body. I could feel him harden through his trousers, and my core ached with need as I gyrated against him.

As ashes rained down from the swirling purple vortex above, the world around us transformed into a surreal dreamscape of desire and magic. Thunder reverberated through the depths of our bones, adding an untamed energy to the air. My hands explored the sinuous landscape of his back, fingers tracing the contours, worshipping the body that had thrown itself in harm's way to keep me safe.

The kiss broke, leaving me breathless and yearning for more. I gazed into his eyes, captivated by the depth of worlds that seemed to float within them. His chest rose and fell with every breath, a steady rhythm that resonated with mine. The flame burning between us seemed fueled by an otherworldly force, an enchantment that defied explanation. Yet, the allure was undeniable, *irresistible*.

His dark eyes searched mine, ravenous ... dangerous as he slid my dress down from my shoulders. The humid air kissed my exposed breasts as his gaze slowly wandered down. Time seemed to suspend, and I found myself lost in the vastness of our connection. The magic that flowed between us was unlike anything I had ever experienced. It whispered promises of passion, companionship, and unspoken understanding. Though uncertain of its origins, I surrendered myself to its intoxicating pull, fully immersed in the magnetic embrace of the flames that consumed us both.

With a hunger that could not be denied, our lips sought each other once more, a magnetic pull that drew us into a passionate dance. The world faded away, leaving only the intoxicating taste and touch of our mouths meeting in a fervent union. He pulled me close again, and his kiss was an inferno that consumed me, igniting every nerve in a blaze of desire within my core. Our lips moved with a desperate intensity, a wordless declaration of our shared longing. Nothing else mattered.

I reached down, unlacing his trousers. Time blurred as we got lost in the depths of our connection. His hands roamed, tracing the curves of my body with a reverence that set my skin ablaze. A symphony of sensations cascaded through me, a harmony of pleasure and longing intertwining in a crescendo of desire. I stroked him, exploring and appreciating his length and girth before guiding him to my entrance.

Every brush of his lips against mine sent sparks of ecstasy shooting through my veins. The soft graze of his tongue was a tantalizing invitation that deepened the intensity of our kiss. Our mouths danced with an insatiable hunger, a dance of souls. I gasped, slowly lowering myself onto him

The world around us faded into oblivion as we surrendered ourselves to the intoxicating passion. His touch, his taste, his very essence became the sole focus of my existence. In that embrace, I felt a completeness, a union of hearts and bodies that defied explanation.

We melded together, a seamless connection beyond the physical realm. Heat radiated between us as our breaths mingled in a soft song of desire that echoed through the chamber.

As I rocked my hips against him, the world spun around us, a whirlwind of sensations and emotions. Our bodies moved in perfect harmony, and the boundaries of time and space faded away. We were alone in our passion, a universe of two souls locked in an intimate embrace. Pleasure undulated through my core, ebbing and flowing until we both reached a climax. Waves of energy pulsed through us, between us, and all around us.

As our lips finally parted, we remained locked in a gaze that held the weight of unspoken words and centuries of unexplored desires. The energy between us flickered, an eternal spark of longing and possibility. With a shared hope that our journey had only just begun.

Pulling the blankets over us, I lay down beside him, and he curled his body around mine. Staring into the storm in the distance, there was nowhere else I would have rather been. No matter what the future held, in that moment I felt safe, and I never wanted to let go of that feeling.

HALE

I wasn't aware of the gaping void in my life until Echo's magic touched it. Beneath the jaded façade was a glimmer of hope, a person who felt the weight of the world on her shoulders because her greatest joy came from helping the people close to her. I'll never know why she decided I was worthy of that.

As her mouth welcomed mine, our tongues danced in a passionate embrace, her lingering touch leaving tangible memories on my skin, the warmest and most tender thing I'd ever felt. The natural scent of her skin and the perfume of her hair intoxicated my senses as I pulled her body against mine. Her hands on my back sent desire surging through my veins as the sounds of our mouths, wet and worshiping each other, echoed off the towering pillars and the arched canopy overhead.

It was perfect... and when it ended, I pulled her close, placing a kiss on the back of her shoulder as I pulled the blanket up to bundle her against me. Her breaths grew steady and deep as the thick veil of her lashes drifted downward, blinking more and more slowly as she drifted off. Even though I knew it couldn't last, I wished I could hold her there forever.

Sleep was harder to find now that I had a past and dared to hope for a future. But sleep did eventually find me, but the world I woke to ... wasn't the one I expected.

I recalled the moment that tattooed bastard lunged for the girl. The rage that welled up inside me was cold and exquisite, and the violence I enacted came as naturally to me as breathing. For as long as I could remember, all I knew was pain and darkness and the smell of rancid blood. But as I floated toward consciousness, I dreamed of something else. I dreamed of Echo.

I dreamed we were lying together at the top of a bell tower, soaking in the ambiance of an infinite swirling purple storm. Like bodies floating in a river, old memories began to surface, blurred and distorted at first, but as I let them in, they became clearer. Images of people who had died at my hands, not all of them violent men like the tattooed torturer.

I could feel the weight of my actions, the heavy burden of a life stained with bloodshed and merciless killings. Each life I had taken, all in the pursuit of coin, flashed before my eyes with a chilling clarity. There was no hesitation, no remorse as I ruthlessly carried out my tasks. The faces of my victims, diverse in age, status, and gender, merged into a haunting nightmare of forgotten souls. It was the damning consequence of my accursed profession, a path that ultimately led me to the clutches of the necromancer.

The sadistic madman loomed at the edge of my thoughts, cloaked in darkness. He held sway over the land with an iron grip when I entered his castle with every intention of taking his life, but in the end, it was he who would take mine. Not once, but thousands of times. In that pitch-black chamber beneath his castle, he eviscerated my body and soul until there was nothing left of me, but this ... shadow of the elf I was.

I wouldn't have grieved my own demise, even if I could have. The killer who died in that dungeon didn't deserve any pity, and I can't imagine anyone missed him after he was gone. The thought that was most upsetting, the one that turned my stomach and filled me with dread, was whether or not there was still any part of him left in *me*.

Was my soul so irredeemable that an afterlife was forever beyond my reach, and was there no peace to be had? The gaps began to fill themselves in. The Ashen Fields. Nox Valar ... and the search for the sorcerer, Surrak Dradon. A pit formed in my stomach as I wondered if Echo would be able to see me in the same way if she knew the monster I really was.

Of course, she wouldn't. How could she? It was the polar opposite of everything she stood for. As the cold mountain air rushed into my lungs, I realized that Echo was no longer next to me, but I could hear something moving.

The blinding light of dawn reflected off the crisp, white layer of snow that covered the ground outside. Shielding my eyes, I blinked and sat up, registering that my side was soaked in dark, congealed blood. No... I'm dreaming. This has to be—

My eyes adjusted to the light, following the burgundy-smeared snow toward the trees, a massive owlbear sank its beak into Echo's limp body. I gasped, my stomach flipping as the beast crunched into her ribcage sending a spatter of red in every direction.

"Gods, no..." The breath stole from my chest at the sight. Coils of intestines spilled out and yellow bones jutted out against the frosted backdrop of the frozen mountain landscape.

Echo's once beautiful face was now a slack, grotesque mask of flesh partially hanging from her skull. Grief unlike anything I'd ever known crashed over me like a rockslide, and I wonder to this day if that was my greatest sin.

Not the lives that I'd taken but the pain inflicted on grieving friends and families left to live with the crushing sense of loss. I was on my feet before I even realized what was happening. Crouching, I charged, sword in hand, as the massive animal barreled toward me. Its blood-stained beak snapped, claws swiping at the air to defend its meal.

With a swift sidestep, I felt the gust of wind as its paw barely missed me. I lunged forward, my sword slicing through the air in a diagonal slash across the creature's flank. It connected, cutting across the owlbear's thick fur, drawing a spatter of fresh red to paint the snow.

The beast roared, whipping around and snapping at me. I barely managed to evade the attack, my body contorting in a nimble backflip to avoid its deadly reach. I landed with a thud, my bare feet sinking into the snow.

Its yellow eyes fixed on me, beak open and tongue panting as it sniffed the air. We circled each other, the frost-bitten wind tearing at my skin as I moved between Echo's body and the hungry animal that had unwittingly taken her away from me.

Something crunched, like the sound of a horse biting into a carrot, and the owlbear's eyes shifted to something behind me. Its throat flashed with each breath, and it tilted its head with what I can only describe as a bewildered expression on its stupid face.

My rage turned cold as I slowly turned to look over my shoulder. Echo's corpse was *moving*. Twitching and convulsing like something out of a nightmare. I didn't mean to lower my sword, but suddenly, the owlbear no longer held my attention. Sick, wet sounds made bile rise in my throat as bones snapped into place and flesh knitted itself back together.

Though her tunic was shredded and stained with blood, the milky skin showing from beneath was flawless and unmarked. Her eyes had rolled forward, and she sat up, sucking in a wet gasping breath. I held up my sword toward her, unsure of the particular flavor of undead she might have become.

"Fuuuuuck!" she screamed, coughing violently as she slouched forward, crossing her arms across her chest.

Zombies don't generally speak ... let alone swear. I breathed a sigh of relief before another thought ripped my focus back to the current threat. *Owlbear!*

I launched myself forward, my sword aimed at the owlbear's exposed side. The blade met its mark, cutting through fur and muscle. The bear screeched, limping backward, before turning to run into the woods.

"Hill giants." Echo's eyes filled with tears. "So many hill giants. Wh-Where am I?"

"You're safe." I rushed to her side, stripping off my shirt and putting it on over her torn garment. "Do you remember me?"

With heavy panicked breaths, her black eyes darted around as she examined my features.

"Yes," she finally said. "I... I do remember you."

"Echo." I took her hand and kissed the warm tender palm. "I thought you were..."

No... I couldn't say it. *You were dead.*

I'd seen enough death to know the difference between devastating injuries and an hours-old corpse. Now that I had time to think about it, her coloring looked as though she had passed sometime in the night and the owlbear was just scavenging for an easy meal. *How then ... was she sitting up, talking to me?*

"We need to get you out of the cold." She put a hand on my bare chest, and I chuckled.

"I think I'll be alright. But maybe we should make camp somewhere else."

CHAPTER 11

RIVKA

Unforgiving shackles kept my fists at my sides, fastened to anchors on the stone bench. The whole place radiated cold that penetrated clothing, fur, and skin, but I forced my muscles to relax… I couldn't let them see me shiver.

"We've been kind until now, Rivka Stonewell." The guard's ragged voice assaulted my ears. A second guard stood silently beside the door. "Where is Surrak Dradon?"

"I don't know." I kept my eyes firmly fixed on the floor at my feet.

"Are you sure about that?" The human guard sat on a wooden stool and placed the lantern on the floor. It cast his shadow across the grimy wall of the cell. "In his notes, he mentions that odd-looking associate of yours. The elf with creepy eyes. What's his name?"

I shrugged. "The elf and I haven't been formally introduced."

"Now, you're toying with me." He grinned, exposing surprisingly white teeth. "I heard things ended badly between the professor and his old apprentice. Is she trying to continue his research outside the sanctions of the Requiem?"

His questions came like sharp arrows, aiming to extract information about Dradon's whereabouts, Hale's involvement, and Echo's research. I remained silent, my feline eyes narrowed with defiance, refusing to give them the satisfaction of an answer.

"Something tells me these friends of yours don't deserve such loyalty." The guard removed a knife from his boot and plucked a piece of fruit from inside a small leather sack on his belt. "Are they out there fretting about you, do you think?" He cut into the tender flesh of the fruit and put the chunk into his mouth. "Looked like it was pretty much every being for themselves when we busted in."

"She's a soldier," the second guard whispered to the one seated, his menacing voice tinged with aggression. "You're not going to get anything out of her without breaking some skin."

"Hmmm." My interrogator nodded. "Think their secrets are worth losing a few fingers, pet? Hope they're paying you well enough."

Doubt flickered in my mind, but my heart pounded with the defiance of a war drum.

"If you're planning to carve me up, then get started," I snarled. "But I don't know where the Professor is, and the people who hired me to find him are even dumber than you are. You've already given me more information than I've given you, so *by all means* ... continue."

Dripping water sounded through the chamber, a constant reminder of the weight of the situation. My fur bristled slightly against the touch of the cold stone, and the flickering flame within the lantern wavered.

The guards exchanged glances, a mix of frustration and unease evident in their eyes.

"Let's see how long that smug attitude lasts when we bring in the warden." The big man picked up his lantern, and the two of them left me alone in the dark.

 ECHO

"Dinner!" The pale elf's voice made me jump as he emerged from between two trees carrying a dead rabbit. "I wasn't going to light a fire, but if we're to outrun the necromancer, we'll need more than nuts and berries in our bellies."

"I *am* hungry." I looked around and started gathering dry sticks from under the cover of the conifer trees. "I'll get wood and start the fire if you want to finish butchering the rabbit."

"It's already gutted." He shook his head. "The fire will burn off the hair, and the skin makes for a crispy texture on the outside."

"I'll take your word for it." The thought of eating something with the skin still on sounded disgusting, but my stomach was beyond empty, and I was in no position to be picky.

As I gathered twigs, leaves, and dry moss, carefully arranging them in a small mound at the center of the fire pit the elf had dug out with a flat stone. Picking up a brittle gray stone, I handed it to the elf. He struck it against the flat side of his knife a few times and sparks ignited the tinder. Flames flickered to life, casting a warm glow over our faces.

The fire crackled and popped, offering both warmth and a means to transform my companion's hard-earned catch into sustenance. The elf meticulously carved thin sticks from beneath a nearby tree that served as impromptu skewers to hold the rabbit pieces as they cooked over the fire.

Apparently, this man's skill with a blade went beyond fighting and killing. His movements were precise. With a steady hand, he dismantled the rabbit, impaling various pieces onto the skewers, and positioned them over the fire.

I wrinkled my nose as the stench of burnt hair and smoke wafted into my face. As we waited for the meat to cook, I studied the elf's expression. His dark eyes glanced up at me, and he smiled.

"I'm sorry, I don't mean to stare." I returned my gaze to the flames. "I'm just trying to figure out how we know each other."

"I couldn't say." He shook his head, shrugging as he turned the skewer over slowly. "Yours is the first... the only friendly face I can remember."

I frowned, biting my lip. "I can't even imagine what that must be like."

The fire's warmth and the crackling symphony served as a backdrop to our quiet conversation. We revisited the previous day's events, our voices mingling with the whisper of the wind through the trees. Finally, the skin began to brown, the sight growing more mouthwatering with each passing moment.

"That looks done." He carefully removed the skewers from the fire, the rabbit cooked to perfection—juicy and tender beneath the crust of blackened skin.

I could barely contain my excitement as I lightly touched the freshly cooked morsel with my fingers. As soon as it was cool enough, I eagerly raised it to my lips, my mouth watering with anticipation, I could almost taste the flavorful succulence that awaited me. With a small, satisfied smile, I took a bite, fully expecting a burst of deliciousness to flood my taste buds.

But the moment my teeth sank into the meat, the flavor that greeted my tongue was the unmistakable taste of rot, a foul bitterness that coated my entire mouth. My face contorted into a grimace, the excitement and hunger that had filled me only moments ago vanishing in an instant.

"Oh gods, that's foul." I spat out the spoiled meat, but the taste lingered. "I think that thing must have been diseased."

"No." The elf frowned, setting his aside. "The berries I found taste exactly the same. Here…"

He took a few dark indigo berries out of his pocket. I recognized them, perfectly ripened and juicy, but he was right. The moment they touched my tongue, my stomach turned, and the taste and smell of advanced decay overwhelmed my senses.

"I think it has something to do with what we are." He looked down at his hands. "I don't think we belong here."

"What are you talking about?" I shifted my weight, leaning away from him. "What do you mean what we are?"

"My skin… I don't think this is normal." He raised his gaze to meet mine. "And your eyes…"

My stomach clenched.

"*My* eyes?" My fingers instinctively raised to touch my cheekbone. "What's wrong with my eyes?"

He tensed, shifting uncomfortably. "I … assumed you knew."

"I don't exactly have a mirror!" I fanned myself, unsure if the burning in my eyes was just because tears were welling up or if it was something else. "Tell me what you're seeing."

"It's okay." He took my hand. "It's nothing bad."

I slowed my breathing, forcing myself to calm down as I squeezed his hand. "Just do your best to describe them. I won't get upset, I promise."

He took his time, gathering his thoughts before he spoke.

"They're incredibly dark…" he said, "Black as the deepest part of the ocean. And there are lights that move around like little flecks of gold in a bottle of oil. Th-They're beautiful."

He could have been describing his own eyes. That was the moment when I realized that whatever happened to him was also happening to me. My lower lip trembled as the tears brimming on my lower lashes finally spilled down my cheeks.

"They used to be green." My voice cracked as I tried to hold myself together.

The elf's forehead creased with sympathy as he put his arms around me, pulling me close. Maybe it was because I was so scared and disoriented. As much as it should have unnerved me for a man I barely knew to touch me with such familiarity, it didn't. In fact, I welcomed it as the sinking feeling of exhaustion overpowered my senses.

 ECHO

But the moment I surrendered to the sweet embrace of sleep, I woke up in the belfry. At first, I was alone, but just as I started to panic, Hale appeared beside me.

"It happened again." I blinked.

"I only remember it happening once." He grinned. "But I wouldn't mind another round."

"Hale!" I slapped him on the bare shoulder. "When we sleep here, we wake up there. And when we sleep there."

"I'm pretty sure we die." His brow furrowed.

"No, we're—"

"Echo, I saw you dead." He put his hands on my shoulders. "That owlbear had eaten half of you when I woke up and saw— gods, it was horrible."

"Interesting..." I bit my lip, drumming my fingers on my chin. "So, maybe our souls leave our bodies. So there, we look like we're dead, but the moment we wake up—"

"We heal." Realization dawned on his face. "I think that was part of the magic the necromancer was trying to work on me. I remember him talking to someone else in the room. Something about experiments nearly finding a breakthrough. And ... someone was running out of time."

"You're remembering more." I raised my eyebrows. "That's incredible. What else?"

He ran a hand through his white hair and shook his head. "It's all in pieces. But when I was there, it was like … I was starting to remember you."

"Because we met in the dungeon there?"

"No, I mean, I was getting glimpses of you *here*." His expression was almost worried. "Of our time together in the Sunless Crossing."

That struck a nerve. My thoughts raced as I tried to wrap my head around what he was saying. It wasn't possible. People don't get to keep their memories when they get resurrected back to the material plane. That was one side-effect that Dradon tried and failed to work around for years.

"Wait…" I stood up and paced. "It can't be a coincidence, can it?"

"What?"

"One of the Professor's most bitter failures was in regard to retaining memories after resurrection."

"What does that mean?"

"I don't know yet." I scrubbed my hands down my face. "If someone is holding him captive and trying to use the Godless Monarchy's research so that they can go back and forth without losing memories…"

"To what end?" Hale put his shirt back on.

"We have more questions than answers, right now." I chewed absently on my thumbnail. "First, let's find Finn, Rivka, and Hyperion. Then we can figure out who is behind this and why. In the meantime…" I pulled one of Hale's daggers from his belt.

"Hey, what are you—"

"Sending myself a message." I curled my tongue as I carved words into my forearm. *His … name … is … Hale.* Beneath the words, I carved a symbol that I'd used as my signature since I was a child in the temple of Azuth. "If it's still there when I wake up on the other side, we'll know we can use this as a way to make ourselves remember things."

"And if not... you'll just have my name scarred into your skin for all eternity." He pressed his lips together in a flat line.

"Calm down." I rolled my eyes. "There are healers that specialize in treating scars. Now, let's go. We need to get out of the city."

In the midst of our scattered paths, the urgency to regroup weighed heavily. We knew that finding sanctuary within the confines of Nox Valar was an impossible task. The Nyxian Guard prowled the streets with ruthless determination, hot on our heels.

We moved in silence through the perpetual darkness of Nox Valar, our footsteps absorbed by the cobblestones. The absence of celestial bodies denied us the comforting glow of the moon, plunging the city into an eternal abyss. Yet even without the guiding light, I sensed the approaching guards, their heavy boots stood out from the rest of the bustling crowd. Hale's hand motioned for me to follow as he led us into a narrow alley, our bodies pressed against the cold stone walls, concealed in the shadows.

We held our breath as the guards passed by the alley entrance, their gazes fixated ahead, oblivious to our presence. The veil of darkness offered us a fleeting respite as I felt Hale's warm breath caress my cheek. Even this soon after enjoying him, being this close made my chest flutter.

A soft smile on his lips made it feel like he was reading my mind. Heat radiated between us, and my mouth watered, longing to kiss those lips. The danger passed, and we lingered for a moment longer than we needed to. Emerging from the safety of the alley, we hurriedly crossed the square, evading the treacherous pools of light cast by flickering lanterns. But our movements did not escape notice, for one of the guards snapped her fingers, signaling to the others to follow us.

"Go!" I whispered.

Adrenaline surged through my veins as we sprinted through winding streets and narrow passageways. Guards shouted orders for us to stop as we maneuvered through obstacles. Panic welled up at the sight of a stone wall, but Hale guided me to step on his thigh and jump for the ledge. I pulled myself up with grace that defied my previous strength.

We rushed into an indoor market pushing through the crowd and causing barrels to topple.

My heart raced as we darted past vendors peddling their wares, their eyes flicking up in surprise as we dashed by in a blur. The guards were hot on our heels, their shouts echoing through the enclosed space of the market. A crate of fruit lay scattered on the ground, and I stumbled, Hale's strong arms catching me before I fell.

"Keep moving," he growled, pulling me up and propelling us forward. His hand was warm and strong around my own, his grip never faltering, even as we weaved through the maze of stalls and tables.

Fear and adrenaline coursed through me as we raced toward the market's exit, our breaths coming in ragged gasps. I could hear the guards getting closer, their heavy footsteps thundering in my ears.

Just as we reached the door, a hand shot out and grabbed my wrist, wrenching me backward. I screamed, but Hale spun around and delivered a powerful punch to the elven guard's face.

My would-be captor stumbled back, and we darted through the exit. Just when we tasted the freedom of open air, a mesh, metal net encumbered us, and we fell together on the hard cobblestone.

"Shit..." Hale struggled, trying to rip the net off of us, but it was heavy, and the tiny barbs dug into our skin.

I called to Azuth, but I couldn't feel him. Without the Ethereal Weavers, it was as if our connection was once again severed.

Just then, an instinct stirred within me, something that felt dark and forbidden. A call from a new power that I'd dare not acknowledge. The guards descended on us, and Hale's eyes met mine as we fought to keep the silver chain blanket from touching our faces.

"Wake up," I said to Hale.

"What?" His brow creased with confusion.

"Remember where we are on the mortal plane." I locked eyes with him, and he searched my expression. "We need. To wake. Up."

Understanding flickered in his eyes, and he nodded. Despite the laws of nature clearly stating that mortal beings weren't meant to travel freely between the realms of the living and the dead, the mortal realm beckoned, and we knew if we didn't answer the call, our quest would end then and there, on the ground outside the back exit of a flea market.

Hale and I closed our eyes and allowed the void to sweep us away. I focused on the sensation of falling, of being ripped from the Sunless Crossing as we plummeted through eternity.

<Echo...> Azuth's voice rumbled like thunder. <What have you done?>

My heart sank, heavy with guilt as I realized that by embracing this dark ability, I was forsaking my faith.

"What choice did I have?" My voice cracked, swallowed up by the emptiness. "I couldn't find you. I couldn't get you to answer me ... Azuth?"

An eerie silence surrounded us, and I sensed a subtle shift in the air that signaled a change in our surroundings.

As we opened our eyes, we found ourselves in the winter woods of those mountains, lying next to the dying embers of our campfire.

Immediately, my memories of Nox Valar began to fade, like the details of a dream that seemed so important, but then suddenly ... they were *gone*.

CHAPTER 12

~ RIVKA ~

I don't know how long I was held in that cell. It could have been days, but it was hard to tell. Periodically, they would come in and question me. But their threats of torture seemed mostly empty since the worst they subjected me to was a stiff beating punctuated periodically by buckets of cold water splashed into my face.

Ultimately, I never had the privilege of meeting the warden. After what seemed like ages, a couple of the guards roughed me up a bit and then tossed me out onto my backside like a common thief. It should have felt like a victory, but despite my fingers all remaining intact, those fools had wasted my valuable time.

I needed to find Nev, and Finn was still my best chance at doing that. More humiliated than physically injured, I headed out to scour the city for any trace of my business associates. After losing the three guards they sent to tail me, I circled around and started returning the favor.

Watching the movements of the Nyxian Guards throughout the city, I had an entire spy network at my fingertips. When they started signaling each other and moving with purpose, I knew it was time to stay close on their heels. Keeping to the shadows, I saw Hale and Echo.

They were moving quickly through the square, hand in hand with a dozen guards closing in on them. As they darted into the indoor market, I rushed along the rooftops toward the backside of the building. If they didn't escape, I would need to make a choice … either drop in and help them or allow to be taken the way they had done to me.

As they burst through the back door, three guards deployed a silver net, not unlike the one they'd used to capture me.

Shit… I thought, placing my hand on the hilt of my sword. Like it or not, we were all in this together. As tenuous as our alliance might have been I didn't have it in me to abandon them. Keeping to the shadows, I prepared to drop down and take the guards by surprise, but the silver mesh net fell flat to the cobblestones. The guards picked it up, exchanging confused glances.

What in all hells? I blinked, backing away from the edge of the roof. I had overheard them talking about the "accidental" resurrection. But no one was lucky enough to accidentally resurrect themselves to evade capture by the Nyxian Guard.

I had a great many questions and a strong suspicion that my new associates weren't being forthcoming. What I needed to do was find the halfling, ply her with alcohol, and find out what the hell was going on.

ECHO

His name is Hale. I gently wiped the blood weeping from the fresh cuts that formed the words carved into my arm. Just beneath the wound was my arcane signature symbol. Something that no one would know unless I told them.

"Hale?" I said.

The pale elf rolled over and looked at me. "What did you call me?"

"I think your name is Hale." I propped myself up on my elbow and held out the arm with the cryptic message on it.

"Hale…" He said slowly, reaching out to touch the partially healed cuts on my arm. "It sounds right somehow."

"It feels like there's another part of me … just under the surface, trying to get free. Is that what it feels like for you?"

"I don't know." He shrugged. "I feel like my soul knows you. From where or when I can't say, and if I'm honest, I don't really care that much. I'm more concerned with keeping you as far away from that necromancer as possible."

My stomach fluttered because, for reasons I couldn't grasp, I believed him. Through some twist of fate or perhaps a pre-written destiny that I was yet to understand, our souls were linked, and that thought brought me more comfort than fear.

 ECHO

Outside the city of Nox Valar, there existed a haven, a gathering point for those who walked the path of the fugitive. A place where the lost, the outcasts, and the hunted could seek solace in their shared struggles. *The Cavalcade of Strays*, whispered of in hushed tones, held the promise of reunion and respite from the ever-watchful eyes of the authorities.

In the shadows of the city, we plotted our course, our minds fixed on that singular destination. It was a beacon of hope amidst the darkness that enveloped us, a refuge for those who dared defy the oppressive grasp of the Nyxian Guard. In our hearts, we clung to the belief that within the embrace of the Cavalcade of Strays, our paths would converge once more, and together we would stand against the forces that sought to destroy us.

Hale maneuvered through the labyrinthine sewage tunnels with practiced ease, a glimmer of determination in his eyes. The haunting memories of our previous encounter with legions of spiders were absent this time, filling me with a sense of relief. As we finally emerged from the dim underground passage, the stale air gave way to the invigorating breeze that swept over the outer wall of the city.

The vast expanse of wheatfields greeted us, their golden hues dancing and swaying in the wind as far as the eye could see. The endless stretch of grain seemed to whisper stories of resilience and hidden secrets, capturing the essence of an untamed landscape. We embarked on our journey, the soft rustling of the wheat accompanying our every step, blending with the rhythmic beating of our hearts.

Days melded into one another as we pressed forward, united by a common purpose. Along the way, I couldn't help but notice a subtle transformation in Hale. His once-guarded demeanor had softened, and the flicker of change in his eyes spoke volumes, revealing a depth of character that I had yet to fully comprehend.

The winds whispered secrets of the world, and in Hale's unwavering presence, I found strength amidst the uncertainty that surrounded us. Together, we ventured forth, bound by a connection forged in adversity, ready to face whatever awaited us beyond the horizon.

But now he was also withdrawn. Following his lead, I gave him the space he seemed to want, sleeping under my own blanket and walking an arm's length away as we attempted to head off to the Cavalcade. Ashen dust swirled around us, carried by a listless breeze, creating an eerie haze that obscured our vision. The suffocating silence was broken only by the distant whispers of the wind. That was, until a bone-chilling groan pierced the quietude, freezing us in our tracks.

The hairs on the back of my neck stood on end as a figure emerged from a cluster of trees, its gaunt and pallid visage revealing its unholy nature. A wight, a creature of death and undeath, had found its way into our path. Its sunken eyes glowed with an unnatural malevolence, its tattered cloak billowing around a skeletal frame.

You died one too many times... The stench of decay hung in the air, mingling with the scent of ash, as the wight advanced, its gait slow yet purposeful.

A cold dread settled deep within me, but we stood our ground, determination etched upon our faces. Without warning, the wight lunged at us, its ethereal touch an icy chill against our flesh. Hale swiftly drew his daggers, blades glinting with desperate resolve.

The clash of steel reverberated through the air, resonating with a symphony of metal upon metal. The metallic tang electrified the atmosphere, heightening the intensity of the moment. Each parry sent sharp notes echoing, the blades meeting with a resounding impact. The sound of steel filled the space, intermingling with the heavy thuds of the wight's strikes.

The wight lunged, swiping a clawed hand along Hale's arm. Blood welled from the wound, staining his sleeve as he clenched his teeth. Hale's daggers traced elegant arcs, the polished steel glinting extensions of the elf himself.

I gasped, clasping a hand over my mouth. Gazing inward, I could sense that I didn't have the power to heal him. My connection to Azuth felt weak, like an old garment fraying at the seams. Hale's agile footwork evaded the wight's lunges, his boots scraping against the ashen ground. The calculated maneuvers thwarted the wight's desperate grasp. Tension lingered, each nimble sidestep evoking anticipation.

The rapid barrage of strikes whooshed through the air, blades slicing with lethal intent. The rush of displaced air caressed my skin, a tactile sensation amidst the symphony of sound and motion. The wight's assaults grew more erratic, claws swiping through the air with chilling hisses.

Malevolence emanated from the spectral form, and amidst the duel, the wight whispered, eerie moans and raspy exhalations haunting the air. The unsettling echoes accompanied the clash of blades, amplifying the eerie ambiance. Hale's daggers moved with precision, metallic kisses against the wight's spectral form as they sought vulnerable points.

Each puncture resonated with the intrusion provoking protests from the creature. Hale's daggers converged, delivering a final strike, and the wight's spectral form dissipated into a wisp of fading darkness. Silence once again settled upon the desolate expanse, broken only by the sound of Hale's ragged breaths.

Wiping the essence from his daggers, he sheathed them, and we marched on. Only I and the Ashen Fields bore witness to the struggle, and Hale asked for no thanks as we pressed on. It was what I estimated to be the third cycle since we'd left the city when we finally spotted it in the distance.

Finn had told me of her visits to the Cavalcade, but seeing it in person was nothing short of spectacular. A seemingly endless line of colorful wagons adorned with bright twinkling lights rolled to a stop alongside a winding dirt road. Knowing that they never stayed in one place for more than a few hours, Hale and I ran through the fields toward the sounds of drums, laughter, and the chatter of people haggling over trading goods and services.

The scent of aromatic stews and honey-drizzled pastries made my mouth water as we approached the kaleidoscope of colors and sounds. Wandering down the rows of tents, we walked through a cloud of fragrant incense smoke, nodding to a fortune teller who offered a seductive smile to Hale. If he noticed, he'd pretended not to, and in the light of how distant he seemed, I appreciated the gesture.

A troupe of acrobats, their bodies intertwined in a breath-taking display of strength and balance, formed a towering structure resembling a colossal humanoid figure. My eyes widened with delight as this living sculpture, crafted from interlocked limbs and unyielding determination, loomed over us. With graceful strides, the towering marvel paraded through the fairgrounds, extending its colossal arm to greet the awe-struck onlookers.

In a whirlwind of vibrant movement, dancers twirled and twined like ribbons caught in the wind. Their rhythmic steps were accompanied by the melodic notes of flutes, weaving a tapestry of enchantment that filled the air. Each dancer's skirt, adorned in a changing display of colors, unfurled like the blossoming petals of exotic flowers, adding a splash of vibrancy to the scene.

Amidst the spectacle, my gaze landed on the renowned Roaming Roadhouse, a marvel in its own right. This mobile inn continued its journey through the Sunless Crossing. It offered respite and comfort to weary travelers, its wheels rolling ceaselessly while ensuring guests' every desire was fulfilled. It was a haven on the move, a sanctuary where dreams met reality and wanderers found solace amidst the ever-changing landscapes of the realm.

A sense of awe washed over me. The Sunless Crossing was a place of perpetual wonder, where imagination and reality merged, and the extraordinary became ordinary. I marveled at the boundless creativity and ingenuity that thrived within this realm.

"Excuse me." I hailed a man wearing a smartly tailored patchwork coat. "I'd like to rent one of your ... rooms?" I gestured toward the boxcars.

"Sorry, luv." He took off his hat. "I'm afraid we're all booked up for the moment. If you're planning to travel alongside us for a cycle or two, I can put you on the list and let you know when something opens up."

"That's alright." I shook my head with a wavering smile. "Just out of curiosity, you wouldn't happen to know a Professor Dradon would you? An elf sorcerer with long gray hair and a flair for the alchemical arts?"

"It's been a good ten cycles since I seen that fella." The man scratched his head, and my eyes widened.

"Ten cycles?" My chest inflated with excitement. "You're sure it was Surrak Dradon?"

He's alive ... or was as of ten cycles ago. He'd been missing for months, and the thought of him being in the Cavalcade meant that he was, in fact, on the run, or at least in hiding.

"You're the second person in the last week to ask about him."

My stomach dropped as I pictured the Nyxian Guard riding in full force across the plains. How long would it be before they came looking for us here?

"Echo?" Finn's voice snapped me out of my anxious thoughts. Her smiling face illuminated the window of one of the boxcars. "Guys, they're here!"

Thank Azuth... My heart flooded with warmth as Finn burst through the door, clearing the steps in a leap as she ran and threw her arms around my legs. She was the best and most loyal friend I'd ever had, and I knew it even then. Rivka peered out the window, offering a feline smile and Hyperion leaned nonchalantly in the doorway.

"I told you they'd turn up." The tiefling grinned.

"I thought the guards might have caught you." Finn wiped the moisture from her eyes and looked up at me.

"Not yet." I looked back at Hale and found him smiling for the first time in days.

"Gods, you look ... different." Finn forced a smile.

Glancing down at my hands, I rubbed my arms self-consciously. I'd been trying not to think about the way my skin had been getting drastically paler ever since our last resurrection.

"Did you catch that Dradon was here recently?"

"We're staying in the same room he rented." Finn beckoned us toward the car. "Come in and have some stew and bread. We need to figure out our next move."

We exchanged brief explanations of where we had all been since we'd last seen each other as we settled into our new surroundings. Bright, red velvet couches lined the edges of the room. At the center was a round oak table decked out with a small feast. Finn asked the attendant for two more bowls and dished us each up a ladle full of hearty mushroom stew.

Vases of fresh flowers decorated the space, and on the far wall, a tall cabinet was stocked with a variety of spirits and beers. Every seat came with its own pile of colorful fluffy pillows, and the warm, soothing colors made the setting warm and intimate.

Settling into one of the comfy nests of pillows, I accepted a bowl of stew and finally allowed myself to relax. Hale sat across from me with his bowl, and Hyperion scanned the cupboard, reading off the labels of various wine bottles.

"What happened after the lab was raided?" I leaned back into the cushions and sipped the dark savory broth.

"I headed back to the apartment where we'd originally planned to bring Dradon." Finn stretched out, taking a sip of wine from her wooden cup. "Hyperion showed up a couple hours later. Then we headed over to the Rancid Skull and found

Rivka. After that, I scouted out a few of our old haunts, but the guard already had the same idea."

"It looks like they've been following us longer than we realized." I sighed. "Did you get word to the leader of the Chantry that the secretary is working with the guard?"

"Left a coded letter on his desk." She shrugged. "But there's no guarantee that he's not in on it as well. Best to steer clear of the guild until we know for sure."

"Isn't there a saying about honor among thieves?" Rivka had finally taken off her armor and changed into a lighter set of clothes.

"There are plenty of sayings about honor among thieves." Hyperion uncorked a bottle of port, filled a glass, and handed it to the feline. "Some of them are even true." He lifted his glass in a toast. "To us ... and our daring escape."

The cat woman smelled the contents of the cup, took a deep breath, and then surrendered, toasting the tiefling and taking a drink. Hyperion passed out cups of port to the rest of us, and the mood of the evening lightened as the alcohol did its work—all inhibitions and worries dimmed in the light of good company.

After a round of particularly vulgar jokes and a healthy fit of laughter, Finn held out her cup for Hyperion to refill it and asked, "What is your worst fear?"

"My worst fear?" Hyperion set the bottle of port aside, swirling the contents of his glass as he propped his feet up and crossed his ankles. "Centipedes."

"Centipedes?" Rivka raised an eyebrow.

"Centipedes." He nodded. "I hate them... Nothing should have that many legs."

"My greatest fear is probably falling overboard in the middle of the ocean." I shivered. "I never liked traveling by boat knowing the things that lurk at the bottom of the sea."

"What about you?" Hyperion smiled at Rivka. "What's your greatest fear?"

"The only thing to fear is fear itself." She turned up her nose. "If you spend too much time thinking of things to fear, you risk freezing up when the time comes to face it."

"What about you, Hale." I looked over at my companion who had been quiet for most of the evening. "Do you fear anything?"

He sighed, lowering his gaze to the contents of his cup. "Eternity ... I suppose."

"Eternity?" Hyperion chuckled. "After what you went through, I'd think you'd be more afraid of running into that tattooed friend of yours."

Rivka and Finn chuckled, but Hale just offered a half-hearted smile.

"When you're mortal and you're alive—fighting, fucking, and surviving as best you can—you know there's only so much time." Hale's expression grew somber, and we all listened intently as he continued, "Every moment is precious. When eternity stretches out in front of you, it's easy to lose sight of that."

The four of us sat in relative silence listening to the merriment and music outside as we mulled over Hale's statement. Lifting my glass in a toast, I smiled at him. "To treasuring the moment, even when facing eternity."

"Here, here." Hyperion raised his glass, and the others followed suit.

After we all drank, Rivka spoke up. "I do have one fear..."

"Just one?" Hyperion teased.

"Only one *great* fear." She glared at him and then softened her expression. "I'm afraid that I sacrificed everything for a man who might have taken my life."

Tears brimmed on her lashes, blurring her split pupils until she blinked it away. The three of us looked at her, stunned by the sudden moment of vulnerability.

"I'm not even sure I want to know anymore." She laughed, shaking off her emotions as she took another drink. "I don't suppose it matters anyway since I'm dead."

"It matters." Hyperion's brow furrowed with sincerity, and he nodded to her. "The truth always matters."

"If we manage to get through this without getting thrown into prison..." Finn added. "We'll help you find out exactly what happened, and if that son of a pig did double-cross you, he'll get what's comin' to him."

Rivka smiled, a genuine one that reached her eyes, before yawning and turning over on her side to sleep. Hyperion set his cup down and crossed the room to spread a blanket over her before taking a seat at the opposite end by her feet.

"I'm sorry, Rivka." Hyperion crossed his arms. "For accusing you of being a turncoat before. I misjudged your character."

"It's alright." She smiled at him, but didn't open her eyes.. "I didn't trust you either."

The tiefling's white teeth glinted as he chuckled, lying his head back and resting his eyes. Finn's empty cup fell to the carpet as her mouth dropped open, and she started snoring softly. Soon it was only Hale and me lying on the floor facing each other, just out of arm's reach.

"Can I ask you a question?" Hale folded an arm under the back of his head.

"Of course." My heart skipped a beat. *Are we going to talk about what happened? Does he want to kiss me again?*

"Why are you so determined to help the Professor if you haven't seen him in so long?"

I exhaled, smiling and covering my face with my hands.

"You don't have to answer if you don't want to."

"No, it's not that." I shook my head and laughed softly. Taking a moment to gather my thoughts, I looked over at him. "As you know, I was the healer for my party, and I got us all killed because I ... wasn't skilled enough."

"If a party dies, it's not the healer's fault alone." He frowned.

"Well, they didn't see it that way. They all managed to get resurrected, and I ... got left here. Dradon saw potential in me. He taught me to be better so that I wouldn't ever be put in a position to watch my friends die again. I owe my competence to him."

"I suppose it's a safe bet that what happened to me isn't the same as what happened to Dradon," he whispered. "I'm sorry you put so much time and energy into a dead end."

"I'm not." I propped myself up on my elbow. "We learned that the power of life force can be used to enhance magical abilities. That would explain why the soul eater is after Dradon. He has centuries of magical knowledge and experience because of how long he's been in the Sunless Crossing. Maybe this killer thinks that by absorbing Dradon's power he can move between worlds."

"What if we don't find him?" he asked. "What if it's too late?"

"Well..." I sighed. "Then I'm still glad I found *you*."

A smile played at the edges of his lips, and he gave a barely perceptible nod. "Me too."

Taking a deep breath, Hale rolled over to face the wall of the boxcar, and eventually, I too fell asleep. Maybe it had been impulsive to make love to him that night in the bell tower. Had he only reciprocated out of some misguided belief that he was indebted to me for freeing him? The thought made my heart sink.

If that was the case, it would explain why he'd been acting so strange since we left the city. I owed him an apology and hoped it wasn't too late to clear the air between us. For now though, I needed to rest and meditate on my healing spells. I had a feeling we were going to need them.

 FINN

My father always said that drinking your troubles away always seems like a good idea… until you wake up the next morning. Or… I imagined he would have said something to that effect if I'd ever met him.

It wasn't just the splitting headache and rotten guts that got to me, but the way all the troubles you avoided come crashing right back down and you realize that all you did was delay the inevitable. Groaning, I scrubbed a hand down my face and looked up at the ceiling. The Cavalcade was on the move again, and our boxcar room rocked back and forth as it rolled along the dirt road.

Rivka was stretched out on the couch at the front end of the car with her feet resting in Hyperion's lap. The tiefling had his head propped on a pillow in the corner, where he slumped to one side. On the floor, Echo and Hale lay a little more than an arm's length apart, facing each other, and I wondered why they wouldn't have taken the couches.

Hale seemed like the kind of fellow who was so used to sleeping on hard ground that it only felt natural to find the hardest most uncomfortable surface to lay on. But Echo … she was used to turning in for the night on a plush mattress. I couldn't help but think she might have chosen the floor as either a show of solidarity, or she simply wanted to be a little closer to him without looking like she wanted to be closer to him.

I shook my head, staring up at the ceiling. As my blurred vision cleared, a small white triangle became visible behind one of the overhead beams. *What in all hells…*

I nudged Hale, and he stirred, shaking off the fog of sleep and reaching for his bow.

"Relax, ranger." I held up a hand, pointing at the ceiling. "Look up there."

"We didn't disappear?" He blinked. "I thought that when we slept—"

"Hale!" I let out an exasperated chuckle and pointed up. As soon as I heard that Dradon had rented this boxcar, I searched every nook and cranny. But apparently, I missed something.

"Look closer," I insisted. "See if you can reach that."

Hale stood up to his full height, reaching over his head. He was even taller than the Professor, but not by much. Curling his fingers around the top of the beam, he brought down a dusty, folded piece of paper. Echo's eyes fluttered open, and she yawned, looking up as Hale turned the small, yellowed square over in his hand.

"What's that?" She sat up. "Why are we still here?"

"I don't know." Hale unfolded the paper, furrowing his brow at the contents before passing it over to me. "Obviously the rules aren't what I thought they were.

On it was a diagram of a man, divided into pieces like a patchwork quilt. Each piece was labeled with some alchemical formulas etched around it.

I shook my head and handed the paper to Echo. "What do you make of this?"

"Strange." She winced, blinking rapidly as she looked over the drawing. "Part of it is in Dradon's handwriting, but part of it isn't. Some of these equations are way too complicated for me. I'm not sure what he's trying to do."

"Looks like necromancy if I ever saw it." I took the paper back and folded it up. "I know an old necro in the Crimson Quarter that might be able to take a look and at least give us an idea of what Dradon is trying to do."

"Finn, we can't risk going back into Nox Valar." Echo's posture stiffened. "Not after what happened. Besides, now that we know Dradon was here, we can ask around the Cavalcade to see if anyone knew what he was up to."

"Echo, I know you're scared." I put my hand on her shoulder. "If I thought laying low would make us safer, I'd be for it, but this world isn't all that big, and it's only a matter of time before the Nyxian Guard close in on us."

"So your solution is to walk back into the city?" She shoved my hand away. "Finn, you'll get caught."

"The dumb bastards think we have something to do with the missing souls." I tucked the paper into my lapel. "If we're going to clear our names, we have to track down the soul eater and put a stop to the killing. Otherwise, who knows how long we could end up rotting in the Sovereign's Cells in the Onyx Requiem before they realize their mistake."

"The authorities in the Sunless Crossing aren't exactly known for their speedy and efficient clerical system." Echo's shoulders sagged. "Alright, let's do it."

"Ha!" My voice woke up Rivka and Hyperion. "If all five of us waltzed into the city, they'd catch us for sure. Especially bright-eyes over there..." I gestured to Hale who gave a quizzical look. "No offense, but you're a little easy to spot."

He shrugged.

"You need someone watching your back." Echo frowned. "I'm going with you."

"Echo, I love you to death, but you'd only slow me down. I'll take the hired muscle to keep an eye out from a distance."

"Can do." Hyperion gave a mock salute.

Echo looked hurt but nodded as Rivka strapped her sword to her hip. We approached the Cavalcade Innkeeper, exchanging coins for another night's stay in the boxcar. Promising to catch up with him later, we bid him farewell and watched as the

Cavalcade continued its journey. Hale and Echo stayed behind, choosing to explore the moving spectacle, engaging various vendors in conversation, seeking any information they could gather about Dradon.

Rivka, Hyperion, and I trudged through the desolate Ashen Fields, my senses on high alert. The eerie silence pressed heavily upon the air, sending a shiver down my spine. Beside me, Rivka prowled with feline grace, her eyes scanning the surroundings like a predator. Hyperion flexed his fingers, ready to conjure at a moment's notice.

A flicker of ethereal light caught my attention, and I tensed. Spectral guardians emerged from the shadows, their translucent forms melding seamlessly with the ashen landscape.

"We've got company." Rivka lunged forward, claws extended to strike, but her attacks passed through the specters as if they were illusions.

Hyperion's voice resonated with otherworldly power, his draconic incantations weaving through the air like a haunting melody.

Waves of arcane energy emanated from his outstretched hands, pulsating with an aura of mystic might. The ethereal beings, enveloped in the rhythm of his incantations, wavered in response. Yet, their spectral resolve held steadfast, undeterred by the warlock's attempt to disrupt their essence.

Their incorporeal forms shimmered as if fortified by an indomitable will that defied mortal comprehension. Despite Hyperion's relentless efforts, the specters stood firm, their determination echoing through the air, resolute in their spectral purpose.

I darted between the spectral guardians, but my strikes passed through their ghostly forms. Adjusting my strategy, I aimed for the spectral energy that bound them, seeking to weaken their ethereal essence. Whispers of forgotten voices filled the air, an unsettling chorus intended to unnerve me, but I steeled myself.

Rivka's lithe form lunged into the midst of the specters, her claws slashing through their ethereal forms with lethal precision. The ghostly entities turned their attention to her, their incorporeal eyes fixated on her agile movements. With each swipe and fierce roar, she commanded their focus, drawing them away from me.

Her feline grace created a swirling vortex of chaos and confusion. Their ghostly forms shifted and swirled, momentarily disoriented by Rivka's diversion, allowing me a brief window of opportunity to exploit their vulnerabilities and strike without their haunting gazes upon me.

Dark tendrils erupted from Hyperion's outstretched hand, snaking through the air with an otherworldly grace. They coiled around the spectral forms, weaving through their translucent bodies and causing momentary disruptions in their ethereal composition. In those fleeting moments of vulnerability, I seized my chance to strike, my blade slashing through the ghostly figures.

The specters closed in on me, but with a surge of adrenaline, narrowly escaping their chilling, ghostly grasp.

The frigid sensation lingered in the air, a chilling reminder of the spectral nature of my foes. Rivka's ferocious roar rippled through the ethereal forms as Hyperion's hands wove intricate patterns in the air, channeling arcane energy with practiced precision. Arcane tendrils surged forth, crackling with eldritch power, colliding with the specters.

The collision caused a violent reaction, the clash of opposing forces sending tremors through their ghostly essence. The specters flickered and wavered, their translucent bodies momentarily disrupted by the arcane assault. Shimmers of spectral energy scattered in all directions. It was a brief disruption, but in that moment, their ethereal forms faltered, opening a fleeting opportunity for me to press my advantage.

With unwavering resolve and precise strikes, I attacked. My daggers passed through the specters, and I sensed their ethereal essence weakening with each blow. As I landed a final blow, the specter before me shuddered, its ghostly form growing faint and translucent. It seemed to flicker like a dying candle, tendrils of spectral energy swirling around its fading figure.

The once-intense gaze of the specter dulled, its ethereal eyes losing their unearthly glow. And then, in an ephemeral instant, it disintegrated, dissipating into nothingness and leaving behind only a lingering chill in the air. I turned my attention to the next specter, my heart racing with anticipation.

With each strike, as I engaged the remaining specters, each confrontation an intricate dance of blades and shadow, I witnessed the gradual dissolution of their incorporeal forms. It was as if they were fading echoes of a forgotten melody. Their spectral bodies fractured and fragmented, wisps of ethereal essence dissipating into the ether. The once-menacing foes now diminished, reduced to mere echoes.

Finally, the last ghost stood before me; its form trembled, and with one decisive strike, I shattered the remaining fragments of its essence. Like a mirage evaporating under the sun's gaze, it dissolved into nothingness.

A profound stillness settled over the battlefield, broken only by the soft rustle of the ashen grass. I stood amidst the remnants of the specters, their presence entirely erased. The Ashen Fields regained their desolate tranquility, their secrets locked away once more. Rivka and Hyperion exchanged triumphant glances, silently acknowledging our victory.

Rivka moved through the fields with a swiftness and grace only rivaled by the storm. The falling ash provided the cover we needed to make our way back in through the open sewage drains and once inside the city, we kept a good twenty paces apart from each other to avoid attracting attention.

The guards were on high alert, the white and purple uniforms visibly scattered throughout the crowds. Avoiding detection wouldn't have been easy no matter what, but with Hale, it would have been damn near impossible. Hyperion watched me, and Rivka watched him, each of us carrying a few miniature smoke bombs for a speedy escape should things go sour.

Just on the opposite side of Whetstone Bluff, Crimson Quarter was a little quieter than usual. Narrow and winding, the cobblestone paths twisted through the district, suffused with a crimson glow cast by the stained-glass windows and the glowing embers within the buildings. The air was heavy with a sense of anticipation, mingled with the scent of smoky incense and the faint undertone of spilled ale.

Gargoyles, stoic and watchful, perched upon the gothic stone arches of the cathedral, their stony gazes surveying the nocturnal activities of the district's seedy denizens. Shadows danced and whispered in the corners as the Crimson Court's headquarters loomed imposingly nearby. Amidst this murky ambiance, I found myself standing before what appeared to be the entrance to a crypt, its weathered stone structure signaling the presence of an old acquaintance, biding his time until fate beckoned him to the afterlife.

Glancing over my shoulder, I spotted Hyperion, hooded and blending into a crowded patio drinking a cup of tea. I took a deep breath and knocked on the door of the crypt. There was no answer at first, but after I knocked a third time, the small stone window, only big enough for his eyes, slid open, and Gideon Grim peered out at me.

"Is that Finn the Halfling, come to visit after all this time?"

"I agree." I held up a bundle of black candles and artisanal incense I'd picked up from the Cavalcade. "It's been too long."

His eyes lit up as the window slid shut and the heavy wooden door crept open, stringing cobwebs as it did.

"You really need to get out more." I swatted the dust in the air as I stepped inside. "I thought you said you were starting a book club."

"No one showed up." Gideon shrugged accepting the gift with an appreciative gesture as he led me down a spiral staircase lit with goat-horn torches. "I've never been very good with the living."

"Ironic since the vast majority of the population here are *dead*." I glanced around as we entered the dimly lit parlor. Paintings depicting death and decay adorned the walls and several display shelves, and tables held various taxidermied creatures and antique medical devices.

"You know what I mean," he sneered as he took a seat in one of the armchairs and rang a small bell that sat on an end table. "I much prefer to have more agreeable friends."

"Mm." I nodded, forcing a smile as I sat down in the chair across from him. "I can't imagine they make very good conversational companions."

The maid shuffled into the room, her tattered uniform hanging loosely on her emaciated frame. Her dull, lifeless eyes stared blankly ahead, and the candlelight danced on her plaid, gray skin as she shambled to stand next to her master.

"Tea please, Beatrice." Gideon threaded his fingers together. "And some of those delightful almond biscuits you made the other day. Would you like anything to eat, Finn?"

"Tea sounds lovely." I settled into the armchair. "Thank you."

A dry wheeze escaped Beatrice's lips as she turned to head through an arched doorway into the kitchen, and I did my best not to stare.

"It must be hard to find someone willing to import corpses into the Sunless Crossing." I crossed my legs. "I'm surprised you were able to get one in such good condition."

"She was ... expensive to be sure." Gideon's bushy red eyebrows that stood out starkly against his pale skin lifted toward his receding hairline accentuating his prominent brow. "But, in all honesty, I would have paid double if I had to."

"Everyone needs a hobby." I pressed my lips together.

"Enough about me, Finn." He leaned forward. "Tell me what you've been up to since our last visit. How's business?"

"Business is good." I leaned on the arm of the chair. "I've mostly been trading in communication with loved ones. With one exception, I haven't even had to steal anything since I moved here."

"One exception, eh?" He chuckled. "You can take the halfling out of the Hovels, but you can't take the Hovels out of the halfling. I have always appreciated your transparency."

"You're one of the few people who knew me back before I had an honest trade." I winked at him. "It wouldn't feel right to lie to you."

"No judgement here." He stroked his beard and sat back in his chair.

Beatrice staggered in, holding a silver tray of tea and biscuits. She placed it on the coffee table between Gideon and me before pouring us each a cup. Though her movements were somewhat disjointed, there was an intensity to her focus, as if some part of her still took great pride in her work.

"That smells lovely." I accepted the cup from her, and she responded with a shallow wheeze.

"She really has been a gods-send." Gideon smiled at Beatrice, glancing at her backside as she waddled back into the other room. "Having spent so much time focusing on my studies, I'm afraid I've neglected the social aspect of my afterlife. I'd be so lonely without her."

"Yeah," I said under my breath as I stirred my tea, segueing into my real reason for visiting. "Speaking of your studies, I came across something I thought you'd find interesting. I wonder, would you give me your assessment?"

"Oh?" His long, pointed fingernails were fanned out from the handle of his teacup as he took a sip and set it down. "An artifact? Or a book perhaps?"

"Not a book, exactly." I took the folded page from my lapel and extended my hand to Gideon. "More like a page of notes."

Gideon's brows lowered, knitting together as he unfolded the paper. "Oh, you *have* been running with an interesting crowd, haven't you?"

"They have their moments." I drummed my fingers on the arm of my chair. "Can you make any sense of those equations?"

"They're alchemical." He stroked his beard. "Definitely dabbling in some dark stuff."

"The diagram almost looks as though he's collecting body parts which doesn't really make sense in the Sunless Crossing, unless he's importing corpses, which ... as you said, would be ridiculously expensive."

"No, these spells aren't for physical bodies." He shook his head, tilting the paper so I could see. "Look here at the use of powdered onyx gems and ghostly essence."

"Gideon..." I took a slow inhale. "You know I have *no* idea what that means."

The old necromancer rolled his eyes.

"It means, old friend, that whoever wrote this is using the souls of the dead to create something else." He handed me the paper and a chill ran up my spine.

"To make what?"

"I can't be sure, and frankly, I'm a little afraid to spend too much time on it." He shuddered, which wasn't a gesture I was used to seeing from the creepy old bastard. Nothing usually spooked him, and the fact that he seemed put off made me nervous.

"So, whatever he's up to... it's bad." I folded the paper and tucked it away.

"I avoid using moral perspective when it comes to science." He grinned. "I will say that those spells look experimental. Nothing like that has ever been done in my experience, and that type of endeavor would obviously be highly frowned upon in a society where the average citizen is dead. Whatever your friend is up to... they'd better not get caught."

Nodding, I allowed the conversation to drift back to our time traveling together. As odd and admittedly unsettling as he is, he was always an interesting character. We'd had each other's backs more than once, which would always mean something, even if his company wasn't something I could stomach very often.

Echo's tolerance of the professor lasted far longer than I would have liked. She made plenty of excuses for him, saying that he just wasn't good with people, or that not everyone knew how to appreciate his brand of honesty. But this was beyond mere social ineptitude.

The man was unkind and, at times, downright cruel, especially when it came to Echo. If he was frustrated or overwhelmed, he would fire off a string of insults, so well-tailored that they were meant to cut deep and leave lasting scars. When she finally walked away, I was shocked, not because I couldn't understand where she was coming from, but because I was beginning to think she enjoyed the abuse.

The constant humiliation and cutting down of her self-worth likely reminded her of what it was like growing up surrounded by religious zealots. *Can abuse be nostalgic?* I shook myself out of the thought tangent, refocusing on what it could mean if the professor was using the souls of people in the Sunless Crossing for his experiments.

Was he somehow responsible for the shift in the laws of nature? Had he unwittingly created the soul eater, and now it was out of his control? There were too many possibilities to consider without first talking to Echo. Knowing the general nature of the magic he was attempting, maybe she could figure out the missing pieces.

With the remnants of warmth lingering in my cup, I set it down gently on the saucer and glanced at Gideon, our conversation nearing its end. The lines etched on his face softened, a subtle satisfaction gleaming in his eyes as he realized our visit had stretched into an extended stay. Sensing my impending departure, he rose from his seat, his movements graceful as he guided me back toward the staircase.

As we ascended, the murmur of voices and clinking of glasses replaced ambient noises of the crypt. Emerging from the iron door, I caught a glimpse of Hyperion, his eyes meeting mine for an instant before he discreetly dropped a few coins onto the table, acknowledging our readiness to depart. With silent understanding, we moved in unison, meandering through the labyrinthine streets until we reached the entrance to the sewers, our next destination shrouded in darkness and uncertainty.

CHAPTER 13

HYPERION

In the depths of my being, hidden behind the façade of a cunning and opportunistic nature, lay a glimmer of something unexpected. It was a seed that had taken root, slowly blossoming into an emotion I thought long lost to me—care.

As a tiefling warlock, I had traversed the realm with a singular focus on my own survival and agenda. I had walked the fine line between shadows and light, never fully trusting anyone or revealing the depth of my true intentions. But in the company of these unlikely companions, something shifted within me, altering the course of my heart.

These connections, these fragile threads of trust softened the edges of my cynical nature, prompting me to question the purpose of my solitary existence. In this realm, where deceit and treachery ran rampant, where alliances could shift like shadows, these bonds became my anchor.

For the first time in a long while, I found myself caring. Caring for their well-being, their dreams, and their pain. The flicker of compassion that I thought had been extinguished within me was reignited, and I slowly came to terms with the vulnerability it brought.

But amidst the growing affection, a lingering fear remained. It was the fear of losing them, of betrayal or abandonment. It was the fear that the fragile web we had woven would be torn apart, leaving me once again alone in the abyss.

Yet, despite these fears, I was willing to face the unknown alongside my newfound companions. For in their presence, I had discovered a sliver of light that guided me through the darkest of times. Perhaps, the strength of these bonds would guide me toward redemption and a chance to forge a new destiny.

Rivka certainly knew how to blend into her surroundings. Wherever she was, I couldn't see her, but I kept a close eye on the crypt, waiting for Finn to re-emerge. When she did, I paid my tab and moved swiftly into the crowd, keeping an eye out for anyone potentially tailing the halfling.

I could only hope my feline companion was watching my back, likewise. The uncanny beauty of the city charmed me as I made my way through the narrow winding streets. Dark twisted spires seemed to writhe with the flickering red light coming through the red stained glass windows, and a dense fog had begun to accumulate, curling around my ankles as we made our way toward the entrance to the sewage tunnels.

As a gust of chilly wind nipped at my exposed skin, I instinctively raised the collar of my coat, seeking refuge from the biting cold. Glancing over my shoulder, my eyes scanned the dimly lit street until they settled on the familiar figure of Rivka, her blue cloak blending seamlessly with the shadows. We had become adept at navigating the intricate web of alleyways and corners that concealed our movements, and now, as we turned the corner that led us closer to the canal, our destination beckoned in the distance.

Finn, standing beside me, seemed to sense the weight of the upcoming venture. Her gaze swept the surroundings, her eyes darting with a mix of caution and determination. With a deep breath, she drew in the frigid air, fortifying her resolve for what lay ahead. The hood of her cape shielded her face and cast a veil of mystery around her as she prepared to step into the yawning mouth of the catacombs.

The little halfling's voice echoed in my mind, her words still fresh from the animated tale she had regaled us with. I couldn't help but wonder how much of her account was embellished regarding the retrieval of the elusive philosopher's stone from the clutches of a wraith. Regardless of how true it was, her story raised our spirits at the time.

Now, it made me hesitant to re-enter the sewers beneath Nox Valar. I'd grown fond of Finn. Despite her stubbornness and constant need to be right, she was quite entertaining and loyal to her friends to a fault. Even Rivka had slowly been coming around to the spirit of our little company. I dared to hope that if we all managed to get through this that we might stay in touch after going our separate ways. Finn and I waited fifty paces inside the tunnel, and Rivka joined us soon after.

The three of us walked together the rest of the way to the broken duct that led through the outer wall of the city. Traversing the fields without being spotted by the guards along the wall was another task altogether. Once we were a safe distance from the city, the three of us stopped to rest.

The Ashen Fields stretched before us, a desolate landscape bathed in the pale light of the vortex. The air hung heavy with the scent of brimstone and earth, a mingling of otherworldly elements that stirred a sense of unease. My senses heightened, attuned to the subtle crackling of arcane energy resonating in the silence.

"What is that?" Rivka narrowed her eyes.

Four sinister presences materialized amidst the swirling ashen mist. The first, a Night Hag, draped in tattered black robes, her skeletal hands adorned with sharp, elongated talons that glimmered. Thin, stringy strands of graying hair clung to her pale and wrinkled scalp, framing an expression of wicked delight.

"Fleeeeeshhh." Her eyes glistened, murky pools of darkness punctuating her sinister snaggletoothed grin.

"Nope." Finn drew her daggers. "Nothing to eat here, you dried-up old twats!"

"Such a filthy tongue." Draped in a cloak of shadow, the second Night Hag towered above her counterparts, exuding an imposing presence that sent a shiver down my spine. Her form was hunched and twisted. Every inch of her elongated limbs ended in gnarled, clawed fingers that twitched with unnerving anticipation.

"Ladies..." I cracked my knuckles. "This isn't a fight you want. Believe me."

The tall hag cackled. "Tongues... Yes, they all have tongues, sisters."

Beneath a hood that partially concealed her face, a grotesque, jagged grin emerged, revealing a set of teeth that seemed plucked from nightmares. Decaying, yellowed flesh framed this macabre display, giving her visage a ghastly countenance. Thick, matted hair poured down her back, a tangle of untamed strands that added to her feral appearance.

Rivka, Finn, and I clustered together, prepared to fight as the trio twirled in their shadow-infused garments, their bony fingers extended into elongated claws that hungered for the touch of mortal flesh. Each step they took sent shivers through the air, their movements mirroring a macabre dance. Shadows seemed to coil around their forms, trailing behind them like remnants of the darkest nightmares.

The third Night Hag, the smallest but by no means the least dangerous, possessed an air of deceptive elegance. Her form was draped in a flowing gown, its midnight-blue fabric seemingly woven from the night itself. Her long, bony fingers ended in sharp, manicured nails painted a deep, blood-red hue. Her face, a mask of unnaturally youthful beauty, held an unsettling charm, its porcelain-like complexion belying the malevolence that simmered within. Wisps of raven-black hair framed her face, accentuating her piercing, ice-blue eyes that held the coldness of a winter storm.

The fourth figure stood silently behind the hags, tall and lean with broad shoulders. His infernal aura spoke to me.

"A Shadow Demon... prowling the Ashen Fields with a little pack of hunting dogs?" I sneered at the silent figure. "I've never known your kind to be generous enough to share."

His laugh was a low rumble as the Shadow Demon held his arms out wide. "Work smarter, not harder, little tiefling. Besides, I love hunting here. Endless mortals killing themselves makes easy meals for my legions... It's only a matter of time before the Nyxian Guard fall and we swarm through the streets of Nox Valar and gorge ourselves like kings.

An eerie silence settled over the Ashen Fields, broken only by the whispers that drifted on the wind. Unwilling to wait for them to make the first move, Finn sprang into action. Her daggers gleamed as she unleashed swift strikes upon the Night Hags, each movement accompanied by the sharp sound of metal meeting ethereal flesh. Her blades sliced through the air with lethal precision, leaving trails of spectral energy dissipating into the ashen breeze.

Rivka's muscles rippled beneath her fur as she launched herself at the Night Hags, claws unsheathed and fangs bared. The primal roar that echoed through the Ashen Fields seemed to stir the very essence of the land. Her ferocious assaults were met with the hiss of the Hags, their incorporeal forms recoiling under the weight of her savage prowess.

I focused my attention, channeling the arcane power that surged within me.

The magic surged through the air, creating an almost tangible prickle against my skin. I wove intricate incantations, tracing symbols in the air with my fingertips, as bolts of eldritch energy streaked against the ashy backdrop of the fields. The collision of my arcane forces with the Night Hags caused their spectral forms to flicker and waver, the impact sending ripples of distortion through the ethereal fabric.

Finn's blades sliced through the air with lethal precision, leaving trails of shimmering energy in her wake. The Hags, momentarily drawn to the rogue's relentless assault, became momentarily vulnerable, and Rivka pounced into action. With feline grace and lightning reflexes, her claws unsheathed and her muscles coiled with raw power. Like the majestic predator she was, she lunged at the unsuspecting Hags, her savage ferocity unleashed. The impact of Rivka's onslaught reverberated through the air, as her claws found purchase in the ethereal flesh of the Night Hags.

Fur and flesh met shadow and smoke, creating a whirlwind of frenzied combat. Her relentless attacks forced the Hags onto the defensive, and their attempts to retaliate were reduced to desperate parries and futile curses. I stood poised at the edges of the battlefield, my arcane powers pulsating within me.

The Shadow Demon drew back, seemingly unsure of whether or not it wanted to assist its pets.

I tapped into the raw energies of the Ashen Fields, channeling the essence of the surrounding desolation. With a focused mind and outstretched hands, I conjured bolts of eldritch energy that streaked through the air with a crackling intensity. The dark tendrils of my arcane magic collided with the Night Hags, sending shockwaves of disruption through their spectral forms.

Each impact caused their ethereal bodies to flicker and waver, their essence momentarily destabilized. It was in these fleeting moments of vulnerability that Finn and Rivka struck with calculated precision, exploiting the weaknesses I had created. Together, we moved in perfect synchrony, a harmonious trio of blade, fang, and magic.

Finn's swift strikes drew the attention of the Night Hags again, allowing Rivka to circle around and unleash her primal fury upon them. With my arcane powers, I alternated between unleashing bolts of dark energy and weaving protective barriers to shield us from their insidious hexes.

Finn's blades glinted in the light of the storm clouds overhead as she evaded the Hags' desperate counterattacks, always one step ahead. Rivka's claws tore through the ethereal flesh of our adversaries, leaving trails of shimmering essence in her wake. And I, with my spells and incantations, continued to disrupt the Hags' spectral forms, weakening their grip on our reality.

The clash of steel and claw, the crackling of arcane power, and the haunting whispers of the Ashen Fields merged. Blow after blow, strike after strike, our relentless assault wore down the Hags, pushing them to the brink of defeat. Whenever they focused on my companions, I seized the opportunity to exploit their vulnerabilities, casting spells that disrupted their magic and weakened their spectral defenses.

Amidst the chaos, the landscape shifted. The static electricity prickled against my skin, a tingling sensation that accompanied the unleashing of my powers. Shadows twisted and warped, responding to the arcane forces at my command. The air seemed to cool as raw power surged through me, fueling my incantations.

With weariness tugging at our muscles, we pressed on. Finn's calculated strikes each hit their mark with deadly accuracy. Rivka lunged forward with feline grace, her claws unsheathed and her muscles coiled with raw power.

The Night Hags, sensing the threat, swiftly retaliated, conjuring dark tendrils of magic that lashed out toward Rivka. She evaded the oncoming tendrils with a swift leap to the side, her lithe body twisting in mid-air. Rivka's claws lashed out, leaving trails of shadowy energy as they found purchase. A guttural screech pierced the air as the wounded Hag's form flickered and distorted, its malevolent essence momentarily weakened.

Rivka and I exchanged a playful smile.

"Still think you've found an easy meal, friends?" I winked at the Shadow Demon who stepped forward, gritting his teeth as he lifted his hands to cast, but then … he hesitated, roaring in infernal tongue for the hags to earn their keep.

The Night Hag nearest to Rivka lunged with claws poised to strike. Rivka's instincts kicked into overdrive as she ducked and weaved, narrowly evading the Hag's vicious attack. The wicked claws grazed her fur, leaving a shallow cut along her flank. Undeterred, Rivka retaliated, her claws rending through the Hag's spectral form with primal ferocity.

The wounded Night Hag writhed in pain, its ethereal body fragmenting and flickering as it struggled to maintain its coherence. Sensing the impending defeat, the final Night Hag unleashed a torrent of dark energy, a malevolent spell aimed directly at Rivka. Caught off guard, Rivka took the brunt of the assault, a surge of unholy energy crashing against her and sending her sprawling to the ground.

Gritting her teeth against the pain, Rivka forced herself to rise, pouncing once more, her claws slashing through the air. The weakened Hag attempted a feeble counterattack, but

Rivka was quicker, evading the strike and delivering a final, decisive blow.

A final screech reverberated through the air as the Night Hag dissipated into a wisp of ethereal energy, vanishing into the ashen mist. Rivka, wounded but undeterred, stood panting, her chest heaving with exertion.

I channeled my magic, my focus unyielding despite the fatigue, I delved deeper into the well of mystic power that resided within me, drawing upon its potent reserves. With every incantation and gesture, I felt the raw vibrations of magic resonating through my veins.

Mystic vibrations coursed through my bones and muscles, electrifying my senses and heightening my connection to the ethereal currents. The air shimmered with an otherworldly luminescence. Each word I spoke and every motion I made sent ripples of energy cascading outward, imbuing the atmosphere with a tangible presence.

Fatigue threatened to slow my movements, yet I refused to succumb to its seductive embrace. With each spell I cast, I became more attuned to the arcane energies that flowed through the Ashen Fields, and I embraced their essence and allowing them to guide my actions. *It was so ... fucking addictive.*

Through the haze of weariness, I felt a surge of exhilaration, the thrill of wielding the raw power of the arcane. It was as if the very fabric of reality responded to my touch, resonating with the energy that emanated from within me. In that moment, I transcended the limitations of mortal flesh, my spirit soaring alongside the currents of magic that danced through the air.

"Hyperion!" Rivka shouted over the roar of my magic. "Slow down, you're exhausting yourself."

"I've got this," I said through gritted teeth.

The mystic vibrations became a part of me, interwoven with my very existence. They fueled my determination, pushing me to summon spells of greater potency and allowing me to manipulate the energies of the Ashen Fields to my advantage. Despite the physical toll it exacted, I reveled in the raw beauty of the arcane, embracing its exhilarating presence and surrendering to its unyielding call.

With every ounce of my being, I channeled the arcane energy, letting it flow through me like a conductor guiding a symphony. The mystic vibrations resonated within me, a constant reminder of the immense power I wielded. Fatigue became a distant whisper in the face of the overwhelming force that surged through my veins, propelling me forward, deeper into the heart of the battle.

Driven by the harmonious symphony of arcane forces, I pushed past the boundaries. The pain served as my anchor, reminding me of the power that lay dormant within. In this desolate realm, amidst the ethereal mist and swirling ash, I embraced the mystic energies and allowed them to guide my every move, relentless in my pursuit of victory.

"Hyperion, stop!" Rivka turned toward me, distracted by her concern for my well-being. In a harrowing instant, a Night Hag's wicked claws tore through Rivka's defenses, slashing across her side with a brutal force that left a deep, jagged gash in its wake. The sickening sound of rending flesh echoed through the battlefield, accompanied by Rivka's pained cry.

No! Fiend, help us... Time seemed to suspend as the gravity of the injury washed over us, the scene etched into my mind like a nightmare. My concentration wavered, and the well of power I was drawing from dried up. Rivka staggered; her fierce countenance contorted with anguish and her grip faltered on her claws. Blood trickled from the wound, staining her fur and mingling with the ashen soil beneath her.

"You..." My heart clenched, and a surge of dread coursed through my veins. The severity of the wound threatened to extinguish the fire within her, dimming the fierce light that had guided our path.

I needed to act. My thoughts raced, searching for a solution, anything to mend her injured form and restore her strength. But as I watched Rivka, her eyes blazing with determination even in the face of pain, I realized that her resilience could not be so easily quelled.

"I've got you, sis." Finn pulled a healing potion from the satchel on her belt and plucked the cork from its top with her teeth.

I leaned forward conjuring enough magic to keep both hags occupied just long enough for the healing potion to reach Rivka's lips.

In a burst of luminous energy, the healing magic surged into Rivka's injured form. It coalesced around the gash, mending the torn flesh and knitting the wound together. Rivka's breath hitched as the restorative energy washed over her, the pain gradually easing as the wound closed.

With a defiant roar, Rivka's muscles tensed, her will surging like a tempest. She straightened, and a renewed fire blazed within her eyes. The pain that had momentarily clouded her vision now became fuel for her determination as she pushed past the limits of her injury.

Witnessing Rivka's resurgence, a flood of pride swelled within me. Gods, she was magnificent... Her resilience steeled my resolve, and together, we pressed forward.

The final confrontation loomed before us, the culmination of our tireless efforts in the face of insidious darkness. Finn, ever swift and precise, unleashed a decisive strike upon one of the Night Hags. In that split second, the Hag's form quivered and wavered, then dissolved into a chilling mist, leaving behind an eerie absence that hung in the air like a lingering whisper.

Rivka and I joined forces in a synchronized dance of blades and spells, our onslaught converging upon the spectral foes. With every strike, they recoiled, their ethereal forms shuddering and fragmenting under the relentless assault.

The one in black trembled, her dark robes billowing as if caught in a tempestuous wind. Fragmented pieces of her essence scattered into the ethereal mist, dissolving into nothingness. And the last one, with her imposing stature and blood-red eyes, faced the full brunt of my arcane onslaught. My spells collided with her twisted form, causing her to convulse with each impact. Jagged cracks spread across her spectral visage, her grotesque grin contorting into a mask of agony. The demon backed away with a contemptuous glare and dematerialized as the Hag screamed in pain. With a final explosion of arcane energy, she shattered into a myriad of spectral fragments that dispersed into the ashen atmosphere.

The battleground fell silent, save for the rustling of the ashen mist and the resonance of our labored breaths. The last remnants of the Night Hags' malevolence dispersed into the void.

"You didn't want to fight us yourself, you coward?" Finn screamed at the empty space where the Shadow Demon once stood.

In the aftermath, a sense of triumph mingled with the weight of exhaustion. The air cleared, and the ashen mist seemed to thin as if the very landscape breathed a sigh of relief. The scent of brimstone lingered in the air, mingling with the scent of triumph. Our breaths came in ragged gasps, our bodies weary but triumphant.

"I suppose all that's left now is to track down the Cavalcade again." I brushed some of the falling ash from my coat.

"If they're still moving in the same direction at relatively the same pace as when we left, north-northeast should have us intercepting them on the road." Finn took out her canteen, sipped from it, and then handed it to Rivka.

"Did the necromancer tell you anything useful?" Rivka asked, taking a sip and passing the canteen to me.

"I hope so." Finn wiped the sweat at her brow, smearing gray ash through it. "I won't know for sure until I talk to Echo, but I'd rather just tell you all at the same time if it's alright with you."

It had been days since we got a new lead, and I was growing impatient. There were several of my own contacts that I wanted to enquire with, despite Finn insisting that we needed to be more careful about who we trusted going forward—as if *anyone* should be surprised that the integrity of the thieves' guild had been compromised.

Walking on, Finn and I struggled to keep pace with Rivka, but the cat woman slowed down every time she realized we were falling behind. The muscles in my legs burned, and my feet ached, but after an eternity staring out of over the vast empty plains, the orange glow of a massive bonfire illuminated the horizon. It possessed an uncanny resemblance to the final embers of the setting sun.

This time the caravan had made a wide turn before stopping with the boxcars arranged in a massive circle. The wagon train enclosed the whole market, but this time there were no vendors peddling goods or stands at which to buy skewered fowl or honey mead.

This was a time of rest for all of them. At first, I was worried they might not let us inside, but the traveling innkeeper recognized the three of us and welcomed us into the circle with a boisterous laugh and a clap on the shoulder. The people who had been twirling through the air doing incredible feats of acrobatics were now dressed in common clothes.

The music was merry and laid back, and there were several rows of long tables covered with fruits, vegetables, cheeses, and breads that had been saved from the previous day. In our rented boxcar, we found Echo, her mood strikingly somber compared to the libations taking place outside.

She stared intently at a mess of papers strewn about on the coffee table. On them, she'd written out the different clues we'd pieced together over the past week. Finn let out a heavy sigh and sat down next to her. Hale sat on the other side of the table with his arms crossed.

"The stuff he was collecting while he was here with the Cavalcade." Echo's bloodshot eyes shimmered with a sheen of tears. "It just doesn't make any sense. If there was a way to let Dradon know that I'm trying to help him, then he could just explain all of it."

Finn's gaze fell to her lap as she put a hand on Echo's shoulder. I had a feeling that whatever the halfling was about to share with us wasn't going to be good news. Swallowing hard, Finn relayed what the necromancer had told her.

"Echo, I hate to say it, but I think Dradon might have created some kind of monster that feeds on souls of the dead." Finn exchanged a glance with Hale. "I know you don't want to believe it, but—"

"No, you're right." Echo nodded. "The Professor isn't perfect, and as careful as he is, he must have made a mistake, and now he's in over his head and doesn't know how to stop the thing."

"Honestly, I think you're still giving him too much credit." Finn shook her head. "But if you still think he's worth helping, I'm with you."

"As am I," Hale said.

Rivka nodded.

"We all are," I agreed. "But tonight … I think we deserve to join the party *outside* for a change."

Finn smiled at me as the cloud of gloom began to dissolve, and the five of us filed out to join the party. The Strays welcomed us with open arms, and when the drinks flowed and the celebration carried on, Rivka's tail switched in time with the music.

Whether it was the light of the fire, the hypnotic rhythm of the drums, or the strong wine, I found myself swept up in the hedonistic spirit of it all. Striding up to Rivka, I held out my hand. At first, she raised a skeptical eyebrow, but her defensive posture softened, and to my surprise, she took my hand.

Towering over me, she moved toward the fire with a lithe feline grace, her eyes flickering in the firelight. On my first step, I tripped over her foot, chuckling at my own awkwardness, and she smirked, only playfully judgmental. The soft, velvety fur of her fingers tickled my palms as I pulled her close and began to find a rhythm.

As we fell into sync, our bodies swaying to the beating drums, the dance became a playful game. Faster and more frenzied, we twirled into oblivion, exhilarated and intoxicated by the beauty of the endless night.

 FINN

"May I have this dance, milady?" I gave a dramatic flourish as I bowed, holding my hand out to Echo. "If bright-eyes over there isn't going to ask you, I may as well."

Her cheeks flushed with a rosy glow, and she forced an awkward chuckle. "What are you—"

"Come on." I tilted my head, giving her the—*Don't play games with me*—look. "You two have been giving each other eyes all night, and if I'm honest... his lack of backbone is starting to make me feel embarrassed for him."

Echo blushed, pressing her lips together as she took my hand, and we joined the dance. Together, we twirled and spun, our steps light and nimble, like leaves caught in a playful breeze. The ground beneath our feet trembled with the vibrations of the lively tunes, igniting a sense of comfort and trust that flowed between us.

"I can tell you fancy him." I spun under Echo's arm, and she turned, clapping her hands to one side.

"Will you stop it." She rolled her eyes as we stepped forward, twirling in unison as we glided in a half circle to face each other.

"He fancies you too." I lifted my arms, glancing toward the elf who stood brooding next to the table.

"He's not even looking over here." She hissed in a whisper shout.

"Exactly." I laughed. "He's been avoiding looking at you anytime you look at him."

Echo's smile widened as she mirrored my movements, shooting a subtle glance toward Hale, catching his eye as she dipped into a graceful bow.

"I ... sort of ... slept with him."

"You strumpet, you!" I gasped, putting a hand on my cheek in mock disbelief. "Was it good?"

"He uh..." She let out a nervous laugh. "*Yes*. Really good, actually. But he's barely spoken to me since."

"Poor fella." I tsked. "He's caught feelings, and now he's terrified."

"Do you really think that's what it is?" Her brow furrowed as we joined hands then broke apart.

"Trust me." I winked at her. "I have a sense about these things."

Echo's laughter mixed with the melodic notes, a delightful melody of its own. Her contagious joy engulfed my spirit, infusing the dance with an added layer of mirth. I caught glimpses of her radiant smile as we whirled past mirrored surfaces, reflecting like a complex display of shared moments. The distant clinking of glasses added to the symphony of merriment, reminding me of the joyful tapestry we were woven into.

Hale stood a little taller, his chest puffing out as he took a deep breath. Setting down his cup, he strode up to us, offering a shallow bow in my direction.

"May I cut in?" A smile tugged at one side of his lips as Echo and I stopped dancing.

"Well..." I nodded my head in appreciation. "I was wondering what was taking you so long."

Echo bit her lip, a faint rosy glow gracing her cheeks as she smiled. Bowing out, I gave her two thumbs up as I backed toward the tables. Growing up as an orphan in the lowlands, I'd never known what it was to have a family. But since I'd met Echo, I felt a sense of connection and belonging, a bond that transcended blood, the kind of kinship forged by trials endured together.

It made me feel good to see her connecting with Hale. She seemed happier than I'd seen in ages. That night was a celebration of our friendship. The memory of her smiling face would forever linger in my heart, a cherished reminder that as long as we had each other, nothing could hold us down.

 HALE

Do I even know how to dance? My throat was dry as desert sand. Taking Echo's hand in mine, the softness of her fingertips sent a thrill through my body. As my limbs began to move with the music, I breathed a sigh of relief, allowing distant memories to bleed into my muscles.

My mind raced as I guided her into a spin, and she moved gracefully, gliding over the ground. She came close, our bodies nearly touching as a wave of her scent rushed over me. I couldn't stop thinking about what it had been like to kiss her, the taste of her lips and the softness of her skin. I wanted to experience that again, but it felt wrong, now that I knew what kind of man I was.

"You're good at this." Her gaze drifted down to our feet as my body took me through a sequence of steps. "I didn't expect that."

"I didn't expect a lot of things." My fingertips grazed her waist as I circled around behind her, resting a hand on her hip.

Her hand drifted up, reaching back to run her fingertips under my hair over the back of my neck. Gooseflesh raised on my arms at her touch, and I stepped closer, inhaling the sweet scent of her hair. She turned to face me, dancing backward in long steady strides as I advanced toward her.

"I didn't mean to overstep before." Her emerald eyes glistened up at me. "If I made you feel—I... I mean you don't owe me anything."

What? My arms fell loosely to my sides as I looked down at her. *Did she really think, for a second, that I didn't want her?*

"I owe you *everything...*" I looked deeply into her eyes. "But that's not why I asked you to dance."

She shifted her weight from one foot to the other, scrunching her shoulders to her ears. "Then why did you?"

What did she expect me to say? I couldn't articulate what I was feeling any better than I could describe what it was like to die. Sweeping her hair out of her eyes, I cupped her face in my hands and slowly lowered my head to place my lips firmly against hers. I sighed, rested my forehead against hers, and smiled, brushing my thumb along her jaw.

"Oh…" She smiled and bit her lower lip.

Taking her in my arms again, I swung her in a slow circle and dipped her slowly back. She surrendered, leaning into my embrace, and our eyes met in silent understanding. Whatever future the afterlife held, I knew she was a pure soul that deserved every joy and happiness this world had to offer.

"If we ever get separated again…" She cleared her throat. "You know, with all the dematerializing and whatnot. I was just thinking we should meet behind the rose quartz gargoyles at Guardian's Rest."

"Then that's the first place I'll look for you."

I could no more resist the urge to be near her than a meteor crashing to the earth could resist the pull of its gravity. Sooner or later, she would have to see me for the monster I was, but that night, I didn't have the strength to stay away. In the light of the fire, with the effervescent energy of the music flowing through us, I gave up all hope.

My heart … was lost.

CHAPTER 14

ECHO

Hale poured five strong cups of coffee as our group settled back into our little boxcar room. The rich, earthy aroma filled the space with warmth, and the bitter flavor awakened my senses, chasing away the haze of the wine. Rivka reclined on a pile of cushions, her long slender tail switching lazily.

"Alright, so what do we know?" Hale handed a cup to Finn and sat down across from me.

"Uh..." I blinked, taking a long sip before gesturing to the tome on the table. "We know that Dradon was doing research based on the life's work of someone who called themselves the mad alchemist, which should have been a red flag, but I digress."

"We know that he was dealing in black market herbs and ingredients." Hyperion sprinkled some jaffray into a rolling paper, licking the edge to make it stick.

"And the body map has equations on it that illustrate how to convert ghostly essence into some other form of energy." Finn looked around with wide eyes. "That's a bit concerning, considering the killer on the loose."

"Maybe it's not a coincidence that the Keepers came after us right after Hale and I traveled back through the veil." My fingers found the holy symbol hanging on a small cord around my neck. "What if there is no soul eater?"

"What do you mean?" Rivka leaned forward. "Who would make something like that up?"

"If Dradon figured out how to perform resurrections from this side, the Monarchy could be worried that it will spark some kind of ... chain reaction. Imagine all the people who would go back to earth if they could."

"Isn't the entire purpose of the Sunless Crossing to be a waystation for souls that could be resurrected?" Rivka nibbled on a piece of bread. "Why would the Monarchy care if people went back to Earth?"

"I don't know." I shook my head. "Control?"

"They wouldn't have much of a kingdom to rule if it was that easy to bring yourself back," Finn said. "A little unicorn dust and whatever else Echo whipped up, and she was able to do something the Monarchy has said no one would be able to do."

"What would happen if there was a mass exodus?" Hale leaned back with a thoughtful expression. "Would they even be able to find a Sovereign?"

"No Sovereign... No Sunless Crossing," I whispered.

"So maybe the easiest way to explain these people going missing is to make up some tale about a horrible soul-eating monster and let the rumor mill work its magic."

"That would certainly make people wary of illegal magic practitioners." Hyperion lit his jaffray cigarette and took a long drag, exhaling a plume of smoke toward the ceiling. "And it would explain why they raided the lab. With more and more people discovering what's in that book, their best bet is to come down hard on anyone practicing black market alchemy."

I leaned back in my chair drumming my fingers against my cup. "That still doesn't explain why they're still looking for Dradon. If he's resurrected, why not just send one of their contacts in the corporeal world after him."

"I mean, maybe this particular brand of resurrection magic makes you harder to track." Finn opened the book and started absently flipping through the pages. "You and Hale only seemed like you were gone for a few minutes tops, and you two had a whole day-long ordeal. If it's distorting something as rigid as time, I imagine the spatial aspect of it is a hell of a lot more complicated."

"She's right." Hyperion nodded. "This is entirely new territory, and no one has any idea what the rules are. After all, you got resurrected in the same room as Hale, and I'm pretty sure your remains weren't anywhere near his. Does that mean someone scrying would have seen your essence in two different places? Or was your energy signature changed completely?"

"Gods..." I rested my head against the heel of my hand. "I wish I had a lab so that I could run more tests."

"I'm sure Dradon thought the same thing." Finn stood up and started pacing. "So where would he look to set up a new lab?"

"Mmm." A strange expression came over Hale's face, something akin to having eaten bad shellfish.

"Hale?" I met his gaze. "Are you alright?"

He opened his mouth to answer and, without warning, blinked out of existence, his cup of coffee clattering to the floor as everyone erupted in gasps and curses.

"What the hell just happened?" Finn waved her arms through the empty spot where he'd been sitting.

"We're not dead," I breathed.

"What?" Rivka scowled, cleaning up the spilled coffee with a cloth. "What are you talking about?"

"Our bodies..." I gestured excitedly, getting up and putting my hands on my head. "We're still alive. We must have come back here when we fell asleep. The magic. There's something wrong with it. It's like the resurrection didn't take hold completely, and we're still straddling both sides of the veil."

And just like that, the final piece of the puzzle fell into place.

"That's why they're still looking for him here." I smiled. "Dradon is appearing and disappearing every time he falls through the veil, and they can't track him!"

"If the Monarchy really is trying to suppress the truth about resurrection, we need to figure out a way to get the word out."

"Easy..." Hyperion put a hand up. "It's a great theory, but if we're going to call out the most powerful people in the realm, we're going to need some cold hard proof. Or else, we won't have a leg to stand on."

"I know someone," I said.

"Echo, how can you be sure you can trust this person?" Finn set her coffee down and took my hands. "Aren't they the one who told you about the soul eater in the first place? Who even are they?"

"Someone who trusts me." I squeezed her hands. "And I trust them with my life."

"Just ... be careful, will you?" She sighed.

"Work on setting up a platform to get the message out." I grabbed my satchel and headed for the door. "I'll work on getting that proof we talked about. Hyperion, can you and Rivka find a lab where I can work?"

"I think my time would be better spent looking for Dradon." Rivka pulled her hooded cloak on. "I can move faster and more quietly alone, and no offense, but none of you can track worth a damn."

"I beg your pardon?" Hyperion put out his cigarette on a saucer.

"We've tried it your way." Rivka held up a hand. "I need you all to trust me on this."

"Fine." I nodded. "Rivka will look for Dradon, Hyperion will find me a lab, and Finn—"

"I'll be finding out the best way to get a message out to an entire city before the Nyxian Guard can try to silence us."

I smiled at her, and the four of us went our separate ways. On the other side of the circular Cavalcade was a large rectangular tent. The previous day, I'd had seen many of the circus performers emerge with dramatic makeup and colorful outfits. If I was going to enter the city and make contact with my friend, I would need this particular artist's services.

"Excuse me." I called through the open canvas flap. "I was wondering if I might procure some of your *supplies*."

"Today is a day of rest for us Strays," a woman's voice said from somewhere in the shadows.

"Apologies." My heart raced and sweat formed on my palms. "If it was possible to wait, I'd come back tomorrow, but I'm afraid it's a bit of an emergency."

"Emergencies are *expensive*..." said the mysterious voice.

"And I'm willing to pay." Pushing the tent flap open, I entered the dimly lit space. "Please, can you help me?"

A tall slender figure stepped away from the wall of the tent, and I was unsure of how I hadn't seen her before. Her lean muscular body was clad in tan leather armor, and a veil covered her face from the bridge of her nose down.

"So..." She circled me like a shark, looking me up and down as I let my gaze wander over the racks and tables of garments, tools, and strange objects. "Since the matter is so urgent, I assume that you're in the market for more than a simple make-over."

"I need to be able to walk into the city without anyone recognizing me." I looked over my shoulder at her. "It would be even better if I could go completely unnoticed altogether."

"I can't make you invisible." The rogue's eyes smiled as she pulled up a weathered stool. "But I can help. Have a seat, my dear."

I obeyed as she took out a cord and began taking my measurements. She didn't speak but moved with silent grace, rummaging through trunks and laying out various pallets of powdered pigment and gummy clay-like substances I didn't recognize. Gently tilting my face one way and then the other, she meticulously examined my features, assessing every slope and curve like a sculptor preparing to chisel expensive marble.

With careful precision, she began smearing the clay substance onto my face. Once the structure was altered, highlights and false shadows were applied using pigment, thickening my brows and shaping a strong jawline with prominent cheekbones. Patting dark sand onto my cheeks, chin, and upper lip, the rogue's eyes glinted with pride as she, at last, held up a hand mirror.

"Holy mother of Azuth..." The reflection staring back at me was that of a young man who boasted the beginnings of a handsome beard. My jaw dropped as I examined my face from several different angles. "This is amazing."

"We're just getting started, my good sir." She winked holding up a wide roll of bandages. "Now, let's get you out of that dress."

Using strategic padding, she built up the semblance of muscles and subdued the soft curves of my hips and breasts, and by the time she was done, I felt like a different person entirely. The rogue's requested payment was substantial, but it wasn't anything I couldn't afford. A barely-sipped-on bottle of heady mead, a bag of glitter bombs, and the secret of a high-ranking officer of the Chantry of Endless Acquisition that I had gleaned from Finn, and we were settled up.

As I left the Cavalcade behind, the atmosphere shifted. The bright colorful world of the Strays and the lively sounds of laughter and music faded as the Ashen Fields stretched out in every direction. The earth at my feet was tinged with gray, and the deafening silence of a world with no frogs or insects swallowed me up.

A westward wind whispered, swirling through the golden wheat stalks, carrying a sense of foreboding as thunder rumbled in the distance. The smoky smell of ash emanated from the sky as the churning clouds threatened to drop a fresh layer over the hills. In the distance, the dark gates of the city loomed, welcoming me like the open jaws of a smiling crocodile.

Nox Valar stood tall against the bleak horizon, it's imposing height casting long shadows over my path.

"Hail, traveler!" The guard on the right raised a hand and stepped forward. "Anything of note to report?"

Lowering my voice an octave, I made a vague gesture to the landscape behind me. "Lots of wide open spaces... Bit lonely out there."

"I imagine so." The guard chuckled. "Headed to the Crimson Quarter, are ya?"

I chuckled nervously. "Can't seem to stay away."

"Don't let 'em take all yer' Crossway Coins, eh?" The guard jerked his head toward the gates, ushering me through.

I waved my hand dismissively. "Meh, what else am I gunna spend it on?"

The guards laughed, and I told them to have a good shift as I entered the city. *Should I be worried that I play this role so well?*

Striding through the streets, I found myself more confident than I expected. Wearing the skin of a young male adventurer seemed to warrant a different kind of attention.

Somehow it felt like a greater stroke of the ego when I caught the eye of a beautiful woman who passed by.

I blushed, smiling to myself as I made my way to the city's center where the great Etherwood tree towered over the surrounding gardens. The massive, lush wisteria was the crown jewel of the city, in my opinion. It's delicate white blossoms bore veins of gold running through the petals and the tree towered high over the surrounding buildings, reaching toward the swirling vortex above.

Just a short walk from there, I reached one of the many bridges that allowed me to cross the seemingly bottomless ring of clear blue water surrounding the tree. These springs were the ones that filled every well and canal in the city, flowing into the numerous waterfalls that would eventually cascade down the cliffs on the far side of Nox Valar to form the rivers in the Fields.

Serenity filled my consciousness as the vibrant gemstone hues of the water danced under the purple light of the sky. The sound of rushing water filled the air, a symphony of cascading melodies that harmonized with the rhythm of my own heartbeat. The clarity of the water allowed me glimpses into the depths below, revealing a mesmerizing display of aquatic plant life, swaying and dancing in the current like an underwater ballet.

As I crossed the bridge, the air was filled with a subtle, refreshing mist that kissed my skin, carrying with it the invigorating scent of water and moss. The sounds of rushing water grew louder, reverberating through the expanse, while gentle droplets caressed my face as if the springs themselves were reaching out to touch me.

On the other side of the bridge, I reached a grand avenue lined with dozens upon dozens of temples, each one a gateway to a different afterlife. The air buzzed with otherworldly energy as if the souls of the departed whispered their stories from beyond. It was here, at the threshold of the Road to Eternity, that the majority of souls who ventured through the Sunless Crossing found their ultimate destination. Amongst the crowd, I caught glimpses of ethereal beings, shimmering with a celestial glow, while others walked with somber expressions, clad in mourning attire.

People had to bid their loved ones farewell when they were called to their afterlives. I'd thought about this before, but the weight of that reality settled upon me, as I stood at the crossroads between the realm of waiting and those beyond, wondering what that would mean for my company of friends.

All of us were of different races, nations, and honored different entities. Sooner or later, I would have to say goodbye to Rivka, Hyperion, and even Finn and Hale forever. The realization made my heart sink and I did my best to shake off the melancholy shroud that had settled over me.

As I walked along the bustling road, mingling with hundreds of wandering souls, I wondered if I'd ever get to see Professor Dradon again. If I did, I'd be sure to tell him that despite how our friendship ended, I held more good memories than bad, and that I'd never forget the lessons he taught me.

The Onyx Requiem emerged in the distance, looming over the surrounding temples. Its black stone spires and golden domes pierced the sky, exuding an aura of power and ancient wisdom. It stood as the seat of authority for Nox Valar and the Sunless Crossing, where the enigmatic Godless Monarchy held court. The Onyx Requiem was not just a symbol of governance but also represented the various afterlives that converged within its realm.

Caution whispered in the back of my mind. With the convergence of countless pathways and access to multiple afterlives, the need for vigilance was paramount. I observed the meticulous movements of the inhabitants, their purposeful strides and watchful gazes, a constant reminder of the delicate balance that kept the planes in harmony.

The grandeur of the Onyx Requiem came into full view as I neared its entrance. The history embedded within its foundations, predating even the city, lent an air of reverence and ancient power to the cathedral. Within these walls, the Sovereign and Arbiter had held sway for countless millennia, safeguarding the Sunless Crossing and its myriad realms. Every step closer to its gates heightened my awareness of the absolute power bestowed upon those who governed from within these hallowed halls.

The vast courtyard leading to the entrance of the Requiem was covered with vast mosaics of onyx and obsidian forming patterns that shifted and rippled with the light of the vortex overhead. At the heart of the courtyard was its spectacular masterpiece, an intricately carved fountain depicting ethereal beings and mortals of all races intertwined in a spiral-shaped sculpture with crystalline water running down over them.

Nude figures frozen in celestial grace, with each detail meticulously rendered, capturing the delicate interplay of light and shadow, evoking a sense of otherworldly harmony. It wasn't difficult to pretend to be enthralled by the intricate craftsmanship that brought the scene to life. I crossed my arms and nodded thoughtfully to the masterpiece.

The expressions on the celestial and mortal faces seemed to judge my intrusion, and I cleared my throat while leaning to one side as my gaze wandered toward the entrance. Valen, the dashing Nyxian Gargoyle, stood atop the grand steps exuding that enchanting allure that defied the expectations of his stone brethren. Unlike most gargoyles, Valen possessed a captivating vitality, his spirit and features alive and expressive.

His chiseled face was a blend of strength and elegance, characterized by sharp angles and a defined jawline that spoke of resilience and determination. Adorned with a rich sea-foam patina, his jade skin held a sheen as if touched by moonlight, while subtle veins of silver traced intricate patterns across his form. His eyes, vibrant and piercing, shone with an intensity that mirrored a burning inner fire, reflecting a spirit of youthful rebellion that I found absolutely intoxicating.

Valen glanced over at me, and I smiled. It was only when he gave me a perplexed look that I remembered I was in disguise. There was also the fact that my eyes had gone black, and my skin was pale as ash.

His wings, impressive and grand, extended proudly from his back, their sculpted membranes as smooth and delicate as silk. Veins of ethereal blue and glimmers of iridescent colors danced along the edges, giving an ethereal luminescence to his wingspan. I'd be lying if I said I hadn't been somewhat infatuated with him despite his only seeing me as a sister.

Pressing my lips together, I suppressed a chuckle and dipped my fingers in the water of the fountain. Tapping into my arcane energy, I called upon a spell. My god was so far from me that our connection felt more like a fading dream than something tangible that I used to possess.

Come on... I clenched my teeth. *One little spell.*

I dug deep, reaching for the dregs hanging at the edges of my consciousness forming the incantation in my mind. *Prismatic Spray...*

Power surged through my core, channeling through my fingertips in waves of dynamic energy, exploding a kaleidoscope of color into the water as it erupted in a shimmering display. Several people gasped and one woman screamed as the rainbow of light rippled and gushed through the fountain.

Valen's eyebrows drew together, but then as my gaze met his, a hidden smile appeared at the corners of his lips.

"Hey…" One of the gargoyles pointed at me. "That'll be enough of that! This is a sacred place. Where's your respect?"

"Oh, it's just a bit of fun," I said in my slightly lowered voice.

"You'll get a bit of an ass-whoopin'." The human guard at his side put a hand on the hilt of his sword and took a step toward me.

"I'll escort him out." Valen put a hand on his comrade's shoulder. "You can deal with the next troublemaker."

Every movement exuded confidence, and his body moved with a fluidity that hinted at a strength beyond the surface. The gargoyle possessed an air of regality as if he were destined to stand watch over these sacred grounds. But despite his formidable appearance, Valen's demeanor was gentle and compassionate.

"What on earth are you wearing," he whispered as he came near with a warm smile playing upon his lips, revealing his true nature.

"You said it yourself." I put my hands up in surrender as he escorted me toward the gates of the courtyard. "I'm a troublemaker."

In the realm of Nox Valar, Valen was an anomaly—a gargoyle bound by duty like all of them, but his heart was forever in the wind.

"I heard the Monarch ordered a raid on the Professor's old lab. Glad to see you made it out." His voice carried a timbre that resonated with sincerity and trust.

"Barely…" I sighed, glancing over my shoulder as we stepped to the side of the entrance, just outside the gates of the courtyard. "Do you think we could go somewhere quiet to talk?

"One last flight?" His smile turned melancholy. "I have a feeling I might get promoted soon and... honestly, I'll probably have my hands pretty full for the foreseeable future."

"You're not joking." I frowned.

"I've found this job puts a damper on my sense of humor." He arched an eyebrow with a half-smile that showed one pearly fang.

I bit my lip. "Alright... Let's do it, but if I start getting—" I gasped as he scooped me up into his arms.

With a gentle sweep of his wings, we lifted off the ground, ascending into the vast expanse of the darkened sky. The wind rushed against my face, whipping through my hair as we soared higher and higher. The city of Nox Valar unfolded beneath us, a sprawling tapestry of black and white, a realm where light and shadow danced in eternal harmony. The mesmerizing sight took my breath away, and I couldn't help but marvel at the sheer beauty of it all.

Circling around the outer rim of the city, we passed the magnificent Guardian's Rest, where the stoic gazes of the gargoyle sentinels watched over the Sunless Crossing, their presence an ever-present reminder of their eternal vigilance. The archway of the Enduring Threshold beckoned, its grandeur a testament to the countless souls that had passed through its gates.

The cavernous tunnel of Ascension Row snaked through the mesa, leading souls to their first destination within the city and the Gray Vista stretched out before us, offering a breathtaking view of the Ashen Fields and the black horizon beyond. It was a place of reflection and contemplation, where souls found solace in the quietude of the landscape.

As we glided over the fortress of Crag Veil, I marveled at the colossal shield and sword hanging proudly, symbols of strength and protection. The towers of Whetstone Bluff came into view, bustling with training grounds, arenas, and smithies, a hub of activity where warriors honed their skills and competed in tests of prowess.

My gaze shifted to Exora's Belfry, perched at the edge of the city atop a bridge, its bell of black iron swaying gently in the breeze, and I thought of Hale. I would have loved for him to meet Valen. Before I'd gotten him in trouble, we'd had numerous adventures exploring the city.

The Codex of the Mortal Realms stood as a symbol of the city's pursuit of knowledge, its black marble structure adorned with golden beams and maps of countless worlds. It housed the wisdom of the ages, a treasury of information spanning the vast tapestry of existence.

At the center of it all, the Etherwood tree, serenely rooted at the center of the Still Garden, with its vibrant grass and lush vegetation, brought a sense of peace to the city. It looked so much smaller from up here.

With each twist and turn, my heart leapt and I clung to him for dear life. Valen danced with a daring grace, as if he and the sky were locked in an eternal waltz. He flipped upside down, momentarily defying gravity, before righting himself with effortless ease.

As we gained altitude once more, I marveled at the breathtaking vista that unfolded before my eyes. The entire realm stretched out beneath us, a mosaic of shadows and light, where the ebon hues of the city blended with the ethereal glow of the celestial vortex overhead. It was a sight that stirred the depths of my soul and filled me with a profound sense of wonder.

My eyes were drawn to the House of the Dawn, a grand building where souls could indulge in games of chance and revelry, even in the realms beyond.

With a final sweep of his wings, Valen began our descent, gently gliding back toward the endless fields. As we landed gracefully, I thought about what an incredible adventure our friendship had been. In life, I struggled to find my tribe, but somehow in Nox Valar, I'd found several kindred spirits and the realization filled me with gratitude.

"It's so hard for me to take you seriously in that beard." He snorted. "You'll have to tell me how you got your eyes to look like that."

It was easy to forget how much I'd changed. I got a sinking feeling as I contemplated whether or not to tell him everything that had happened.

"Ha-ha, laugh it up." I cleared my throat. "Everyone's looking for me, and what I'm working on is too important for me to risk getting locked up."

"Speaking of which…" He set me down in the middle of the open field, and I stumbled, swaying a couple of times before I could find my balance again. "What's on your mind, Echo?"

"Well," I sat next to him and plucked a piece of golden grass, fidgeting with it. "I think there might be something strange going on with the investigation the Monarchy is carrying out."

"Stranger than a soul-eating madman?" He lowered his voice. "Do tell."

"I don't know if there is a soul eater." I picked the blade of grass apart, tearing it into strips, hoping I didn't sound like a lunatic. "I think it's a red-herring to distract people from what's actually going on. What if the people who are missing were actually resurrected?"

"I don't follow." He blinked. "What would be the point of trying to cover up resurrections?"

"The same reason they're after Dradon. I think he figured out a loophole." I crossed my arms. "I think he's resurrecting people from *this* side."

He chuckled, narrowing his eyes… then when he realized I was serious, his expression grew severe. "That's … impossible.

Echo, a betwixt can't rez from this side, and if they were crazy enough to try, they'd be in a whole heap of trouble. It could have some serious repercussions that we wouldn't even be able to predict yet."

"Of course." Guilt flushed my cheeks, and I bit my thumbnail, shifting my weight from one foot to the other, deciding not to tell him that I'd already resurrected myself *and* Hale.

"If word gets out that Dradon is rezzing people, it's going to change everything." He shook his head. "People would be trampling each other to get to him."

"I know." I put a hand on Valen's arm, and his smooth stone skin was cool to the touch. "I can't be sure that's actually what's happening. But if it is … Valen, I need you to find out if I'm right."

He let out a deep sigh, hanging his head and shaking it before meeting my gaze again. "You realize that I'm already risking a lot just by continuing to talk to you."

"I know." A knot formed in my throat.

"I'd be sitting in a cell if I hadn't taken this deal to join the guard."

"I get it, and I'm sorry to have to ask this of you, but Valen… we can't just let the Monarchy cover this up. It wouldn't be right."

"*Right?*" He blinked. "I helped you leave Nox Valar to poke around those old temples. We could have been swallowed by the storm, all for what? Your research? I bear you no malice, Echo. I was fully complicit in all that foolishness. It made me feel… *alive*. But let's not pretend that your misadventures have ever been about what's *right*."

I held my breath, my heart breaking as I looked up into his eyes. After everything we'd been through together, all the trouble I'd caused him already, I hated myself for asking him to risk his second chance.

"Fuck…" He ran a clawed hand through this dark hair. "Fine…"

"Seriously?" I exhaled.

"Meet me in the hanging gardens near the Etherwood in two cycles." He turned his face away. "I'll find out what I can."

"Thank you." I bounced on the balls of my feet, and threw my arms around his neck.

"I have to get back before someone realizes I'm gone." He stood up and when he turned to take flight, my heart swelled, and I had to see his face one last time.

"Valen?" I called after him, and he looked over his shoulder. "It was good to see you."

He smiled but didn't say another word as he flapped his great wings, lifting into the air. My once carefree companion was no longer the man I knew. I could see that something in him had shifted and despite what he said, he no longer resented his post on the steps of the Requiem. His newfound sense of duty suited him well, even if I didn't care for the authority he knelt to.

I stumbled as a strange sense of vertigo overwhelmed me. I leaned against the wall to steady myself as a strange falling sensation seemed to pull inward at the center of my gut.

"What the—" Putting a hand on my stomach, I took a few deep breaths.

All of a sudden, I seemed to drop out from under the world around me, the stalks of wheat and the thundering of a nearby waterfall blurred together in a horrible hellish vision that seared every nerve ending in my body.

CHAPTER 15

HALE

Each morning, she woke with the same panicked look on her face. Though having a name to call me seemed to put her somewhat at ease. On the trail, we stopped periodically to forage, testing out various edible plants and finding that all of them tasted the same. Rotten, dry, and gritty to the inside of our mouths. We forced ourselves to eat some fruit and allowed the animals to graze for a bit.

The horses whinnied softly as we urged them forward, their breath forming wisps of vapor in the crisp morning air. Our ride was shared in companionable silence, occasionally exchanging glances and smiles of shared understanding as we fell into a steady trot, the sound of hoofbeats reverberating through the forest.

The setting sun cast a warm golden glow over the landscape as we finally stopped to make camp after a long day of travel. Nestled amidst towering trees, their branches reaching toward the darkening sky, I dismounted my horse, my muscles protesting the day's exertion as a weariness settled into my bones.

"Here is as good a place to rest as any." I inhaled the scent of pine and earth that permeated the air.

"I was just thinking..." Echo dismounted gracefully, her resilience evident in every movement. "Do you think we're turning into something like a vampire or a ghoul? I've heard that human food becomes revolting during that kind of transformation. And honestly, now that the sun is down, I feel better than I have all day."

"I don't know." The solid earth beneath my boots grounded me amidst the vast wilderness as we set about the familiar routine of making camp. "We saw a lot of blood fighting our way out of that castle, and I didn't once feel the urge to eat anyone."

"True." She winced.

I gathered fallen branches and dry leaves, creating a circle for our fire. Our journey had forged a bond between us, a connection that transcended the physical hardships we faced. As darkness descended upon the forest, I gazed up at the star-studded sky, a tapestry of twinkling lights that seemed to hold the secrets of the universe.

"What if it has something to do with astral projection or soul teleportation." The bright yellow flames danced in the dark pools of her eyes. "This morning, when I was waking up, it felt like I was traveling. You know that feeling you get when sleep is sweeping you away?"

"Like you're falling or drifting on the wind?" I asked.

"Exactly!" She smiled. "I saw some nightshade bushes back there that were thick with berries. If I look around the base of some of these trees, I know I could find some dreamer's cap mushrooms. We could—"

"Woah, slow down!" I chuckled. "In case you've forgotten, the men from that castle could still be after us. Drugging ourselves to sleep heavy is literally the worst thing we could do."

"What if I were to do it?" she asked, letting out a heavy sigh. "Please, Hale. If you're willing to keep a lookout, I think I might be able to induce a vision and possibly get some answers."

The sound of what I was growing more and more certain was my name on her lips, broke down my defenses. Scratching the back of my neck, I thought about it. It didn't seem wise, but I knew little of magic. My skills were centered on killing, escaping, and basic survival. If anyone would be able to keep watch while she went on some kind of dream quest, it would be me.

"Fine." I nodded. "But I'm trusting that you won't poison yourself to death on accident."

"I know what I'm doing." She nodded, her expression illuminated with optimism.

We ventured into the moonlit forest, our steps cautious and deliberate. The crackling fire cast dancing shadows, illuminating our path as we sought the elusive nightshade berries and dreamer's cap mushrooms. Echo's nimble fingers plucked the delicate flora with expertise, carefully depositing them into a small cloth pouch she'd fashioned from her tattered shirt. Returning to the warmth of our fireside sanctuary, Echo cupped her hands, cradling the collection of herbs.

I watched her intently, with uncertainty etched on my face. Her gaze met mine, a mischievous glint twinkling in her eyes.

"Are you sure about this?" I put a hand on her shoulder.

A gentle smile tugged at the corners of her lips as she gazed up at me, her long lashes casting shadows against her cheeks. Leaning closer, she pressed her lips against mine, a sweet and tender kiss that sent ripples of warmth cascading through my entire being. It was a moment that both soothed and ignited the ache in my chest.

As our lips parted, a sense of anticipation hung in the air. Without uttering a single word, Echo brought her open palm to her mouth, swallowing the gathered fruits and herbs in one swift motion. I watched, captivated by her unwavering resolve and the trust she placed in the concoction.

In that fleeting exchange, a silent understanding passed between us. It was a shared journey, an act of faith in the unknown. And as the mixture descended into her being, I couldn't help but feel the weight of our bond deepening, our connection solidifying amidst the mystical ambiance of the night.

I settled down beside the fire, the flames casting dancing shadows upon my face, and Echo laid down in front of me, snuggling close, her presence a source of comfort and solace in this vast wilderness. The crackling of the wood and the rhythmic chorus of treefrogs and crickets thrummed all around us as I put my arm over her.

I'm with you Echo... Wherever you travel, I will follow.

CHAPTER 16

❧ ECHO ❧

As the ethereal energies coalesced, I rematerialized in the once-empty field where Valen and I had parted ways. A passing traveler yelped at my sudden appearance, and I stammered some nonsense about a patchy invisibility spell.

I was right... As the fog of my memory cleared, I remembered eating the mushrooms and berries. I remembered my return to the corporeal realm... and I remembered Hale.

How long have I been gone? From what I gathered during our previous time in the mortal plane, time didn't move as quickly there as it did here. *Or was it the other way around?* The first thing I needed to do was figure out how much time had passed. If I missed my rendezvous with Valen, there was no telling how long it would be before I could flag him down again.

When I reached the gates, I greeted the guards cordially as I entered and they politely acknowledged me as usual. As I navigated the winding paths, the scent of night-blooming flowers filled the air, their intoxicating fragrance mingling with the cool night breeze. The gentle rustle of leaves accompanied my footsteps.

Approaching a familiar moss-covered stone bench, was Valen, his sea-foam jade practically glowing in contrast to the murky shadows. The vortex illuminated his chiseled features, accentuating the intricate details of his stony form. He sat with an air of quiet contemplation.

"Sorry if I'm late," I said nervously.

His face lit up as he looked over his shoulder, and a sense of comfort washed over me. His eyes met mine, a glimmer of recognition sparkling within them.

"When you didn't show up yesterday, I thought something must have happened to you." He stood, and his wings partially unfurled.

"I guess in a way, something did." With measured steps, I drew nearer to Valen, the vortex casting a soft glow upon us. "I would explain, but it's all really confusing."

"Well, you were right about one thing." Valen sighed. "Something *is* being covered up. In the Lieutenant's office, I found some letters from her superior talking about a mad alchemist."

My eyes grew wide, and I leaned forward, whispering, "What did they say?"

"From what I could gather, the mad alchemist didn't want to leave the Sunless Crossing, believing that the afterlife he was destined for would be one filled with pain and torment."

"I've known a few people who had that worry." I nodded.

"So he spent ages working on trying to find a loophole. A way to avoid passing onto the afterlife by transforming a soul into something else."

"And did he?" I looked around, stepping in closer.

"It was thought that he died in a terrible explosion, but according to the letters, they're unsure. Echo, if what they're saying is true, he figured out a way to travel back to the mortal plane without resurrection. This is some seriously dark magic, the kind that can permanently taint your soul. You shouldn't be toying with it."

"Toying with it?" I asked as anger flushed my cheeks. "Is that what you think I'm doing?"

"Are those black eyes part of your disguise?" He looked at me with an expression that said he already knew the answer.

"I never said my eyes were part of the disguise." I turned away.

"We have a prisoner with eyes like yours, Echo." He put his hands on my shoulders and gave me a single shake. "This magic hides its user from the gods. We don't know why, but it changes your eyes... Don't you see? I wouldn't tell you to back off from this if there wasn't a good reason."

"Well, it's a little late." I crossed my arms. "I already managed to resurrect myself."

He took a step back, eyes wide with terror. "Echo..."

"Look, it was an accident." I held my hands up. "I was trying to fix someone's memory, and we sort of got sucked back to the earthly plane. Now, when my physical body wakes up, I disappear from the Sunless Crossing. It seems like when that body sleeps, it sort of dies and come back here."

"Shit..." His lips parted and he got a distant look in his eyes. "Echo, this is bad."

"Valen, I'm still me." I reached for his hand but he withdrew it from my reach and my heart broke a little. "Please..."

"We have to go to the Monarchy" His gaze fell to the ground, and he refused to look at me. "Maybe there's still a chance they can undo this."

"You can't be serious." A lump formed in my throat and the purple light shrouding the garden seemed to dim. His silence sent a whirlwind of confusion and disbelief rolling through my mind. "You *are* serious."

"I'm sorry..." He breathed. "You've gone too far, Echo, and I can't just pretend it's not happening."

No matter how precious something was and how much trust you placed in someone, friendship should never be taken for granted. The bond we had nurtured over time, built upon mutual respect and shared experiences, crumbled away like sand slipping through my trembling fingers.

"I understand." I forced the words through my parched lips, taking a step back as I nodded.

"No, Echo." He clenched his jaw, and the light cast down from the vortex shifted as the muscle flexed. "I don't think you do."

"Please don't do this..." The warmth that had radiated between us, the effortless flow of conversation, and the shared laughter now felt like distant memories fading into the vast emptiness.

"I have to take you in." Each word struck like a stone as he strode toward me. "It will be better if you come willingly. Maybe if you explain how this all happened, the judge will—"

"What?" I laughed, but tears stung my eyes. "Do you think they'll show mercy and lock me up for the rest of my time in the Sunless Crossing? Or will they just toss me into the storm and be done with it?"

"The Monarchy doesn't execute people every time they mess up." He furrowed his brow. "But this isn't for you or me to decide. You have to take responsibility for what you've done."

"I do." I held my hands up and continued backing away as he walked forward. "And I will. But I have to find Dradon first."

"I'm sorry Echo." He held out his hand. "But your part in this is done."

"I see." I swallowed hard, staring down the man who had been one of my oldest and dearest friends. What I needed to determine was if he was seriously willing to chase me down and drag me into the Onyx Requiem.

"You're thinking of running." He tilted his head. "I wouldn't if I were you."

"What?" I forced a brittle smile. "Worried that I'm going to make you work for that promotion?"

"Echo—"

Before he could say another word, I darted to the right, sprinting full tilt through the bushes. The bio-luminescent plants guided my way through the perpetual darkness as Valen barreled after me, quickly closing the distance between us. Lightning from the vortex illuminated the garden in brief, haunting bursts as I weaved between statues and plants. As Valen's low growl echoed behind me, I leaped over a gurgling fountain and skidded to a stop, feeling the gust of wind from his wingbeats just inches overhead.

My hand brushed against the cold, smooth surface of the edge of the marble fountain as I pushed off and veered around a corner, my breaths ragged with fear and exertion. Between lightning strikes, I dashed from behind the tree, making my way toward the far end of the garden. I prayed the darkness would shroud my movements long enough to reach it.

My heart soared with hope as I spotted the concealed trap door I'd entered through just ahead, the adrenaline urging me forward. Valen lunged, nearly catching me with his out-stretched talons.

With every fiber of my being, I pushed myself, my determination eclipsing my fatigue as I yanked up the trap door and dropped into the narrow passage below. *If he wants to follow me down here, he'll have to leave those big, beautiful wings behind, and last I checked, he was pretty attached to them.*

"Echo!" He roared down into the manhole. "If you come in with me, at least I can vouch for your character."

"That's sweet of you to offer." I panted. "But it's too late for that. And I'm not getting locked up before I can find Dradon."

Looking up, the swirling purple clouds illuminated the dark silhouette of his head and shoulders. If it hadn't been for the confines of the dark drainage tunnel, I wouldn't have bothered running. Part of me hoped this wouldn't be the last time I saw Valen, but I also knew that if I did ever face him again, things would be very different between us.

FINN

As I settled onto the soft picnic blanket just outside the Cavalcade, I hoped that wherever Echo was, she was safe. She'd talked about implicitly trusting her friend who had, through some mysterious course of events, ended up working for the Monarchy. As much as I loved Echo, sometimes she put too much faith in people.

"Fortunately, I found milk." Minerva, the fortune teller I'd befriended so many months ago, took her seat at the other end of the blanket. "Cannot have proper tea without milk."

"Indeed." I arranged the delicate teacups and saucers with care, their intricate designs reflecting the enchanting atmosphere surrounding us. "Milk and sugar are essential for the perfect cup of tea."

Hanging lanterns cast a gentle glow upon our makeshift dining area as the aromas of freshly steeped tea and an array of delectable brunch foods filled the air, transporting us to a tranquil haven away from the ongoing chaos of the never-ending festival. Minerva's robes billowed in the breeze, the dark indigo fabric embroidered with shimmering silver thread.

"Have you decided if you'll look for Logic?" Minerva asked in her thick accent. The fortune teller had given me a lead to follow on, Ritgur Logic, a traveling journalist who comes through the Cavalcade every so often.

"Yes, Ma'am." I reached for a plate piled high with buttery pastries. "As soon as we're done eating, I'm going to head back to the city. If we confirm Echo's suspicions, he might be our best chance at telling the world what the Monarchy is hiding."

"You should exercise caution, little warrior." Dark, wavy hair fell in loose tendrils, framing Minerva's face, adding an air of mystery to her already captivating aura. "These are dangerous rumors surrounding your professor."

"Only if you'll come with me into the city sometime and let me buy you dinner." I flashed her a flirtatious smirk.

"I'm serious."

"So am I." I chuckled. "When are you going to let me take you on a real date?"

"A vision came to me last night that showed you surrounded by a dark energy." She frowned. "I might even suggest you leave the Sunless Crossing as soon as you've fulfilled your promise to your friend."

"Not a chance." I rolled my eyes.

"You're a fool." Her gestures were graceful and deliberate, like a conductor guiding the symphony as she placed a cluster of grapes on her plate. "A loving fool."

The silver rings adorning her hands, glimmered with inherent power, as if they were vessels through which the secrets of the universe flowed. What Minerva didn't and couldn't understand was that my obligation went beyond helping Echo find a way to expose the truth. She needed someone to have her back and see this through.

"I've already told you, Echo's had enough people bow out when things got hard. Her parents, her guildmates..." I lifted a finger sandwich to my lips, its layers of thinly sliced meats, artisanal cheese, and freshly picked greens tantalizing my senses with their vibrant colors and aromas. "I'm not about to let her face this hellish shit-storm alone."

"I think ... perhaps you should take your fruit tart to go, my love." Minerva leaned to one side, her eyes focusing on something in the distance behind me.

I felt a prickling sensation at the back of my neck, and a sense of unease urged me to turn. As I did, my eyes caught sight of a group of men clad in gleaming armor, their billowing white and purple cloaks marking them as officials of some kind. Their voices carried a commanding presence, their inquiries cutting through the jovial laughter and lively music that permeated the air.

Azuth's angular balls... A knot tightened in my stomach as I casually pulled up the hood of my cloak. *This is exactly what I don't need right now.*

My gaze darted around, spotting a patch of tall grass. With a quick, nervous smile, I winked at Minerva, and I slipped away from the bustling crowd, my footsteps muted by the swaying grain around me. The sound of their questioning voices slowly faded as I vanished into the concealment of the golden vegetation, skirting around the edge of the caravan.

Luckily, Echo, Rivka, and Hyperion had already gone back to the city, but there was one problem. My bag containing the philosopher's stone and the mad alchemist's book was still in our boxcar. Of course, Echo would be worried about how we would help Professor Dradon when we found him... but regardless. Echo and Hale had been tangled in some kind of botched resurrection spell. I had to retrieve those supplies before making my get-away or we'd never be able to help them undo whatever magic had latched onto them.

Unease gnawed at my mind, as though eyes unseen were watching my every move. I darted behind a colorful caravan, catching my breath as the murmur of interrogative voices grew louder.

Panic surged within me, threatening to consume my senses. My mind raced, desperately seeking a plan, an escape from the impending danger. *What had we done to draw their attention? How had they discovered our presence amidst the Cavalcade?* Peeking out from behind the caravan, I spotted their light uniforms, contrasting sharply with the vibrant colors of the festival.

I wove between the clusters of trees that dotted the landscape, eyes fixed on the winged gargoyles above. Timing my movements to match the moments when they soared farther away, I waited for a clear path toward the boxcar. Every step was silent, my lithe form moving with a cat-like grace as I left no trace of my presence.

As a group of Strays passed by, I seized the opportunity to blend in with the lively crowd. I kept my head low, effortlessly becoming one with the jubilant revelers, their constant motion masking my movements from the keen-eyed gargoyles. Finally, I found myself within reach of the boxcar. My heart raced with anticipation as the moment of truth arrived. I opened the door, slipped inside, and stepped silently onto the plush carpet.

Shit... I clenched my fists as I heard the guards outside pushing their way into people's tents and banging on the doors of boxcars. Snatching up my bag from under the table, I turned around to make my exit when a dark cloud in the shape of a man formed between the door and me. My heart leaped into my throat, and I couldn't help but gasp, my hands flying to my mouth to stifle the sound. I clamped down on my instinctive scream as the dark shimmering silhouette solidified into Hale.

"You pasty little mother..." I shook my fist, pursing my lips with a deep scowl. "What in hells is wrong with you?"

"I can't always control when my other body wakes up."

"Your other body?" I pinched the bridge of my nose.

"I mean my body on the material plane—"

"Shut up!" I cut him off in a whisper-shout, slapping a floral printed shawl onto his stupid white-haired head and wrapping it up. "Listen, we have to go... *Now*. We have the Nyxian Guard crawling all over this place. I can hear them rummaging through the car next door, so can we catch up later?"

Hale nodded, and I breathed a sigh of relief when he didn't ask me what the plan was. From what I'd seen, the elf was quick to think on his feet, and he needed to be if we were going to get out of this.

Nothing to see here. I opened the door, closing it softly behind us as Hale and I slipped into the bustling crowd. Weaving between stalls and caravans, I ducked behind bustling groups of festival-goers, my small stature affording me an advantage in remaining unseen. As I neared the outskirts of the Cavalcade, adrenaline surged through my veins.

The wheat field beckoned to me like a hidden sanctuary, its golden stalks swaying in the gentle breeze. With a quick glance over my shoulder, I saw a guard point in my direction.

"You there!" He snapped his fingers. "Halt in the name of the Sovereign!" I darted into the field, the tall wheat engulfing me like a protective cloak.

Each step sent a rustling wave through the vegetation, threatening to betray my presence. Suppressing the urge to gasp for air, I kept my breathing controlled and steady as I reached the first cluster of trees.

What the... I glanced around. *Where did Hale go?* I knew he was probably close by, but we were less likely to be seen if we didn't cluster. I watched the gargoyle circling overhead

My heart hammered in my chest, threatening to give away my hiding spot. With bated breath, I dropped to the ground, flattening myself against the earth. The wheat swayed as I fluffed it and made sure it was hiding me from above me. I watched through the narrow gaps as the guards sprinted past, their armor clanking with each hurried step.

Time seemed to stretch, each second an eternity as I waited, the anticipation coiling as every muscle compressed like a spring, ready to sprint headlong into the brush. Once the sound of the aerial searchers circled back the other way, I exhaled a breath. It was now or never.

I darted toward the next cluster of trees, scanning the surroundings for any sign of danger as I cleaved through the wheat field. A triumphant smile tugged at the corners of my lips as Hale peeked out from behind a tree.

"Idiots evaded." I nudged him with my elbow. "Now we just need to track down the others."

"I know where we'll find Echo," he said. "Guardian's Rest, behind the cluster of rose quartz gargoyles."

"Why would she tell you and not me?" I wrinkled my nose at him.

"Probably because she figured you would find her regardless."

I shrugged but still felt a little hurt. A real friend would be happy to see Echo learning to open up to someone else. I just hoped this guy was worthy of her.

HYPERION

The looming structure stood tall and seductive, exuding an opulent glow with its polished red gem-incrusted façade. Gold filigree molding swirled over every surface, and sculptures of gargoyles and nude female merfolk adorned the outer walls. At the front, in the center, tall double doors were carved of fine ebony, and above the entrance, obsidian letters spelled out "The Sinful Siren."

Flanking the entrance were two seductive sirens sculpted from smooth, black marble. They smiled coyly as if they held the key to unlocking the dormant desires of all who passed through the threshold. Meticulously manicured gardens surrounded the building. Lush, deep-red roses bloomed in abundance, their fragrance soaking the air with temptation.

Stone pathways, lined with intricately designed iron lanterns, meandered through the garden, guiding visitors toward the entrance with an inviting glow, and the building seemed to pulsate with anticipation. As I stepped through the lavish doors, the sweet, smokey perfume of burning candles and incense washed over me.

Dimly lit chandeliers cast flickering shadows over the heavy, red velvet drapes, and the hard polished souls of my shoes sank into the lush carpet as I entered the foyer. Stringed instruments played in another room and the muffled sound of melodic laughter echoed through the walls.

"Is that Hyperion Fiorello?" Sorshe Von Tess, the owner of the establishment, a woman of captivating allure and confidence, stood at the center of attention, effortlessly commanding the room.

"My lady, Von Tess." I bowed deeply, extending my hand toward her. "I told you I'd see you again."

"You always were a man of your word." Her lustrous black hair cascaded down her shoulders in elegant waves, framing her delicate features. She possessed an air of authority, a regal presence that demanded respect. She reached out, allowing me to take her hand.

"I do my best." Kissing the back of her knuckles, I grinned and met her piercing gaze. "Though it took longer than I would have liked."

"No one is eager to die twice, Hyperion." She toyed with a delicate silk handkerchief, the fabric whispering softly as it slipped through her elegant grasp.

"This is my third time, actually." I caught the silky swatch before it reached the floor and handed it back to her. "And I think once people find your lovely establishment, death doesn't seem nearly as bad as it's made out to be."

"You flatter me." She took the handkerchief. "Tell me, what brings you in after all this time?"

"I've been looking for someone." I put my hands in my pockets.

"Aren't we all?" A flush of warmth reddened her cheeks, and she smirked.

"Someone specific," I added. "An elven professor named Surrak Dradon. He's an alchemist and a sorcerer who—"

"I know Dradon." She rolled her eyes, letting out a sharp sigh. "He's run up a bit of a tab recently, and I haven't heard from him in days."

"Days..." I straightened my back, lying with practiced ease. "You're the first person I've found that's seen him in weeks."

"Well, if you find him, let him know I expect to be compensated for the mess he left behind."

"I'll take care of it." I took out my coin purse. "How much does he owe?"

She arched an eyebrow. "A high Crossway Coin or so."

"Really?" Mimicking her, I raised my eyebrows then locked eyes with her. "Tsk, tsk, tsk... I hope none of your workers were harmed. What happened?"

"He wasn't here for the girls ... or boys. I don't always rent rooms, but he was the quiet sort... or so I thought." She sighed as I counted out the Crossway Coins equal to the ranking and placed them in her hand. "Did one of his experiments and caused an explosion of black tar. Took ages to clean up."

"Why would Dradon rent a room here if not for the *amenities*?" I tilted my head.

"She shrugged. "He said it made for a convenient spot to stay between his lab outside the city and the shop where he purchased supplies. I made a rule that he wasn't supposed to do any experiments in the room but ... obviously, he didn't listen."

"Did you know the Nyxian Guard were looking for him?" I watched her put the coins into her own purse, tucking it back into a pocket concealed in the folds of her massive ruffling dress.

"I stay out of all that." She fanned away the notion. "He usually came and went through a passage in the back garden if you'd like to see. Right takes you under the wall and out of the city, left takes you to the market district."

"You know what?" I smiled, offering my arm. "I would *love* to see that. I'd also like to see the room where he stayed."

"I'll do you one better." Her ruby-red lips curved into a smile. "You paid his tab, so you can have the box of junk he left behind."

"You are an absolute doll, Sorshe."

CHAPTER 17

⟨ ECHO ⟩

I needed to get back to my friends, but the heaviness in my chest made every step harder than the next. *I should be used to this… It's not as if I haven't had friends walk out of my life before. These things happen. It's better to accept it and move on.*

No matter how my logical mind tried to convince me, my broken heart didn't find any comfort in understanding. I ascended the sandstone staircase, my footsteps crunching softly with the soft leather soles of my boots. The cool touch of the stony wall sent a chill through my fingertips, and as I reached the ledge where the pink stone gargoyles stood, I closed my eyes, allowing the solitude of Guardian's Rest to envelope me.

Taking my hair down from the warrior's knot the rogue had tied it into, I let it fall loosely around my shoulders, and sat on the ground between two gargoyles overlooking the city in the distance. Despite the ageless gloom, there truly was a beauty to this place that couldn't be captured in any other realm. The warmth of the breeze was a welcome sensation on my skin after spending time on the cold mortal plain.

"Echo?" Hale's voice made me spin around to find his handsome chiseled face catching the flickering light of the candles that lined the stairs. "That is an incredible disguise, but I can recognize your walk anywhere."

Emotion welled up within me, and I rushed into his embrace, tears rushing down my face in steady streams.

"Hey…" He lifted my chin with the edge of his finger. "What happened?"

"My friend inside the Requiem…" I wiped my tear-streaked cheeks, pulling off the wig. "He won't be helping us. He confirmed that there is some kind of cover-up going on. But then he tried to arrest me… so who knows?"

"I meant your skin." Hale's brow furrowed. "What's happening to you."

"My…" I shook my head, looking down at my hands that had gone ghostly white. "I… I'm still changing."

"Maybe we should go see another healer." He took my hand. "Someone in the Cavalcade. You don't want to be stuck like—"

"No." I planted my feet. "I need to hole up until I can think clearly. My friend—I mean my *former contact* said that the mad alchemist figured out a way to travel between realms without resurrection. If we're not resurrected when we travel over there, then what are we?"

"I don't know." His eyes searched mine.

"I don't know either," I whispered, rubbing my sore eyes. "I'm so tired, Hale. I just need to rest for a few hours."

"Thanks for leaving me behind, asshole!" Finn trudged up the stairs, and the moment I saw her, I felt the turmoil and uncertainty dissipate, loosening its grip on me. "You look… weirdly attractive with a beard," she said when she saw me.

She didn't mention anything about my skin or my eyes, and I was grateful. I chuckled, tears still falling as I leaned down to hug her.

"What are you doing here?" I wiped my cheek. "I thought you were going to wait for us at the Cavalcade."

"The guards showed up." She sighed. "I got our stuff and bolted, but they are intensifying their efforts. If you need to rest, we should probably camp somewhere in the Ashen Fields. Someplace with minimal traffic."

"Good plan." I nodded.

Finn patted me on the back, her smile warm and genuine as she pulled away. "Let's get the hell out of here."

I smiled at Hale, and he smiled back. But there was a sadness in his eyes as he looked away, which made me wonder if he was hiding something. The vortex overhead swirled and rumbled, and a light snow of ashes began to fall, and the lightning illuminated our path as we made our way across the fields to a small cluster of trees.

We had found our sanctuary, a place where we could rest and regain our strength before continuing our journey. Hale scouted the perimeter, strategically positioning our bags and supplies to blend seamlessly with the surrounding environment, further ensuring our hidden status. His presence reassured me.

"I'll take first watch," he said.

"I won't argue with you." Finn stretched out, yawning as she shifted around and got comfortable.

Not only were Hale's senses accustomed to living as a ranger in the Sunless Crossing, but he also seemed savvy in evading capture. He would sense any threat long before it reached us.

We'll be okay... at least for now, I told myself. A small, meandering stream glimmered nearby, its gentle babbling creating a soothing symphony amidst the stillness of the night.

Taking a seat next to Hale, I allowed my thoughts to drift. After everything, there was one thing that kept nagging at the back of my mind.

"Are you alright?" Hale asked.

"I will be." I shot him a glance from the corner of my eye and smiled softly. "I just need to gather my thoughts for a bit."

"Do you want to talk about it?"

I lowered my eyes to my lap and shook my head. "Not really."

Hale nodded, and I leaned on his shoulder. As the elf put his arm around me, I let out a long, weighted breath. No matter what Finn and Hale might try to say to the contrary, Valen was right to cut ties with me. I'd been reckless and senseless pulling my friends into this, and for what?

I still wanted to find Dradon and help him if I could. But I never meant to sacrifice Finn or anyone else to do that. The weight of Hale's arm lifted off my shoulder, passing partially through me as he dissolved into thin air, and I realized all at once that his body on the corporeal plane must have woken up.

The transition was so gentle... so subtle that wasn't sure if it had actually happened at first. I looked back at Finn who was curled up on her side, snoring softly. Still wide awake, I went over to where the bags were carefully positioned and started going through Finn's pack.

Taking out the body map, I held it up to the light of the vortex and saw indentations in the paper that I'd missed before. It was as if someone had drawn on a piece of paper on top of this one, a minimalistic map of the Ashen Fields. It showed a small square near the Storm of Broken Worlds. A temple that I had researched when I was still an apprentice under Dradon.

Is that where Dradon would have set up his new lab? In a spot that was so dangerous and unpredictable that no one would be crazy enough to look for him there?

Well... almost no one. I found a pad of parchment and a stick of charcoal. Hale and Finn would feel like I betrayed them, but it was better than asking them to follow me into this. I'd leave them a note to let them know that I was okay, but I couldn't let them endanger themselves for me... not again. I'd take the book and the stone and finish this myself. It was the right thing to do.

 HALE

I woke to a frosty winter forest; the world around me was shrouded in darkness. My eyes slowly adjusted to the faint moonlight filtering through the canopy, casting ghostly shadows on the forest floor. My heart pounded in my chest, the ripples of some forgotten nightmare still reverberating through my veins.

As my senses sharpened, I realized that I was not alone. Beside me lay Echo, her form eerily still, bathed in the soft glow of the moon. The sight sent a jolt of fear through me, and I reached out to touch her.

"No... Echo!" *Cold... she's so deathly cold.* "Wake up. Please wake up."

The night was alive with the gentle rustle of leaves and the thrum of insects. A soft breeze caressed my skin, carrying the scent of earth and the sweetness of the nightshade berries Echo and I had gathered earlier.

My heart wailed like a man in hell, tearing the skin from his own bones. I was an assassin. I dealt in death like bakers dealt in bread. I never got so close to anyone that I'd have to grieve when they died.

Yet, as I carefully cradled Echo's lifeless body, feeling the chill of her skin against my own, desperation gnawed at me. I gnashed my teeth, hoping to force the pain down into the abyss, but it was no use. Tears gathered in the corners of my eyes, brimming on my lower lids and trailing down my cheeks in warm, stinging streams.

"I can't ... lose you." I forced myself to draw in a shaky breath. "Please, come back to me."

An image flashed through my mind, one of us dancing by a bonfire. She smiled against the backdrop of a swirling purple vortex in the sky. The smell of falling ash and the taste of Echo's skin... A whole lifetime of memories came flooding back.

I thought back to the owlbear's attack and Echo's miraculous regeneration. A flicker of hope ignited within me, *She's not dead ... not truly.*

With these unpredictable powers of traveling between the world of the living and the dead, I couldn't be sure that she was able to return to me here. I needed to go where *she* was. Picking her up, I headed for a rocky outcropping and found a narrow crevice in the ground. I carefully hid her form inside, ensuring that no one would stumble upon her.

In the dim light of the forest clearing, I set out to find more nightshade berries and dream cap mushrooms. The forest seemed to close in around me, the shadows playing tricks on my mind as I hunted for the elusive ingredients. As I gathered the potent components, my fingers brushed against the delicate mushrooms, and I felt a surge of hope knowing that this was the doorway that would lead me back to Echo.

Returning to her side, I laid down in the crevice and held her close, feeling the weight of her body against mine. The falling snow had already begun to cover us, and I took a moment to listen to the rustling of leaves and the distant call of nocturnal creatures. With trembling hands, I put the medley into my mouth. The nightshade berries released their potent fragrance, and the texture of the dream cap mushrooms felt strangely airy as I chewed.

I took a deep breath, my heart pounding with anticipation and fear. If I ate too much, the cocktail would kill me. But if not, it would take me back to the Sunless Crossing, where I could find Echo. I held her close, and closed my eyes, surrendering to the effects of the concoction.

Colors intensified, and the forest around me seemed to shift and blur. Reality melded with a dream-like state, and I could feel the pull of the Sunless Crossing. The sensation was both surreal and comforting, as if the realm was welcoming me back. I drifted off into a deep, swirling sleep, clinging to the hope that I would see her smiling face the moment I opened my eyes.

 FINN

"Finn." Hale's voice pierced through the haze of my dreams, and I blinked, swatting him away.

"It's Echo..." His frantic tone shook the sleep from my consciousness. "Finn she's gone!"

"What?" I snapped upright. "What do you mean, she's gone? Like she disappeared again?"

"No, like she left us." He stocked over to my pack and snatched up a piece of paper. "She took the stone and the book, and she—"

"How could you let this happen?" I darted toward him and snatched the paper from his hand.

Hale's eyes bore into mine, filled with remorse and understanding. "My body on the earthly plane woke up again."

As the storm of emotions raged within, I knew deep down that it wasn't Hale's fault. It wasn't anyone's fault. Echo's actions, as reckless as they may have seemed, were driven by a desire to shield us from harm. Silence hung heavily between us, the weight of Echo's absence casting a somber pall over our shared grief.

"Just…" I scrubbed my hands down my face, anger surging like a tempest. *How could Echo just leave without telling us? How could she leave us behind, alone and defenseless?* "Forget it. Where would she have gone?"

"What is…" Hale's brow furrowed as he squinted at something in the distance. "Is that Hyperion?"

I turned around, following Hale's gaze to a figure in the distance moving steadily through a field with a box in his arms. Putting two fingers in my mouth, I let loose a loud whistle. "Hyperion!"

He looked up, and I waved my arms at him. What were the chances? My spirits lifted as I scooped up my pack and hurried toward him. I wasn't always sure I believed in fate or destiny, but I would have liked to. Because if there was some unseen force bringing our group back together, it meant that we would find Echo, and we'd do it before she got herself hurt.

"I take it you two are also looking for Dradon's lab?" Hyperion dusted the pollen off the sleeve of his coat.

"We … weren't, but we can." I gave a questioning look. "What did you find out visiting your friend?"

"Dradon was renting a room at a high-end brothel in the Crimson Quarter until a few days ago." Hyperion glanced down at the box in his arms. "Apparently, there was a nasty accident. No one is sure if there was someone in the room with him when it happened because there was a private entrance."

"What kind of accident?" Hale caught up to us.

"Alchemical, probably?" Hyperion shrugged. "A squid ink type of explosion, from the sound of it. I hate to be the one to point this out… but has anyone considered that the professor might be the soul eater?"

My heart sank a little, but another part of me was relieved that someone else was willing to say it out loud.

"I've been suspecting that for a while, actually." I shifted my weight from one foot to the other. "Echo is pretty convinced that he's somehow a victim in all this."

"Perhaps he didn't mean for this to happen." Hyperion took a deep breath. "But all signs point to him being at the center of the mess. Why else would he be in hiding?"

"How can he be eating souls without meaning to?" Hale frowned. "I can't imagine that being unintentional."

"Echo didn't mean to turn herself into ... whatever you are." I gestured to Hale. "No offense. But obviously, it's possible to alter the essence of a soul if you're screwing around with alchemical elements. Maybe Dradon has turned himself into something else."

"Alchemy *is* all about transformation." Hyperion rubbed his chin. "Perhaps he's accidentally transformed into something that has to feed on souls in order to survive. Now he's in hiding, trying to figure out how to undo it."

I nodded, letting out a heavy breath. "It's possible."

"It's going to break Echo's heart when she finds out." Hale hung his head. "She talks about the man like he's some kind of father figure to her."

"If I'd told her what I thought before, I would have been risking her pushing me away." I huffed. "Now that she's gone off on her own to try and save the old bastard, we don't exactly have a choice. The only question now is where would she have gone."

"My friend said that Dradon had a lab somewhere just inside the Storm of Broken Worlds." Hyperion pointed in the direction he'd been walking.

"Is he out of his mind?" Hale's eyes grew severe. "The storm is unpredictable. Even if it doesn't kill him, the energies surging through it are…"

"Terrifying beyond all reason." I raised an eyebrow. "So, to answer your question… *Yes*, he *is* out of his mind, and before anyone asks, *yes* we're going after Echo, or she will absolutely get herself killed trying to save that asshole."

The Ashen Fields stretched out before us, a vast expanse of desolation and solitude. The air hung heavy with a faint scent of burnt earth, and it wasn't long before Echo's footprints appeared in the crisp layer of gray ash that had fallen. The storm raged up ahead, swirling with ominous gray clouds.

I adjusted the straps of my backpack as we soldiered on, its weight reminding me that I was, in fact, planning to come back from this. My eyes scanned the barren landscape searching for Echo's slender silhouette on the hazy horizon. Part of me was furious with her for abandoning us like that, but mostly, I just felt hurt… Hurt that she didn't trust me to have her back when it mattered most.

The warm breeze turned into forceful wind as we neared the storm, carefully navigating around craggy rocks and fissures that dotted the landscape. A low chant, barely audible, escaped Hyperion's lips, a whispered invocation to the unseen forces that shaped their warlock powers, a silent plea for guidance. Hale's focus remained fixed on Echo's footprints as he stepped lightly, graceful like a woodland animal that easily avoided the treacherous terrain that could have easily tripped up someone less dexterous.

Echo… You'd better be ready for an earful when we get to you.

CHAPTER 18

ECHO

I knew it was reckless when I researched the latent energies lingering in this temple. Dradon scolded me for it. What would possess my old mentor to come to this place? The Storm of Broken Worlds emanated a sense of madness... essences of fractured realities swept through the air, but along with it the promise of answers. Dradon's obsession with the mad alchemist's work had led him down an uncertain path. Maybe he followed that path here.

As I ventured deeper into the shrouded realm, far beyond the familiar confines of the city, the landscape transformed into a gray tapestry of mystery and foreboding. A dark mountainous shape loomed in the murk, and I steadied my nerves as I stepped forward. Before me stood the remnants of a once-proud temple, dedicated to some long-forgotten god.

It made my heart ache to see such grandeur, now reduced to a haunting silhouette, its pillars and arches worn by the ravages of time and neglect.

"Professor!" I tried to call out, but my voice was swallowed by the roar of the storm. The temple's entrance beckoned me forward, a gateway to secrets untold and the possibility of finding Dradon's laboratory.

As soon as I stepped inside the stone archway, I could finally hear my own thoughts again. My eyes wandered upward to the high vaulted ceilings, where vines clung desperately to the cracked stone as if seeking safety within the ancient ruins. The shattered stained glass windows cast an eerie mosaic of colors upon the decaying floor, and the air carried a chill, raising goosebumps along my skin.

Scents of damp earth and moss mingled with the distant echoes of forgotten prayers. *What was this place doing all the way out here? Did the Monarchy even know it existed?*

"Hello?" A sense of reverence and caution enveloped me as I ventured deeper into the forgotten sanctum. "Is anyone here?"

Shadows flickered amidst the remnants of crumbling stone, jousting with the light cast by the vortex that was visible through the broken roof. Dust danced in the beams of purple light, giving an illusion of ethereal life to the desolate halls. I stepped over fallen debris, careful to avoid the treacherous gaps that yawned within the floor. Cobwebs draped across forgotten alcoves, hinting at the passage of time and the abandonment of this once-hallowed place.

Stopping in a darkened doorway, I stared down the curve of a spiral stone stairway that led down into an unlit room below. Holding my head high, I put my hand on the wall and began making my way down, one careful step after another. As I turned the corner, a sickly green glow pulsed somewhere at the bottom of the stairs.

The passage opened into what had once been a storeroom. Amidst the decay, a subtle aura of power lingered, whispering of the mad alchemist's hidden secrets. The faint but familiar scent of bubbling alchemical potions greeted my nostrils as I entered. *This is it... I found it.*

In the heart of the chamber stood a sturdy wooden table, worn by countless hours of alchemical pursuits. Magical ingredients and spell supplies were scattered over its top, bottles and vials, their glass surfaces etched with mysterious symbols. Picking up the empty bottles, I read the labels.

They contained rare and potent ingredients: crushed moonstone, powdered dragon scales, and essence of starlight, each waiting to be blended into concoctions of untold potency. The table bore stains of vibrant hues and scorch marks. Further proof that even Dradon made mistakes. I sighed... I'd spent so long idolizing him, sometimes it was nice to be reminded that he, too, was fallible.

Candles strategically positioned under beakers and burners slowly heated the concoctions within. Around the table, shelves filled with neatly organized vials and jars reached toward the low ceiling, their contents shimmering with a mesmerizing glow. Crystalline powders and sparkling gems glimmered in the faint glow of the candles.

Books and scrolls, their pages yellowed with age, lined the shelves, and the air was charged with a faint crackling energy. Maybe it was a residue left over from Dradon's most recent experiments, but the air seemed heavy with a stagnant malevolence that tied my stomach in knots. As uneasy as I was, I didn't hear the footsteps approaching behind me.

The cold tip of a blade pressed against my throat, sending a shiver of fear coursing through my limbs. The metallic scent of the blade mingled with the musty odor of decay, creating a disconcerting combination that assaulted my senses. My body tensed, but I forced myself to remain calm.

"Professor..." My voice caught in my throat as I held up my hands, remembering that I still looked like a bearded ranger. "It's Echo. I'm here to help you."

"Echo..." The pressure exerted from the blade lightened. "Is it really..."

"It's me." I put my hand over his and found it ice cold.

"Stay back!" He quickly pulled away, and as I turned to face him, he backed into the shadows.

"Surrak, please." I frowned. "You know me well enough to realize I'm not walking away."

"Why not?" He hissed. "I seem to remember that you're quite good at it."

My hands dropped to my sides, his words hitting me like a kick to the ribs. I nodded and pressed my lips together. "And you're still good at lashing out at the people closest to you."

A weighted silence hung between us for what seemed an eternity before he spoke again, his voice horse and gravelly. "Your eyes... What's happened to your eyes?"

"I guess you're not the only one who could use some help." My fingers drifted to wipe the blood from the small cut on my neck. "What do you say we figure this out together?"

The sound of his ragged breath slowed as he stepped forward. Emerging from the darkness, Dradon's form took shape as it touched the candlelight. My eyes widened as my breath caught in my throat at the grotesque sight before me.

My old friend, whom I'd loved like a father, had transformed into a twisted amalgamation of torn flesh and stitched remnants of himself. Captivated and repulsed, unable to tear my gaze away, I looked upon the once-familiar features, now twisted into a grotesque caricature of the man I knew. I thought back to the map ... and the sketch of the body that now bore an uncanny resemblance. Stitches, like intricate webs, traced a map of pain and suffering across his body, revealing the magnitude of his transformation.

"Surrak..." I reached for him, tears rushing to my eyes. "What happened?"

"It's … complicated." His hollow eyes, devoid of their former brilliance, met mine with a haunting intensity before he once again hung his head, shoulders sagging from the weight of his secret. "I'm begging you, if our friendship ever meant anything, leave this place and don't tell anyone you saw me."

My mind reeled, trying to reconcile the memories of the elf sorcerer I had known with this horrifying reality. A tempest of compassion, revulsion, and sorrow swept through me, knowing that trapped within the stitched exterior was my friend and teacher. He was facing a darkness I couldn't begin to comprehend, and because of how our paths divulged all those years ago, he'd been facing it all *alone*.

"Dradon…" I held back a deluge of tears and years of regret for our lost friendship. "I don't even care anymore about who was right and who was wrong. Regardless of what you might think of me, I never gave up on you. So, screw your pride… and screw mine too. I'm not leaving."

"Do you," Dradon's words, laden with a mix of longing and doubt, sounded brittle as they fell from his lips, "really think you can help me?"

The plea in his eyes tugged at my heart, and for a moment, I thought for sure that my stoic exterior would break. Reaching into his cloak, he produced a piece of folded parchment and extended it with a trembling hand. Despite the instinctive fear of his appearance, I forced myself not to hesitate as I accepted the paper. The paper unfolded with a delicate whisper, stirring the air like the flutter of a moth's wings as the page unfurled.

Intricate symbols and cryptic text danced across the yellowed stationary, evidence of the twisted knowledge he'd gleaned from that damn book. It was not only a tantalizing glimpse into the realm of alchemical secrets but also a reminder that the danger had only just begun. The complex patterns and formulas dancing before my eyes wove a tangled web of arcane knowledge that held the key to undoing the dark magic we'd cast on ourselves.

The question was... after everything that had gone wrong, did I dare?

"In case I don't get the chance to say so..." Dradon's disfigured face drooped into a frown. "I never meant to hurt you, Echo. I won't pretend to agree with you about before, but it wasn't worth losing you."

As halfhearted an apology as that was, it was more than I ever would have expected from the proud and stubborn sorcerer. A flicker of warmth touched my heart, and I couldn't suppress the smile on my lips as I put my arms around him and pulled him in close. The bond between us had meant something, and after what happened with Valen, I had to believe that even the most broken friendship can still be salvaged if there's love in it.

Tears poured down my cheeks in a cathartic release as we held each other, a mutual understanding shared in the embrace. We had put our differences aside and together we would get through this. As we pulled back and locked eyes, a renewed sense of purpose filled the room.

With hearts aligned and our friendship reforged, we would find a way to restore our former selves.

 HALE

Echo's footprints led us through the untamed terrain toward the Storm of Broken Worlds. The air crackled with a sense of urgency, mingling with the whispers of the wind that rustled through the sparse patches of trees. The wide open fields slowly descended into dense underbrush, and soon, ancient trees sprang up amidst the rocky terrain and the gray fog of the storm began seeping in amongst the foliage.

A few paces in, Hyperion set down the box, abandoning it as he turned up the collar of his coat. Despite the flesh-rending winds, he seemed almost at home in the chaotic element of the outskirts of the storm. Ancient, gnarled branches reached toward the sky, as if yearning to touch the gaping void within the storm, and the trembling ground beneath our feet seemed to sense the danger in the air. Finn, nimble and swift, followed closely behind, her steps light and calculated.

She moved with a grace that belied her halfling stature, her keen senses ever alert for any signs of danger that lurked amidst the untamed wilderness. Her gaze met mine, a silent understanding passing between us. Despite our differences, a mutual respect had taken root. Both of us were there for Echo, and neither of us would stop until she was safe.

A massive, ruined temple rose before us, its weathered stone sentinels taking shape in the darkness. As we approached, a sense of ancient power mingled with the weight of anticipation that hung in the air. Echo's footprints, already half swept away from the storm, disappeared at its entrance, and I knew we were close.

The air shifted, charged with an energy that hinted at the potent magic contained within the temple's walls. Distant whispers danced on the breeze, a haunting chorus that beckoned us inside. I stepped over the threshold, my senses immediately assailed by a strange smell.

Finn's eyes narrowed as she examined the surroundings, her keen perception noting the subtlest details. Her fingers brushed against the worn stone, tracing the carvings that depicted scenes lost to time.

"Charming decor." Hyperion's voice, low and resonant, broke the silence. "Though I'd hire a new maid."

The Storm of Broken Worlds churned just outside, thunder rumbling, its ethereal winds, devastating and ravenous as we ventured deeper. Our steps echoed through the corridors, mingling with the distant whispers of forgotten voices. The damp air grew heavy with an unspoken warning.

"There." Finn pointed to a dark alcove.

A closer inspection revealed the gaping mouth of a descending staircase. Indeed, there was some residual light coming from somewhere deep below.

"Stay behind me." I drew my bow, knocking an arrow as I led my companions down into the bowels of the temple.

The weight of our mission pressed upon my shoulders, urging me to move with stealth and precision. Finn followed closely, her footsteps barely a whisper against the ancient stone. Hyperion, ever watchful, matched our pace, his keen eyes glancing back for any signs of danger.

As we neared the green glow of the chamber, I slowed, and my companions followed my lead, melding in with the shadows. Echo's voice resonated off the stone walls, and my pulse quickened. Another voice... one that was strained and distorted. While I was relieved she didn't sound like she was in distress, it was likely that she had no idea what kind of danger she was in.

Pausing just above the bottom of the stairs, I took a deep breath and interrupted.

"Echo..."

Two figures standing next to a table turned to look at me.

"You treacherous wench." The tall figure stepped back, drawing a dagger and pulling Echo to his chest. "You almost had me fooled."

"Easy." Arrow nocked and ready, I stepped into the dimly lit cellar. "Let her go."

"Stop it, all of you!" Echo, in an almost tender gesture, put her hand on Dradon's forearm as he clasped it across her chest. "Hale, lower your bow."

"Sorry, Echo." Finn stepped out from behind me, dagger in hand. "There's no peaceful resolution to this."

"Finn." Echo frowned. "It's Dradon. What's wrong with you?"

"Dradon's the soul eater, Echo!" Finn's tone was desperate. "He's the real mad alchemist that's been behind everything."

"He'd never hurt anyone." Echo's brow furrowed. "He's scared, and you're all just making it worse. Hale, after I help him, Dradon can restore your memories. He's already got a plan."

"I don't *want* my memories back, Echo." My chest felt like it was caving in as I forced the words out. "The man I was in my mortal life... I wasn't a good person. I was a murderer. I'm sorry, but I'd rather let that man stay dead."

She blinked, disappointment marring her expression as she let my words sink in.

"We don't have to be pulled spontaneously between worlds..." she said. "I may not be able to bring Dradon back to normal, but I can stabilize him."

"Can you make it so that he's no longer able to consume souls?" I glanced at Dradon.

"I can ... make it so that he can survive without having to consume souls as often." She put her hands up. "That will buy us the time we need to figure out how to reverse the process altogether."

"I don't think he intends to reverse the process." Hyperion's voice came from across the room. He pulled a small book from inside the breast pocket of his coat. "According to his notes, this was quite *the happy accident*."

"No." Echo shook her head. "You're wrong. You don't *know* him."

"He's only ever cared about power." Finn threw her hands up, gesturing toward Dradon with her dagger. "For gods' sake, Echo, he's holding a knife to your throat!"

"He won't hurt me." Echo pleaded, "Just lower your weapons, and you'll see."

"I absorb the power of every soul I consume." Hyperion flipped the book open to a page and pointed to a passage as he read. "'I no longer need to fear the hereafter or resurrection. I am grounded in existence, and my memories are forever intact. I've won...'"

"Shut your filthy mouth!" Dradon turned and pointed the dagger toward Hyperion. But the tiefling merely turned the book around so that its pages faced Echo.

"Right here, he wrote about how much he wanted to take *your* soul, Echo." Hyperion turned the page and held the book closer, though it was likely too dim for her human eyes to behold. "He talks about how your restorative powers would prove useful, but not as much as your talent for making subtle adjustments to his brilliant recipes. He needed your help to stabilize the soul stitch so that he could more easily control his new powers. Dradon was a monster long before he turned himself into this *thing*."

Echo frowned, grief and disappointment etched onto her brow as the truth crashed over her like a tidal wave. My heart broke for her, but there was nothing more I could do. The damage had been done.

CHAPTER 19

ECHO

It's true... The realization dawned upon me like a dark cloud, and my heart sank. The pieces of the puzzle fit together with painful clarity, forming a picture I wished I had never witnessed.

Dradon, the friend I'd trusted so blindly, had been using me all along. My mind raced, connecting the dots that revealed his true nature—evil and manipulative. How could I have been so stupid? How could I have allowed myself to be a pawn to a murderer?

The weight of my sins pressed upon my chest, suffocating me as a whirlwind of emotions raged within. I mustered the courage to confront Dradon, to unveil the monster lurking beneath his façade.

"He's right, isn't he?" My voice was laced with rage and anguish as my legs trembled under me. "You've never cared about anything or anyone, have you? You've only ever taught me what I needed to help with your work!"

"You should be *grateful*." Dradon's ragged voice sent a chill down my spine, and even Hale flinched at the sound.

"Stop!" Finn's brow furrowed, her eyes burning into Dradon like flames.

"You..." Dradon glared at Hale. "I've got what I needed from you, and now I'll put you down like all my other failed experiments."

"That voice." Hale's lips parted as his expression went slack. "You were there... With the necromancer on the other side."

"Of course I was, you bleached sack of bones!" Dradon hurled me to the floor, and my knees and elbows slammed onto the grimy stones with a *crack*. "It was my work that made all this possible. Do you think that sadistic philistine could have accomplished any of this without me?" For the first time since I'd met him, I saw true fear in Hale's face. Hyperion yelled for him to snap out of it while Finn slung a flurry of curse words at Dradon.

I was a fool... Now everyone I cared about was going to pay the price for my misplaced trust.

Something's not right.

The musty scent of ancient stone mingled with the acrid tinge of burning candles and shadows danced upon the walls, their movements mirroring the chaotic turmoil in my heart. As Dradon loomed above me, he delivered another swift kick, sending me tumbling farther from my friends. His malevolent presence felt like a suffocating weight as the atmosphere constricted around me, the pain becoming sharper nestled deep within my chest. *This isn't normal...*

I looked down, clawing at the invisible wound when a golden light erupted from the center of my ribs without warning. The radiant tendril writhed and twisted with a mind of its own, each movement feeling as though the fibers of my soul were all being pulled, leaving a burning sensation behind. The air turned rancid, mingling with the metallic tang of blood at the back of my throat as I opened my mouth to scream, but there was no air in my lungs.

My eyes bulged as the life force drained from me, and I turned to look toward Dradon. The soul-stitched sorcerer held his arms out as if he were conducting a symphony of torment. A cold, violent wind stirred within the stagnant chamber.

The golden thread strained against the pull of the wind, but it was no use. The delicate wisp of light flowed toward him like a delicate spiderweb drifting on a breeze, and I was powerless to resist. Beneath the weight of his twisted smile, I glimpsed the twisted pleasure he took from my suffering, and the realization ignited a fury within me, a fire that burned brighter than the agony ravaging my body.

"You ... can't ... have ... me." I dug my fingernails into the palms of my hands, gnashing my teeth as I strained to pull my soul back into my body that looked less ... present. More translucent than what was normal for a soul.

Even with all the defiance I could muster, his power was so much stronger than mine. The sound of my pulse rushed in my ears as the world around me grew dim and distant. My mouth, and throat grew parched, cracking like the crust of desert sand. Tears evaporated along with every drop of moisture in my skin. My eyes felt like they were full of powdered glass.

So this is where it ends... My life force flickered like a dying ember as the weight of mortality pressed upon me. Each breath was a fading struggle against the encroaching darkness. Falling on the flat of my back, I closed my eyes, accepting my fate, when suddenly, a fierce battle cry resonated through the chamber.

In a blur of dynamic movement, Finn charged into the fray, leaping through the air with the courage of a thousand lions, dagger glinting in the light cast off by the golden thread. Finn collided with Dradon, plunging the blade into his chest.

A grimace twisted across Dradon's face, a flicker of pain that swiftly gave way to a malicious grin.

With his focus on me disrupted, the fine golden ribbon began to return, subduing the burning that filled my nerves with a refreshing, cool sensation. Things began to refocus, my breath coming easier as I watched the attack on my former professor, unable to assist or call out to those wishing to protect me.

His undead nature and dark magic granted him resilience beyond natural limits. With a surge of energy, he gripped Finn's biceps and slowly pulled her away from his chest. The dagger slowly withdrew, leaving a dark slit. Black ooze pumped from the wound.

A flurry of arrows whistled by, and Dradon sidestepped to avoid them, whipping around to lock eyes with Hale who was advancing quickly. I watched with growing unease as Dradon's gaze locked onto Hale, a sinister grin etching across his lips. A knot formed in the pit of my stomach, a sense of impending danger coursing through me. The air crackled with malevolence as Dradon raised his hand, his fingers emanating a sickly green glow.

Dradon's voice rumbled like thunder as he spoke his incantation, channeling his dark power. The atmosphere grew heavy with the weight of his malefic energy, and my heart raced as I anticipated the impending strike.

A beam of putrid green light shot forth from Dradon's fingertips, hurtling toward Hale. He attempted to dodge, but the ray struck his leg with a sickening impact. The sickly green energy coiled around Hale's limb, seeping into his flesh and spreading its toxicity. A pained grimace contorted his features as the poison invaded his veins, sapping his strength. I could almost feel the insidious influence taking hold, weakening his muscles and draining his vitality.

The area around Hale's leg turned pallid. Hale stumbled, his movements growing sluggish and unsteady as the poison took its toll.

With my energy returned but my strength sapped, I directed my power toward Hale, begging that I could do *something* in this situation. *Azuth, cure these wounds... Azuth, cure these wounds.* I channeled my cleric abilities, but to my dismay, where I should have felt a warm healing energy, there was only a cold dark void. My hands trembled as I felt the weight of my diminished connection with the divine. *I... I'm useless. Powerless.*

"Your precious Azuth won't help you anymore." Dradon's sinister voice dripped with venom as my heart sank.

"Don't listen to him, Echo." Finn grunted. "He's just mad that he looks like a hobo's lucky underpants."

Dradon's lips twitched as he dug his fingers into Finn's arms. The halfling struggled, but couldn't get free.

"You'll never comprehend Azuth," I said through clenched teeth. "He would never forsake me."

Dradon's face twisted as he let out a laugh that sounded more like a gurgling drain.

"How can such a brilliant little acolyte be so stupid?" He looked down at Finn, then back at me. "He didn't forsake you... You forsook *him*."

"Shut up." I shook my head, searching for any remaining traces of my divine connection, hoping to find a spark of healing power. "You're insane. You—"

"*You* embraced your unhallowed nature." Drops of spittle escaped his lips with each word. "Consciously or unconsciously, you took to it like a merrow to water."

I sent forth another feeble attempt to mend Hale's wound, but with each attempt to channel my healing magic, I felt the tenuous thread connecting me to divine power slipping through my fingers. The once radiant spark within me dimmed, casting shadows of doubt and uncertainty upon my efforts.

I dug deeper, drawing upon my own diminishing life force to fuel my healing spells, I felt a heavy weariness settling upon my spirit, dampening my resolve. The warmth that once surged through my fingertips during healing now felt distant, as if my touch had lost its sacred glow. With every passing moment, my limitations weighed me down like an anchor.

Waves of weakness and despair washed over me like an unrelenting tide. The room seemed to close in around me, suffocating me with the gravity of my waning powers.

As the healing spells left me drained and depleted, a sense of foreboding filled my mind. Maybe he's right... *After everything I've done, the lines I've crossed, maybe I'm no longer worthy of my divine connection, and my bond with Azuth has faded beyond repair.* I sank back to the ground in a pathetic heap.

Finn, fueled by the defiance of a feral cat, kicked and flailed, wriggling free from his grasp. She hit the floor and rolled, dodging the low swing of his long arms.

The professor faltered, briefly touching the wound on his chest, his face scrunching into a snarl as Finn slashed at him. Each swing of her dagger was met with a calculated counter from Dradon, his movements fluid and precise. Hyperion channeled eldritch magics, sending bolts of crackling energy hurtling toward Dradon, each strike carrying a touch of otherworldly power.

The soul-stitched maniac dropped to the ground, his limbs contorting like the legs of a spider as he evaded the eldritch blasts. He reached an open hand toward Finn, and her dagger found purchase once more, slicing through the gray skin of his palm. Necrotic energy pulsed around his mangled fingertips as dark magic surged toward Finn, and she leaped backward, narrowly avoiding its destructive path.

"You're fast," he snickered, drawing upon forbidden reserves, his aura pulsating with an ominous glow. "But that won't save you."

With a menacing smile, Dradon whispered an incantation and shadowy tendrils erupted from the ground, ensnaring Finn in a writhing mass of dark, constricting force, their grip tightening with each futile struggle. Hale dropped to one knee, nocking another arrow and aiming with deadly precision as Hyperion summoned a swirling vortex of shadows surrounding Dradon.

The soul-stitched wizard vocalized a low ethereal note, conjuring a shimmering iridescent shield, deflecting arrows and dark magic all at once. Finn darted in, stabbing and slashing as Dradon swatted her away with the back of his hand. She stumbled backward, fighting to regain her footing, her strength waning, but her will unwavering.

Launching a final desperate assault, Finn's strikes rained down upon Dradon with furious precision. For a fleeting moment, it seemed victory was within reach, as the sorcerer's defenses faltered.

But the darkness that encased Dradon seemed to swell with an unholy surge of power that defied all reason. With a terrifying burst of necrotic energy, he sent Finn hurtling across the chamber. Her back folded against the edge of the table with a sickening crack and she fell to the floor, gasping for breath.

No! Please Azuth... Save us. I tried to lift myself from the floor, but my limbs were dead weight. A wave of force swept over us as Dradon unleashed a spell of dark power that reverberated through the chamber.

My muscles tensed and locked in place, and a surge of panic overwhelmed my body and mind. Finn stared at me from across the floor with wide terrified eyes. I could see Hale and

Hyperion in my periphery, frozen in place. Even Hale's arrows hung motionless in the air.

"Finn," I croaked. "I'm so sorry."

A single tear rolled down her cheek. Then that low whistling wind began again. Finn's mouth gaped as a gold light emerged from her chest. The golden thread of her soul shimmered, flowing, light, and wispy toward Dradon.

Azuth, save us. Please, come back. I beg you... But it was no use. The moan of the wind reached a deafening crescendo as Finn's lips trembled and grew paler with each passing second. As the golden wisp of her life force departed from her chest, the spark of life faded from her violet eyes, leaving a gray milky film.

The world felt a little colder, and in my heart, I knew. There was nothing left of my friend but an eerie shell. An unnatural decay took hold of Finn's corpse as the vibrant colors of her once lively attire faded into muted shades, and her skin paled to an eerie ashen hue. Wrinkles crept across her face, deepening with each passing second, and her limbs convulsed with the rapid rot.

Her flesh withered and sagged as if decades of aging were compressed into mere seconds. Bones cracked and splintered as her joints contorted in unnatural angles, and the smell of putrefied death filled the air. This was true death. Her very existence was erased before my eyes, replaced with the darkness of Dradon's malefic power.

And then, in an instant, it was over. All that remained of the friend I loved was a pile of ash. There were no words... My ribcage held a gaping void that consumed any light that had been left in me. I'd never felt so broken, and I knew that I'd never be whole again.

A guttural, primal sound tore itself from my throat, a piercing cry that seemed to encapsulate all the pain and frustration that coursed through my veins. It was a voice that I didn't even recognize as my own, born from the depths of my shattered soul.

As my anguished wail faded into the surrounding darkness, my tear-filled eyes locked with Dradon's gaze. His once familiar irises had transformed, now shimmering with an unsettling beauty, a haunting shade of violet. It was as if, in the act of taking Finn's soul, he had absorbed not only her essence but her very power and consciousness.

Finn had been utterly consumed, her existence assimilated into Dradon's being. His twisted smile widened, his new eyes gleaming with sadistic delight. In the depths of despair and with my spirit teetering on the edge of desolation, a surge of raw power coursed through my veins. My heart, heavy with grief and fury, unleashed the greatest force within me.

Tears streamed down my face as I called upon the divine energy that resided far across the sea of the cosmos. The air sparked with an electric charge, resonating with the intensity of my anguish as a radiant glow enveloped my form. Divine power pulsed and swelled within my center as if gathering all the pain of Finn's loss.

A torrent of energy surged, ripping through the magical conduits of my outstretched hands, an ethereal tempest of divine wrath unleashed. The force of my attack blasted through the air, and the chamber quaked as the cataclysmic wave washed over Dradon like a flash flood. Flames of divine fury licked at the soul-stitched form, searing through his defenses and scorching his gray patchwork flesh.

Where was this power when I needed it? Where was Azuth when Finn could have been saved? A thousand anguished cries reverberated through the chamber as my attack tore through him. Dradon recoiled in pain and surprise, his façade of confidence crumbling, twisted into a mask of horror and desperation. I don't remember getting off the floor... It almost felt like floating.

The power abruptly ended, my body utterly spent. I felt haggard and hollow, as if sheer rage was the only thing that kept my heart beating.

As Dradon lay sprawled before me, his once imposing figure was now reduced to a pitiful heap. Wisps of smoke curled upward from the singed remnants of his hair, the acrid scent of burnt flesh, a haunting reminder of the violence I'd unleashed. Tattered garments exposed large patches of his blackened, bleeding flesh, but I felt no pity for him.

I picked up Finn's dagger and limped across the space between us. The dim light cast by the potion bottles sent eerie shadows across the contours of his face, accentuating the twisted lines and jagged scars, and I thought, *It would be so easy to end him if I want to.*

And, *Yes* ... I wanted to.

"You vile parasite..." Digging my fingers into what burnt hair remained in his scalp, I yanked his head back and pressed the tip of Finn's blade to his exposed throat. "You have finally fallen beyond redemption."

"Oh, sweet Echo..." He smiled, exposing his black, blood-covered teeth. "I never asked for your redemption."

How I longed to spill every drop of his blood on the cold stone floor. My hand trembled, my stomach turning at the stench of burnt flesh. *Just one quick motion ... like opening a letter.*

"Echo." Hale's hand on my shoulder radiated a subtle warmth that diluted my rage, a gentle anchor in the storm of my grief. "You're not a killer."

"I think today I am." My breaths grew fast and shallow as black blood beaded up under the tip of the knife. *Do it... Do it, damn you!*

But Hale was right... I wasn't a killer. And the justice of the Godless Monarchy would be far worse than any suffering I could inflict on Dradon.

"Everyone, just stay calm, alright?" Rivka appeared at the bottom of the stairs, holding her hands out as if she was talking to a frightened animal. "Everything will be alright if you just surrender."

"What?" Hyperion chuckled.

"Drop your weapon!" A Nyxian Guard wielding a crossbow came down the stairs behind her.

Hale reached for his bow, but I stopped him, placing a hand on his forearm.

"Rivka..." Hyperion's hands fell limp at his sides. "What have you done?"

Rivka's eyes, once warm and filled with camaraderie, now held a weighty shame. Her steps were hesitant, her movements marked by a reluctance that mirrored the weight of her decision. The betrayal cut deep, but her choice, though painful, had been motivated by a desperate belief that it was the only way to protect us all.

"It's alright." My voice cracked as I dropped the dagger.

The sound of steel clattering on the stone floor punctuated the end of our adventure. Hale's gaze met mine, and I forced a weak smile. It was over... For better or worse, it was done.

CHAPTER 20

HALE

I leaned against the cold bars of my cell, my gaze fixed on the adjacent cell where Echo seemed lost in her own thoughts. My heart yearned to hold her, those soft eyes carrying the weight of so much grief. Nothing could be done. Nothing could be said that would dull the pain.

Finn's absence loomed, a void that seemed impossible to fill. The echoes of her laughter and the warmth of her presence felt like distant memories, overshadowed by the anguish of her sacrifice. *How will Echo carry on without her?*

Flickering torchlight cast dancing shadows on the rough-hewn walls, creating an eerie play of light and darkness. It painted a haunting tableau that amplified the sense of isolation and confinement, a stark contrast to the wide-open fields surrounding the city. Muffled conversations drifted through the prison corridors, a small reminder of the guards and prisoners navigating the labyrinthine depths of the Onyx Requiem.

Would we ever see freedom again? Or were we to be entombed for all eternity within these walls, forever waiting for judgment that may never come?

"She knew," Echo's voice was barely a whimper. "Finn knew what a monster Dradon was but I... I wouldn't listen."

"You endeavor to see the best in people." I shrugged. "It's part of what drew Finn to you in the first place."

"I may as well have killed her myself." She hung her head, grimacing as tears began streaming.

"Stop it," I ordered. "Finn fought like a barbarian and went down like a gods-damn hero. Don't you dare cheapen her sacrifice by acting like she didn't know exactly what she was doing."

Echo blinked, her chest still jumping with suppressed sobs. A moment of silence passed, and then she nodded weakly.

"You're right. She was..." Echo pressed the heels of her hands over her eyes. "Gods, I just can't believe she's gone. Not just *dead*. Truly gone. I can't even fathom living in world where she doesn't exist."

"Nothing in the Sunless Crossing is supposed to last forever." I sighed. "But... Finn lived and died on her own terms, and those of us that are still here will never forget her. So in that sense, she'll never really be *gone*."

"But she is!" Echo kicked her plate of unwanted food across the floor, and the metal dish clattered against the stone wall. "She's fucking gone, and it should have been me."

"Not everything is about you!" I snapped. "I realize that all you can feel right now is your own pain, but—"

"You have no idea what I feel." She scowled at me, her red eyes still shrouded in tears. "But you're right about one thing. Nothing in the Sunless Crossing lasts forever."

The weight in my heart deepened as the cell seemed to get smaller. The cold pressed in, and I welcomed it, numbing myself to her words. Because even though I wanted to reach out, to hold onto her, it was clear that whatever love was shared between us ... had reached its end.

Days turned into an agonizing blur, marked by the absence of words exchanged between us. Echo retreated further within herself, her once vibrant spirit dimmed by the memory of losing her friend. She moved away from the front of her cell, seeking solace in the darkness that clung to the farthest wall. The torchlight no longer reached her, and with each passing day, unspoken words hung heavy in the air.

The heavy footsteps of the guards resonated through the dimly lit corridors, each thud a somber drumbeat that made my stomach sour. My heart clenched in my chest as the familiar sound of cell doors creaking open reached my ears.

"Up with you." The guard nudged me with his boot. "Time for your trial."

Don't lose your temper... Taking a deep breath, I reminded myself that this poor sod was just doing his job and bouncing his head off the floor wouldn't accomplish anything. Getting to my feet, I held out my hands for the heavy iron manacles. As he pulled me out into the hall, I exchanged a quick glance with Echo and Hyperion, our eyes speaking volumes of the apprehension that coiled within us.

Hyperion, though disabled from languishing in his cell, looked no worse for the wear. But Echo... once vibrant and full of life, had lost any glimmer of hope. The inky orbs that peered back at me from behind the wall of silence between us seemed less human than ever, and there was a faded gray layer of despair encasing her like a layer of glass.

The weight of our collective fate pressed upon my shoulders, and with a steady resolve, we left the darkness of our cells behind and stepped before the massive wooden doors leading into the courtroom. The guards stepped aside, and the doors opened as they ushered us forward, the courtroom unfurling before us.

Positioned on a raised platform, a revered and empty seat made of neon blue bones that shimmered with an ethereal blue light stood tall and resolute. The regal back stretched high as though trying to touch the ceiling. Before the raised platform, a modest bench and chair sat, waiting for our judge. To the right of the room, seated in pews were the representatives of the Godless Monarchy. On the left, sat the members of The House of the Sovereign.

As the courtroom fell into a hushed silence, a figure strode confidently through the grand entrance. This esteemed judge, a being of remarkable presence, commanded attention with every step. Tall and statuesque, the Aasimar woman possessed an ethereal beauty that captivated all who beheld her.

"Prosecutor?" The judge nodded to an androgynous, robed gargoyle standing off to our right. "Will you lay out the charges, please?"

"The charges brought against the defendants encompass a series of grave offenses..." The gargoyle prosecutor moved with deliberate grace, their stone limbs navigating the space with an elegance that belied their sturdy form. Their voice, a resonant and commanding baritone, filled the room, demanding attention and respect. "...*including* forbidden alchemy, unsanctioned death magic, evading the lawful pursuit of justice, actively obstructing the duties of the Nyxian Guard and, let's not forget, murder within the Sunless Crossing, which bears more permanent consequence than in the material plane. These are offenses that demand a thorough examination and a just resolution."

"One at a time, I will ask each defendant how they would plead." The judge's sapphire eyes shifted, settling on Hyperion. "Hyperion Fiorello?"

"Not guilty on all accounts, your honor." Hyperion held his hands out. "We were all merely concerned citizens trying to aid this investigation, and obviously … the soul eater has been apprehended and justice will be served, largely because of our diligence and willingness to put ourselves in harm's way. Who knows how many lives we saved by doing what we did."

The judge tilted her head, and her alabaster skin seemed to glow softly, adorned with a delicate luminescence that hinted at her celestial lineage. Her gaze drifted to me. "And you, Hale… Do we have a surname?" She leaned toward the bailiff who whispered in her ear. "No surname. Since many investigators have been referring to you as *the Unhallowed*, that will serve as your official surname for now. Sir, your very existence is proof that some sort of unsanctioned death magic has been at work. Do you also profess your innocence?"

"I'm hardly innocent, your honor." A soft smirk tugged at the edge of my lips. "Evading capture … sure… It's not in my nature to submit to being caged. But the death magic that made me what I am was not the doing of myself or anyone in this room."

"How *did* you come to be … as you are?" Her lashes fluttered as she tried to be as delicate as possible.

"Best I can figure… I was resurrected repeatedly and killed … repeatedly. Something went wrong. Honestly, I think whatever gods I was beholden to, if there ever were any, must have abandoned me long ago."

"So you fell through the cracks?"

"Yes, your honor." I lowered my gaze and nodded. "Beautifully said."

"And you…" The judge looked to Echo. "What was your role in all of this?"

Echo's lips parted, and she took a deep, trembling breath, not lifting her eyes to meet those of the judge. The dark circles under her eyes told of the sleepless nights spent building up to this moment.

"I…" She choked on the words but stayed composed. "I was reckless. Searching for a means to save my former mentor, believing he was my friend."

"During your experiments, is this when your appearance changed?" The judge leaned on the armrest of her seat, bracing her elbow and resting her chin on her knuckles. "Is that when you forsook your god?"

"No." Echo chuffed under her breath, shaking her head weakly. "That part was an accident. I tried to fix what had been done to Hale, not knowing that Dradon's associate had been pulling him back and forth through the veil between realms. In my ignorance, we were both pulled through the loophole he'd created."

"So you plead innocent due to ignorance?" The judge tilted her head. "All this was … just a silly little accident?"

Echo's chin quivered, but she spoke with conviction.

"I didn't realize the monster Professor Dradon was. I watched him consume and extinguish the most loyal friend I've ever known. And it was all because I … am *guilty*."

A chorus of whispers and gasps erupted from those in attendance.

"Echo, what are you doing?" I leaned toward her, my brows pinched together, but the guards behind us stepped forward, preventing me from touching her.

"All of the charges brought against me are true." Echo swallowed hard, visibly shaking as she spoke louder. "I worked the spells in question and ended up getting a good friend killed. My selfishness and pride endangered the very fabric of our realm. And I accept whatever fate you deem appropriate."

The murmurs of our audience turned into an uproar, and in that brief moment, the judge's composure was momentarily shaken. The weight of Echo's words seemed to challenge the foundations of justice she upheld. She held up a hand, and the noise of hushed discussion ceased.

Giving a single nod, she instructed the prosecutor to present all the evidence at his disposal, and over the next several hours, he did so. But in the end, it was Rivka's testimony that rocked the courtroom. She recounted every step of our journey, and to her credit, painted a sympathetic picture of our little company as we pursued our quest.

After all was said and done, the judge retreated to her chamber to deliberate with her advisors. When she returned, we were each allowed to give our closing statements. Hyperion delivered a colorful speech that boiled down to all's well that ends well, and asked if losing Finn was not punishment enough for the mistakes that were made.

When it was my turn to speak, I cleared my throat, blood rushing to my ears as I addressed the judge for the final time.

"Your honor, I understand that things didn't go as planned … for anyone here." I spared a hateful glance toward Rivka. "Mistakes were made, and we paid dearly. We will continue bearing that burden as long as we live."

I looked around at the cold faces peering out from under their hoods.

"But," I continued, "you should know that Echo put herself at risk to pull me out of … what I thought was literal *hell*. If it wasn't for her, I'd still be getting tortured to death and resurrected, over and over again."

Whispered words were exchanged amongst onlookers as I looked for the right words. Glancing over at Echo, I found her grief-stricken eyes staring back at me, her chin quivering with the threat of tears and a sad smile on her lips.

"Yes, she overstepped." I gestured to her, voice cracking with emotion. "The lines between right and wrong got blurry, more than once. That happens when you're trying to save someone you love. But you can believe that everything she does is motivated by a desire to help those who can't help themselves. How can it benefit Nox Valar to lock someone of her talent away?"

Giving a final nod, I thanked the judge for allowing me to speak and stepped back.

"And you, Echo?" The judge tilted her head. "Is there anything you'd like to say?"

Sniffling, she looked at Hyperion and me. "Th-Thank you for everything." She shifted her gaze to Rivka. "And I hope one day you can all forgive me for dragging you into this."

"Is that all?" The prosecutor rolled his eyes, and the judge arched an irritated eyebrow at him.

"Thank you." Echo nodded as tears once again streaked down her cheeks.

"Very well." The celestial judge stood from her seat and looked to my tiefling companion. "In the case of Hyperion, accused of forbidden alchemy, unsanctioned death magic, avoiding arrest, interfering with a Nyxian Guard investigation, and murder, I find you... innocent."

I turned my gaze toward Hyperion, watching as a wave of emotions washed over him. A gentle smile spread across my lips, mirroring his expression of relief and gratitude. It was as if a heavy shroud had been lifted from his spirit, and I couldn't help but share in his moment of triumph.

The court grumbled, but the judge held up her hand and continued without missing a beat. "In the case of Hale the Unhallowed, accused of forbidden alchemy, evading arrest, interfering with a Nyxian Guard investigation, and murder, I find you..." I held my breath, imagining an eternity spent in the dark confines of my cell. "...*innocent!*"

I blinked, trying to process the reality that had unfolded before me. The courtroom seemed to blur for a brief moment, the sights and sounds of the subsequent uproar fading into a hazy backdrop as my mind grappled with the sudden shift in fortune. A subtle smile tugged at the corners of my lips, a glimmer of joy breaking through the disbelief that had momentarily gripped me. *Innocent? I was innocent?*

The once-assertive gleam in her eyes softened, replaced by a compassionate understanding of the gravity of the situation. With a heavy heart, she spoke the words that echoed through the silent courtroom, casting a shadow of inevitability over Echo's world.

"In the case of Echo, accused of forbidden alchemy, evading arrest, interfering with a Nyxian Guard investigation, murder, and attempting to corrupt a philosopher's stone." The judge's voice resounded, and the room fell into a stifled silence, "I find you … **guilty**."

Echo flinched, her gaze fixed upon the ground. I could see the weight of the judge's words pressing upon her, her shoulders slumping under the burden of guilt. She nodded, a gesture tinged with sadness and acceptance of her fate. My clenched fists relaxed, the realization settling upon me that no words could alter the truth.

We had faced so much together, but now she alone confronted the consequences of all our actions. As the weight of judgment settled upon us, Echo's strength, once unyielding, diminished. She carried herself with quiet resignation. I wanted so badly to tell her that what happened to Finn wasn't her fault. But I'd said it before, and I knew she'd never believe me.

Echo turned to me, her eyes reflecting, not defiance, but deep regret.

As we walked through the towering halls of the Onyx Requiem, the weight of battle was still etched into my weary body. Neglected wounds throbbed and festered, demanding attention.

"Come, my boy..." The healer stood before me, a soft-spoken figure draped in flowing white robes that cascaded around his frame. "Let's take care of that leg."

His presence exuded a sense of calm, as if he had transcended the chaos of the world. A smooth, bald head gleamed under the gentle glow of the chamber's light, emphasizing the tranquility that radiated from his being.

Nodding appreciatively, I took a seat on a cushioned bench, wincing as the injured leg bore my weight, the torn flesh stinging. A delicate symphony of scents filled the space, intertwining the aroma of smoldering incense with the fragrant notes of medicinal herbs. Wisps of sandalwood, myrrh, and lavender intermingled, swirling through the air like wisps of ephemeral magic.

Soft hues of muted gold bathed the chamber, casting a warm, soothing glow upon the walls adorned with tapestries of ancient healing symbols. The patterns seemed to dance in the flickering light of tall, slender candles, their flames flickering with a tranquil grace. Soft, plush cushions lined the room, inviting weary bodies to find solace and rest.

"The conditions of those cells are infuriating." With hands glowing in healing light, the healer approached, their touch brushing against my skin. "One would think the court would try to keep their prisoners alive long enough to stand trial."

A soothing warmth spread through my body as they knit my wounds together, easing the pain, and I exhaled a sigh of relief as a hushed sanctity settled around us like a comforting shroud. The walls seemed imbued with whispered prayers, reverberating through the sacred space. Each prayer, spoken in times of pain and hope, seemed to infuse the chamber with a palpable aura of healing.

"There is still one member of our party being held." I leaned in and lowered my voice, "She's suffering the same ... illness that I am. Can you help her?"

"Yes, I've been researching your condition, Mr. Hale." His eyes, clear and serene, held a depth of understanding that seemed to touch the very depths of my soul. "*Unhallowed*, the scholars have been calling it. The cause seems to be associated with resurrection magic being corrupted somehow."

Odd... My brow furrowed as I mulled over the implication. My eyes wandered to a corner where a small altar stood adorned with delicate blossoms, their petals unfurling with vibrant colors. Vessels of aromatic oils, their essence released in gentle tendrils, emanated a soothing ambiance. The flickering candlelight reflected upon a polished silver bowl, brimming with shimmering crystal-clear water that evoked a sense of purity and renewal.

"Echo hasn't been like this nearly as long as I have." I frowned.

"Poor girl..." He shook his head. "I believe she was infected because she opened a channel directly between you and her healing light." Behind those gentle orbs, I sensed a profound wisdom, accumulated through years of tending to the wounded and weary. "I do believe I've found a way to reverse what's happened to her. I'll be seeing her in her cell after we're done here."

"So... if the court is allowing you to help her, does that mean they're going to let her go?"

"I'm sorry, my child." Lines of compassion were etched upon his face, evidence of a life dedicated to healing. "I cannot say what her fate will be. I only know they are allowing me to try and help her so that we can better understand the transformation from a betwixt into the Unhallowed."

My spirit deflated as his words sank in. His hands, weathered yet tender, cradled the essence of healing. They moved with gentle grace, their touch conveying a soothing energy that flowed from his very core. It was as if his fingertips held the power to mend broken bodies and mend shattered spirits.

My eyes settled on a pendant, simple yet significant, that adorned his neck. A polished stone that dangled from a delicate chain. Its earthy hues resonated with the healer's grounded presence, a symbol of his connection to the natural world and the forces of rejuvenation.

"She began a spell on you, didn't she." The soft-spoken healer's voice carried a tranquil melody, each word chosen with care and spoken with a serene cadence. "I can sense the vestiges of her magic. Let's finish what she started, shall we?"

"Wait..." I tensed. "She was trying to help me remember who I was. But after glimpsing my past, I think I'd rather let that man fade into oblivion."

"Of course, the choice is yours." He held up his hands in surrender before resting a warm palm on my shoulder. "Just bear in mind that when we don't face our own demons, they tend to revisit in disguise."

"What?" I let out a nervous chuckle.

He sighed. "It's much easier to be the man one wants to be when he is well acquainted with the thing he doesn't wish to be. Denying parts of ourselves and forgetting our past mistakes may feel like healing. But if you have the strength to bear such a burden, you will have the strength not to let the past repeat itself.

His words settled over me like a warm blanket, and as he started to walk away, I called after him.

"Okay." My voice cracked, and I swallowed the lump in my throat. "Please... Finish it."

He gestured for me to lie back on the cushion, and then he rubbed his hands together. As I lay there, vulnerable and still, the healer's hands moved with a grace that seemed otherworldly. Patterns danced through the air, their purpose known only to the one who wove them. Soft incantations fell from their lips, like whispers of ancient wisdom, carrying a weight of profound magic.

I watched in awe as a gentle luminescence bathed my form, casting ethereal threads that connected the physical and ethereal planes. I felt the boundaries between realms blur, blending into a seamless tapestry of existence. With each intricate gesture, I could sense the merging of my dual consciousness, the fragments of my being drawing closer together.

A surge of power coursed through the chamber as the healer harnessed the forces of balance and transformation. Our eyes locked, a profound understanding passing between us, a silent vow to restore what was fragmented. Time seemed to hold its breath, the universe anticipating the profound shift about to unfold.

The healer's voice resonated through the air, their final incantation stirring something deep within me. Radiant energy cascaded over my body, and the veil between worlds dissolved, merging my fractured existence into one unified whole. I could feel the ebb and flow of ethereal luminosity coursing through my veins, transcending the limitations of mere flesh.

In that transformative embrace of magic, I became both ethereal and tangible, my essence transcending the boundaries of the physical realm. The spell bridged the chasm that had separated my dual selves, integrating them into a harmonious symphony. The healer's enchantment, a conduit between planes, completed the journey Echo had set in motion.

The magic waned, and I opened my eyes, a sense of wonder and clarity flooded my being. The healer's spell had rewritten my story.

In that sacred moment, I stood at the precipice of a new chapter in my journey. I had been reborn. With each breath, I embraced the boundless possibilities that lay before me, forever grateful to Echo and the healer who had woven the strands of my being and guided me toward my true essence.

"Remember, adventurer... Existence is not linear. No matter where we go or how we change form, those who are meant to find each other will."

His words held a profound comfort, despite the fact that I wasn't sure if they were true. Stepping back, the healer's task completed, I rose from the bench, my body renewed, my spirit uplifted. Gratitude swelled within as I expressed my thanks, his kind eyes reflecting a sense of accomplishment.

Leaving the healing chamber, I emerged into the grandeur of the Onyx Requiem, the weight of my past struggles lightening upon my shoulders. Renewed strength coursed through me. With wounds tended to, I knew I needed to find a way to help Echo.

It was our souls entwining that had caused the corruption that transformed her. Unfortunately, I was already too far gone to reverse the process in me, but there was still hope for Echo.

The priest assured me that, once I had a chance to rest and recover, I would be able to continue my travel between the Sunless Crossing and the world of the living... *Though, with Echo gone, what reason did I have to return there, now?*

CHAPTER 21

RIVKA

Guilty? The memory of the guards dragging Echo back to her cell weighed upon me like an anchor. Yet even as my conscience ate me alive, I clung to the belief that my actions were driven by a desperate desire to protect her, to protect all of them.

In my heart, I feared that if I hadn't intervened, the consequences would have been far more devastating. It was a painful realization, the clash of my loyalty to my friends and the betrayal that I had inadvertently wrought upon them. As I stepped out into the courtyard, the weight of my actions settled upon me like a suffocating fog. The grandeur of the Onyx Requiem loomed behind me, its towering spires casting long shadows.

"Are you happy?" As Hale's accusing words pierced the air, anguish and regret washed over me. "Is this what you wanted!"

"I... I thought I was doing what was necessary." I searched Hale's eyes for any sign of understanding, praying that he could see the desperation that had driven my actions. "I didn't want any of you to get killed. If I'd arrived a few minutes earlier, I could have saved Finn."

"Well, you didn't!" Hale's venomous glare spoke volumes as he grabbed me by the collar of my shirt. "She watched Finn die. She thinks all that was her fault, and now she's going to be in there, all alone, for *who knows how long*."

"I never meant to hurt Echo." I pulled his hand off my shirt. "You have to believe me. I'd trade places with her if I could."

"I highly doubt that." Hyperion approached, rubbing his wrist. "You weren't up on the chopping block with us. What kind of a deal did you cut with the Nyxian Guard, not just your freedom, I hope? You could have negotiated for more."

"I didn't betray you for my own gain," I snapped. But just as guilt rose up in my throat, I muttered. "Although, they did agree to work with the clerics in the corporeal realm to get me resurrected."

Hale's features hardened, his voice dripping with disdain. "You betrayed her, Rivka. You didn't trust us to face the consequences of our own choices. You took it upon yourself to make that decision, and now we all have to live with the fallout."

His words hit me like a punch to the gut, a painful reminder of the trust I had broken. I had let fear guide my actions, and the more I thought about it, the worse I felt. By the time we'd reached that temple, Echo had already subdued Dradon. If I'd been with them, we might have stood a better chance of beating him. Finn might not have had to die.

I had hoped to justify my actions, but now, faced with his righteous anger, I saw the weight of my mistakes.

"I'm sorry." I looked down and away. "I can't make it right. I wish I could."

Hale huffed, putting his hands on his hips and pacing away. "Maybe you can..."

"What?" My ears twitched. "What could possibly—"

"We can get her out." Hale's black eyes were wide with hope.

"Come again?" Hyperion crossed his arms. "You realize we got very lucky in there. If we screw up again, they're not going to let us go free."

"We didn't get *lucky*," Hale said through clenched teeth. "We let her take the fall for us."

"You do realize that she was the one who spearheaded this whole thing." Hyperion raised his clawed index finger. "I care about Echo, but we were all just following her lead. Her taking the fall had nothing to do with us. Well," Hyperion glanced at me, "with *most* of us."

I snarled at the tiefling, and he rolled his eyes.

"You know what, forget it." Hale threw his hands up. "If either of you decide Echo's life is worth saving, I'll be staying at the Rancid Skull."

"This was supposed to be a job." I snapped. "I didn't sign up for any of this, and I don't owe any of you a damn thing."

Turning on my heel, I stocked off toward the city center and didn't look back.

As days stretched into an unending abyss, the weight of guilt and regret bore down upon my soul, enveloping me in a shroud of darkness. I was haunted by the faces of my friends, haunted by my own betrayal.

All that was left to do was wait... wait for the Monarchy to make good on their promise to return me to the mortal plane. Seeking solace amidst the perpetual night of Nox Valar, I walked through the shadowed streets, the dim glow of lanterns casting eerie silhouettes upon the cobblestones. The city mirrored the perpetual gloom that hung over me, forever enshrouded in darkness.

Lost in my thoughts, I found myself standing before the entrance of the Rancid Skull, a haven for those seeking respite from their troubles. The flickering torches lining the walls cast dancing shadows, adding to the macabre ambiance of the place. The air was thick with the scent of smoke, stale ale, and desperation.

I stepped inside, the creaking door protesting my intrusion. The atmosphere seemed heavy with the weight of despair and lost souls seeking distraction. The patrons huddled in dimly lit corners, nursing their own sorrows, their speech slurred and their laughter hollow.

Making my way to the bar, I found the worn wooden surface cool beneath my fingertips.

"What'll it be?" The bartender, a grizzled half-orc with a face weathered by a lifetime of hardships, glanced up at me with tired eyes.

"Ale," I replied.

I needed something to numb the pain, even if only for a fleeting moment. The bartender nodded, pouring the dark liquid into a tankard and sliding it across the counter. A nearby table beckoned, the flickering candle casting a feeble glow on my weary face. With each sip of the bitter ale, the weight of my actions pressed upon me, a constant reminder of the irreversible damage I had wrought.

The ale offered no solace, no redemption. Instead, it mingled with the bitterness within me, leaving a sour taste upon my lips. I stared into the murky depths of the wooden mug, lost in the swirling abyss of my thoughts. *How had I allowed myself to be swayed by fear, to betray those who had stood by my side?*

As I sat in that somber corner of the Rancid Skull, drowning in my own despair, the voices around me melded into a distant murmur, their laughter fading into a haunting echo. I realized there was no escaping the consequences of my actions, no erasing the pain I had inflicted upon my friends. All I could do was face the truth.

 ECHO

I was meant to mend wounds and restore life. But my powers were useless, incapable of resurrecting the one person who most deserved to live a full, happy life. I had failed Finn, failed in my duty to protect her. The thought filled me with profound emptiness, and there was nowhere to hide from it.

I thought about Hale... I think I loved him, *truly* loved him. But what good was that love now? Hale, like Finn, was lost to me, and Dradon, the one I had once trusted, a twisted father figure whose insatiable thirst for power, had led me into the darkest moment of my life. The knowledge that I had been manipulated, used as a pawn in his wicked game, only deepened my despair.

How can I ever trust my own judgment again? Locked within the cold and unforgiving walls, I realized this was my rightful place. *I should be punished for the chaos and devastation I caused.*

In the darkness of my cell, I sank to the cold stone floor, my body trembling with exhaustion and sorrow.

Yes... Tears streamed down my face, each drop carrying with it my shattered dreams and shattered friendships. *This is where I belong.*

The sound of footsteps rebounded in the corridor outside, like a beacon cutting through the fog, and a glimmer of light pierced the darkness as the cell door creaked open. I held up a hand to shield my eyes.

"Who's there?" my voice cracked.

"Hello, Echo." Valen stepped into the cramped space, his presence a ray of solace amidst the gloom.

A surge of gratitude washed over me, mingling with the remnants of despair. It was a bittersweet feeling, for while I longed for comfort and reassurance, a part of me believed I didn't deserve it.

Close behind Valen followed a human woman with flowing raven black, her practical attire blending seamlessly with the shades of gray that enveloped the room. There was a silent power in her presence, a sense of importance that I couldn't quite place.

"This is Lady Kiara Lorene," Valen said. "Sovereign of the realm."

Lady Lorene, the Sovereign, the one who held the power to shape the destiny of our world, was here in my cell. The weight of her presence filled the room, infusing the air with a palpable sense of purpose. I stammered, getting to my feet and bowing deeply.

"No need for that." There was a kindness in her eyes, as if she saw beyond my mistakes, beyond the darkness that had consumed me. "Guilty, though you may be, you have suffered enough."

Tears stung my eyes, and I hung my head, clenching my fists at my sides. "I... I don't deserve your mercy."

She lifted my chin, forcing me to meet her gaze. "I have been serving this realm longer than this young gargoyle at my side has been alive, but even if I wasn't older than dirt, it's not difficult to see that things in the Sunless Crossing are changing."

My entire body trembled. *Valen didn't come here to help me. Azuth has forsaken me and It was my hubris that got Finn killed. I deserve to be disconnected, forgotten, and alone. Perhaps that was to be my fate, and eventually, my consciousness would dissolve into oblivion. At least in that way, I could follow Finn.* Overcome, I sank to my knees and wept.

Anguish reverberated through my chest as I let go, sobbing so deeply I couldn't breathe. The man I loved would move on, as he should, and eventually, there would be nothing left of me. Not even a memory.

The Sovereign nodded to Valen, who took a deep breath.

"What you did was wrong, Echo." Valen looked down at me. "But... Dradon was stopped because of you, and your god is calling you home."

Unsure if it could really be true, I looked up into Valen's eyes.

His harsh expression softened. "Close your eyes and *listen*."

Closing my eyes, I reached out to Azuth. My entire body trembled as I strained, desperate to believe it could be possible. For several moments, I felt nothing but emptiness. Then something fluttered at the center of my chest.

It was a whisper, a gentle yet undeniable call that seemed to resonate from deep within. My heart skipped a beat as the truth dawned upon me. The voice I had longed to hear, the presence I had devoted my life to, was now reaching out to me. It was a call from my god, beckoning me to join them in the afterlife I had always believed awaited me.

CHAPTER 22

I stepped into the bustling marketplace, my eyes scanning the shops that lined the cobblestone streets. There, amidst the medley of colorful stalls and mystical symbols, I spotted a quaint establishment with a sign adorned in arcane emblems. It seemed like the perfect place to find what I needed.

Approaching the counter, I was greeted by the warm smile of an elderly woman, her silver hair cascading down in gentle waves, wisps of gray framing her face.

"Hail, traveler." Her eyes, a serene shade of hazel, held a glimmer of wisdom that seemed to surpass the years etched upon her weathered features. "Can I interest you in some Boots of Swift Striding? They enhance speed and agility, allowing you to move swiftly and gracefully in combat or exploration."

"I could see those coming in very handy." I chuckled. "Unfortunately, I'm fairly certain they're out of my budget— Or they will be after I find what I came for."

"Oh?" Deep lines of experience etched the corners of her eyes and mouth.

"I have heard that you considered Finn the living halfling a friend."

"I do." She titled her head and crossed her arms. "Did Finn send you?"

"I'm sorry to bring you this news." I sighed. "But she's gone. Killed by a madman while protecting her best friend."

"I don't believe you." She narrowed her eyes. "That little halfling is far too clever to—" Studying my expression, she frowned. "You're serious..."

"I'm afraid so." Placing a hand on the counter, I sighed. "I'm terribly sorry for your loss."

The old woman blinked away a sheen of tears. "It's a shame. I'd grown fond of that little imp."

"As did I." I nodded. "Now all I can do is honor her memory by saving the person she was trying to protect."

"What do you need?" she asked.

"A map of the Onyx Requiem," I said flatly. I didn't have the time nor the patience to play games.

She raised her eyebrows, fluttering her lashes in a rapid blink. "Ballsy... What makes you think I'd have that here?"

"Finn seemed to think you were the one to come to when it came to rare maps." I shrugged, giving a respectful nod as I headed toward the door. "I can go somewhere else."

"I didn't say I didn't have it." She rounded the counter and walked over to the door, turning the lock. "But it's not for sale, and may not be entirely accurate. I'll let you look at it and copy it if you've got the coin."

Heading into the back room, she retrieved a weathered scroll, its edges frayed from years of use. Glancing at my coin purse, she smirked. I reached in and took out a handful of coins, placing them in a pile on the wooden counter between us. With a gentle touch, she unfurled the map, revealing a rough and crude depiction of the interior of the grand structure, sections annotated with question marks.

My heart quickened as I traced my finger along the intricate corridors and winding pathways, committing the routes to memory to use as a guideline if nothing else. Turning my attention to a display of lock-picking tools, they shimmered under the shop's warm light. I marveled at the craftsmanship, each delicate instrument a perfect medium for the art of unlocking hidden doors.

With the shopkeeper's guidance, I selected a set that felt just right in my hands. She observed my choices, her eyes holding a mix of caution and understanding. With a nod of approval, she bid me farewell.

For several hours, I stood atop the roof patio of the Rancid Skull. The vortex loomed, swirling ominously over the city's center, its arcane energy crackling through the air, creating an unsettling aura of power. Ash fell gently from the sky, whispering secrets of the worlds beyond.

Thoughts of Echo consumed my mind, her absence, a constant ache that refused to fade. It felt unjust, unbearable even, that she should shoulder the burden of Finn's death alone. She had been our light in the darkness, our voice of reason amidst the chaos. Now, as she languished in that cold prison cell, it felt so cruelly unfair.

I can't leave her in there… I won't.

Sensing an approaching presence, I glanced over my shoulder to find Rivka and Hyperion creeping silently up the stairs. The tiefling had replaced his formal ballroom shoes for something practical with soft leather souls. Rivka glanced up from her feet and back down, remorse still weighing down her gaze as I turned to face them.

"Well." Hyperion took a deep resolute breath, putting his hands on his hips. "What's the plan?"

A smile crossed my lips. They'd had a change of heart, and with the three of us, I dared to think we might actually stand a chance at freeing Echo.

 HALE

The streets of Nox Valar seemed to hold their breath, enveloped in an eerie stillness that made the tiny hairs on the back of my neck stand on end. The towering walls of the Onyx Requiem loomed before us, casting long shadows in the dim light created by the vortex. Rivka and Hyperion stood by my side, their eyes reflecting the same mixture of determination and trepidation that coursed through me.

The guards manning the perimeter completed their circuit and took their posts at the entrance. We exchanged a silent nod, understanding the risks we were about to take, and moved around to the side of the building. With each step, I could feel the weight of the task ahead settle upon my shoulders, yet I steeled my resolve and braced myself for what lay beyond those foreboding doors.

I crouched before the side entrance, my fingers working in the dark shadow of the alcove. With each delicate movement, the lock yielded to my touch. I held my breath, straining to hear any sign of the guards patrolling nearby. Finally, with a soft click, the lock gave way, and the door swung open on silent hinges, revealing a dimly lit corridor.

Shadows danced along the walls, casting an ethereal glow on the worn stone floor. I motioned for Rivka and Hyperion to follow, their steps light and cautious. The air was heavy with anticipation as we ventured deeper into the fortress.

My heart raced. Each step forward brought us closer to Echo, and a flicker of hope kindled within me, even amidst the encroaching danger. The weight of each step was carefully distributed, the soft padding of our footfalls a whisper in the darkness.

Despite meeting an occasional dead end, we navigated the maze-like corridors, weaving through the shadows like ghosts in the night. The occasional sconces cast dancing shadows upon the stone walls, urging us to seek refuge in hidden alcoves and doorways, avoiding the gaze of patrolling guards. We moved as one, our movements synchronized, our breath held in anticipation.

A guard's footsteps rounded a corner ahead, and I signaled to the others. Ducking behind several stone pillars, we pressed ourselves against the cold walls, holding a collective breath. One wrong move... One mistake and Echo would be lost to us forever. I gestured for Rivka and Hyperion to halt, their eyes locking with mine in silent understanding.

We needed a distraction, something that would divert the attention of the vigilant guards away from our path. Hyperion grinned, stepping forward, his hand reaching into his arcane pouch to retrieve a small vial of shimmering liquid. With a quick motion, he uncorked the vial and hurled its contents into the air. The liquid transformed into a swarm of ethereal, dancing lights, each one pulsating with vibrant energy.

Shit... I glared at Hyperion. These weren't stupid ettins or gnolls that would follow random dancing lights without question. They were trained guards. But as the lights dispersed, weaving intricate patterns in the air, the guards all exchanged a puzzled glance following the lights down the corridor with mesmerized expressions, and I realized the spell must have had a kind of hypnotic quality. Seizing the opportunity, we moved swiftly.

The mesmerizing lights continued their hypnotic dance, casting a surreal ambiance throughout the corridor. The guards were momentarily enthralled, their senses entranced by the magical display. It bought us the precious moments we needed to take the stairs down into the lower levels of the Requiem.

We slipped away, leaving behind nothing but an enigmatic memory. Careful not to disturb the silence that enveloped the hallway, we scanned the barred cells on either side. The promise of seeing Echo made my heart leap into my throat. My footsteps faltered as I reached the third one from the end, my heart sinking with each empty, desolate chamber.

"She's not here." Rivka whispered.

The realization struck me with a force I hadn't anticipated, and a wave of frustration crashed into me like a charging bull. *How can she not be here?* Had we come all this way, risking everything, only to be met with disappointment? We exchanged wordless glances, the weight of our collective anguish hanging heavily in the air.

"Alright." I ran my hand through my hair, trying to steady my racing thoughts. *We have to find her.*

"The isolation cells." Hyperion gestured to a staircase descending even further into the bowls of the Requiem, and I nodded. It was a long-shot, but it was the best one we had.

The corridors seemed to stretch endlessly before us as we ventured deeper into the heart of the prison. Every step felt heavy with anticipation, each barred window we peered through with bated breath, hoping, praying.

Opening a trap door at the center of the hall, a spiral staircase led down into a pitch-black void. A chill ran down my spine as even my keen night vision couldn't penetrate the dense murk. The smell of rotting flesh filled the air.

"Hale." Rivka put her hand on my shoulder. "We're running out of time."

She was right. For all we knew, Echo's fate was already sealed.

"Give me five more minutes." My tone was authoritative, but my eyes were pleading. Rivka's shoulders rose with a trepidatious breath as we descended one last time. At the bottom of the rickety metal staircase was a circular room and five tunnels leading off in different directions.

"Split up," I whispered. "If we can't find her in the next five minutes, we'll leave and figure something else out.

The darkness of the prison was palpable, and the damp air seeped into every pore. The walls, slick with some kind of algae, made me cringe as I dragged my fingertips along to keep my bearings. Each step carried me further into the abyss, the chilling air gnawing at my bones as the hall slowly descended. The floor must have been just as slick because as I put my weight down, my foot slipped out from under me.

As I stumbled forward, my stomach lurched, and I fell, gasping as I fell through the air. My body tensed, limbs flailing as I flipped end over end before slamming into a pile of putrid filth that I could only speculate the nature of. I groaned, my back aching as I rolled to my side. The pungent smell assaulted my senses, and I wretched, my stomach giving up its contents to the mound.

Echo ... isn't down here. I hung my head in defeat. There was nothing left to do but get the hell out. We would have to do some recon to find out where Echo was before making another rescue attempt.

Coughing and gagging on the putrid stench, I pushed myself up from the heap of garbage, my hands finding purchase on the slimy surface. The foul odor clung to me as I struggled to rise, my muscles protesting against the strain. The garbage pit seemed to stretch on forever, a bottomless abyss of filth and decay.

With determination fueling my every move, I began the arduous ascent. The walls were slick and treacherous, making each foothold a precarious gamble. I could feel the slimy residue clinging to my boots, threatening to send me slipping back down into the repulsive depths below.

Step by careful step, I inched my way upward, my fingers desperately seeking out crevices and protrusions in the wall for support. The darkness weighed heavily upon me, making it difficult to gauge my progress, and the only thing I could hear was the thrumming of my pulse in my ears. Doubt crept into my mind.

Was this climb even possible? Would I need to risk alerting the enemy to my presence by calling out for help? No... I couldn't risk exposing Rivka and Hyperion after they trusted my plan to get us through this.

Clenching my teeth, I made up my mind that I would get out of this myself or die trying. After what felt like an eternity, my fingers reached a flat, solid surface. My heart soared with relief as I realized it was the edge of the pit.

With a final burst of strength, I pulled myself over the edge and collapsed onto solid ground. Gasping for breath, I took a moment to gather my composure before heading back to the rendezvous point.

"Dear gods." Rivka covered her nose and mouth. "What happened to you?"

My shoulders sagged, and I looked down at myself. "I'd rather not talk about it."

Overhead, the trap door opened and the dim light from the hall above, sending a cone of light down over us. What had seemed like dim lighting before was now blinding after growing accustomed to the blackness of the pit.

"Don't move!" A gargoyle guard lifted a crossbow and several others crowded around to offer support.

I sighed, hanging my head as I put up my hands and dropped to my knees in surrender. The jig was up. I'd gambled with all our freedom and lost.

The sounds of heavy footsteps, rustling wings and jangling armor shattered the air, bringing our daring rescue-attempt to an abrupt halt. The guards converged upon us, their eyes filled with disdain. They overpowered us in an instant, displaying their strength and training with swift movements.

Coarse ropes tightly bound our bodies, digging into our flesh with an unforgiving bite. The guards showed no mercy, stripping us of our weapons and tools, leaving us defenseless against the impending ordeal.

We marched forward forcefully, frustration and simmering rage fueling each step. The cold, damp stone walls of the prison corridor closed in, taunting us with their unyielding presence. Desperation pulsed in the air as we exchanged quick glances, silently sharing a determination to escape this wretched fate.

Finally, we were herded into a desolate cell, the heavy iron door slamming shut with a resounding thud, sealing us within its claustrophobic confines. Darkness enveloped us, with only dim light filtering through the barred window. Huddled together, our bound hands strained against the restraints, seeking solace in our shared resolve.

"Rivka, can you bite through the ropes at my wrists?" Hyperion whispered over his shoulder.

"What?" She hissed, "Why me?"

"Well... You do have sharper teeth than Hale."

"How am I supposed to reach them, my hands are tied to yours?" she retorted.

Whispers flowed through the air as we exchanged plans and hopes for liberation. Ideas and strategies fueled the flickering flame of defiance within our hearts. In this dimly lit cell, our voices blended with the faint echoes of prisoners, all yearning for freedom, all grappling with the chains of their circumstances.

The returning guards interrupted our plotting, their heavy footfalls announcing their presence. Our captors led us through a maze of stony corridors, our footsteps echoing in sync with theirs. As we ventured outside, I don't deny, I thought about making an attempt at getting away, but ... in the end, there was no way I could further endanger my companions. If they were going to face consequences for my botched plan, the least I could do was face them as well.

As the temple of Azuth came into view, I could only wonder what punishment they had in store for us.

The atmosphere hummed with serene energy, a palpable presence that permeated every inch of the sacred space. We stood in the heart of Azuth's temple, a place of knowledge and magic, where the clerics of Azuth dedicated their lives to the pursuit of wisdom and enlightenment.

Elaborate pillars rose to touch the vaulted ceiling, adorned with intricate carvings depicting ancient Azuthian saints and arcane symbols. The walls were lined with shelves, filled with countless tomes and scrolls. Soft, golden light emanated from delicate orbs suspended from the ceiling, casting a warm glow upon a serene pool at the center of the room.

Clerics in vibrant blue robes moved with grace and purpose, their steps echoing with solemn reverence as they tended to the needs of the temple, offering prayers and conducting rituals with an air of deep devotion. You could sense their unwavering faith in Azuth and their commitment to the preservation of healing magic through the calm radiating from their presence.

And there, amidst the serenity of the temple, stood Echo. I gazed, wide-eyed and captivated by the sight of her. She filled the room with a sense of hope and possibility, a beacon of light amidst the trials we had faced. The weight of our shared journey seemed to dissipate, replaced by a newfound sense of peace and purpose.

Her face lit up with a smile that reached the depths of her soul. It was a smile that brought tears to my eyes, and in that moment, I knew that somehow, despite what just happened, everything would be okay. Beyond the grand altar, a statue of Azuth stood, nearly twice the height of a man.

His white hair cascaded down to his broad shoulders, framing a weathered face adorned with a majestic, flowing beard. His gray silk robes billowed around him, as if perpetually caught in an invisible breeze.

With a graceful turn, he shifted into the form of a floating pyramid. Lights shimmered, casting a mesmerizing display of colors that danced and swirled in harmony. Though devoid of eyes or mouths, the pyramid radiated an undeniable presence. I could still feel the weight of Azuth's gaze upon me, his divine sight penetrating the depths of my being.

"Echo," his voice resonated through the air, rich and commanding, "take a moment to say what you need to say. You will not be able to return after I transform you into your eventual form."

Echo's smile faded as she took a deep breath and descended the white marble steps to face us. Swallowing hard, she nodded and took a deep breath.

"There are no words ... for the depth of gratitude I feel." Her eyes glistened with tears as she glanced over her shoulder at the pyramid of light. "The three of you risked so much to try and help me. I feel unworthy to have friends like you."

A knot formed in my throat as I felt my heart breaking.

Echo's smile faded as she took a deep breath. Swallowing hard, she nodded, her hand reaching out toward mine.

"Will you take a walk with me, Hale?"

Hesitating only for a moment, I intertwined my fingers with hers, feeling a gentle shiver run down my spine. Together, we exited the temple and descended the white marble steps, the eternal night casting a veil of mystery over Nox Valar.

The clouds above us churned and swirled, driven by unseen forces, as the ever-turning purple vortex loomed overhead, casting an eerie glow on our path. Each step felt like a plunge into the depths of uncertainty, the weight of our impending farewell hanging heavy in the air.

As we ventured beyond the confines of the temple, the wind whispered through the trees, carrying with it a haunting melody. The garden, shrouded in shadows, held a mystic allure, a fragile connection amidst the ethereal darkness.

"You smell much like you did when we first met." Echo smiled, but it didn't reach her eyes. "What sort of mess have you gotten into this time?"

I gave a small sad chuckle, and she laughed softly with me.

"Do you have to leave?" I finally asked. "I mean, couldn't you stay a little longer?"

"I don't belong here, Hale." Echo's voice quivered in the night, her revelations carrying the weight of a thousand stars. "When souls linger here too long... nothing good can come of it."

"I wish..." My heart ached with understanding, knowing that her journey would lead her to realms beyond mortal comprehension. "I wish things could be different."

"I think I'm finally ready to see what comes after this." She smiled. "Maybe we'll find each other again someday."

"I hope so."

Our truth was spoken softly amidst the secrets whispered by the night. With every step, we found solace in each other's presence, our intertwined fingers a lifeline amidst the dark unknown.

We found ourselves at a precipice, overlooking a vast expanse that disappeared into the enigmatic depths of the realm. The ambient glow of the ever-turning vortex overhead cast its violet hue upon our faces, a constant reminder of the cosmic forces at play.

We held each other tightly as the stormy clouds above mirrored the tempest of emotions within us, a symphony of love and sorrow.

In a tender and lingering kiss, we savored the taste of our bittersweet goodbye, a reminder of the fleeting nature of our time together. Hand in hand, we walked back into the temple, our steps guided by a stained glass mosaic of light and shadows. The ever-turning vortex watched over us as she caressed my cheek, placing one last chaste kiss on my lips.

"Safe travels." Rivka placed her right fist across her chest. "My sister."

"Safe travels." Hyperion bowed his head.

As I stepped forward and kissed her forehead, my heart shattered into countless pieces, aching with indescribable pain. "Safe travels, my love."

Tears streamed down Echo's cheeks as she gracefully stepped toward the ethereal threshold of the afterlife with Azuth. The bond we shared, the laughter and tears, the shared moments of triumph and despair—it all felt so distant. I felt guilty to grieve her loss as she stepped away.

How could I be so sad knowing she had found her peace, her rightful place in the embrace of the divine? Though it pained me beyond measure to let her go, I knew deep down that it was what she needed and deserved. For my part, I would honor her friendship. Honor the second chance she gave me by living a life worthy of the love she had bestowed.

The moment was both beautiful and agonizing as her figure gradually faded into the luminous glow, and my heart broke irreparably. I knew that in the void left in her absence, I would never be the same.

CHAPTER 23

⊱ ECHO ⊰

I crossed the threshold of eternity, my heart heavy with regret. The space between realms was enchanting, a kaleidoscope of shifting colors and ethereal shapes. My gaze flickered back to the portal leading to the Sunless Crossing, where I'd said goodbye to the man I loved.

"Cold feet?" The radiant form of my god drew close.

"No, never." I smiled, my breath faltering with a repressed sob. "This is the right thing to do."

"Echo," Azuth's voice was a soothing melody, "you have served me well, and your dedication is commendable. But you should only come with me if it's what you truly want."

He understood the turmoil within my heart, the weight of the choice I had to make. I looked up at him, feeling small yet cherished in his gaze.

"You have a brilliant mind and a compassionate heart, and you shouldn't ignore either one." His words touched my soul, and tears welled up in my eyes. I wanted to be with Hale, but I also feared losing the bond I had with Azuth.

Azuth drew me into a loving embrace, and I felt safe and understood. "You have the strength to make your own choices, Echo. Don't be afraid. Life is not bound by a single path."

His words stirred something within me, a realization that I didn't have to sacrifice one love for another... even if I had to love from a distance.

"Thank you, Father." Taking a deep breath, I stepped back.

As I passed through the portal, Azuth's voice echoed in my mind, offering good wishes and a fond farewell.

 HALE

As the days turned into weeks and the weeks into months, I found myself standing at a crossroad of destiny. I emerged from the darkness of the tunnel, my footsteps echoing softly as they met the stone surface of the promenade. The wind swept through the air, dancing around me, its touch carrying a whisper of the familiar scents of ash and dirt

Stepping to the edge of the promenade, I gazed out across the vast expanse of the Ashen Fields stretching before me. The sight before my eyes was nothing short of awe-inspiring. The land seemed to stretch on endlessly, its vastness merging seamlessly with the black horizon at the Crossing's end. The boundary between earth and sky blurred, creating a surreal panorama that captured my gaze, holding it captive.

A sense of wonder washed over me as I stood there, the enormity of the view enveloping my senses. The ever-turning purple vortex, a swirling nexus of power, hovered in the distance, casting an ethereal glow over the landscape. Its presence reminded me of the mystical forces that intertwined within the Sunless Crossing, where nothing was as it seemed.

The breeze continued to caress my face, its gentle touch carrying whispers of secrets and untold stories. The expanse of the Ashen Fields, with its eerie mist and hidden mysteries, beckoned to me. It stirred a longing deep within my soul, igniting a yearning for exploration, for the discovery of hidden truths and forgotten treasures.

I took a moment to absorb the grandeur before me, allowing the beauty of the scene to permeate my being. The world seemed vast and full of possibilities, ready to unfold its secrets to those who dared to venture further. With a steady resolve and a heart brimming with anticipation, I took my first steps forward, ready to embrace the unknown and embark on my own journey.

As I stood on the promenade, the vortex emanated an otherworldly radiance, its brilliance piercing through the gloom of the Ashen Fields. Like a siren's call, it drew my attention, beckoning me to explore the mysteries concealed within its swirling depths.

The air around me carried a sense of both tranquility and unease, a delicate balance between the known and the unknown. It whispered of ancient secrets and hidden enchantments, evoking a shiver down my spine. The promenade, with its sturdy structure and elevated position, offered a vantage point from which I could admire the enigmatic beauty of this realm.

With each passing moment, the Ashen Fields revealed new facets, as if holding the keys to a thousand untold tales. As I stood on the promenade, taking in the breathtaking view of the Ashen Fields, I felt a presence beside me. Lady Kiara Lorene, the sovereign of Nox Valar, joined me, her regal presence emitting a sense of authority and grace. She surveyed the panorama before us with a mix of admiration and ownership.

"Truly a sight to behold," Lady Kiara Lorene remarked, her voice carrying an air of confidence and power. "Hale, you have proven yourself time and again, demonstrating exceptional skill and depth of character. I extend to you an offer, a position not within the Nyxian Guard but a different branch entirely. With it comes influence, security, and the opportunity to shape the future of our realm."

Her words hung in the air, the allure of her offer beckoning to me. The thought of wielding such power and influence within the realm was enticing, a path that would provide stability and prestige. It was a proposition that many would have eagerly embraced.

But deep within my heart, a fire burned, a yearning for something more than mere titles and authority. The desire for independence, the freedom to carve my own destiny and follow the path less traveled, tugged at my very soul. I looked into Lady Kiara's eyes, my voice steady yet resolute.

"I am honored by your offer, Kiara Lorene." I smiled. "But I fear my nature is a bit too chaotic for that kind of work."

A fleeting moment of understanding passed between us, a shared acknowledgment that the road I sought to tread diverged from the well-trodden path of a sworn guard. Lady Lorene's expression softened, a mixture of respect and acceptance.

"I understand, Hale," she replied, her voice tinged with a touch of regret. "The path you choose is yours to walk. Know that the doors of Nox Valar will always be open to you."

With those words, Kiara Lorene turned and walked away, leaving me to contemplate the weight of my decision. As I stood on the promenade, gazing out at the vast expanse of the Ashen Fields, I felt a sense of liberation, knowing that my destiny was mine to shape, guided by my own choices and convictions. The soft breeze danced through my hair, carrying whispers of promise and possibility. With each breath, I felt a renewed sense of purpose surging within me.

The Ashen Fields stretched out like an infinite canvas, their ethereal mist swirling and shifting in the faded light. The beauty and mystery of this realm beckoned me forward, reminding me that my chosen path was one of resilience and self-discovery.

I'd been given a new life, and I'd be damned if I was about to waste it in allegiance to powers with their own agenda. My journey would be guided by my own principles, not shaped by the Monarchy or by the man I had been before.

I turned away and stepped onto the path that led into the unknown. The last thing in the world that I expected to see … was *Echo*.

Time passed and, despite our insistence on remaining independent, we did consent to embark on several important missions for the Sovereign. Thus, the seed of a new venture was born. One that we didn't want to continue alone.

I pushed open the creaking door of the Rancid Skull, the scent of ale and merriment wafting through the air. As we entered, my eyes scanned the dimly lit tavern, searching for familiar faces. And there they were, Rivka and Hyperion, engrossed in a game of skill and precision. Small throwing knives flew through the air, finding their mark on the wooden target affixed to the wall. The rhythmic thud of metal meeting wood echoed through the room, drawing the attention of the patrons.

A smile tugged at the corners of my lips as I approached them, the clinking of coins and boisterous laughter providing the backdrop to our reunion. Their faces lit up with joy and surprise as they caught sight of me, their games momentarily forgotten. But their mouths dropped open when Echo entered behind me.

"Hale the Unhallowed." Rivka smiled with a warmth I didn't expect. "I was wondering where in all hells you'd been. I guess now I know."

We embraced in a celebratory reunion, and the tavern's lively atmosphere faded into the background as we exchanged tales of triumph and tribulation, laughter punctuating our conversations. It felt as though time stood still, and the world outside the Rancid Skull ceased to exist.

The warm glow of the flickering candlelight painted the walls with dancing shadows, creating an intimate and inviting atmosphere. The sound of laughter and lively chatter reverberated through the smoke-filled room, as patrons raised their mugs together.

"Catch us up, Echo." Hyperion stepped aside, ordering three more tankards of ale. "Tell us all about your journey to eternity."

"I would, but I never made it that far." She smiled at me. "But I think you'd be more interested to learn where we plan to go from here."

"Oh?" The tiefling's mischievous smirk was almost childlike.

Our group made its way to a secluded corner of the tavern, drawn to the worn wooden table and its accompanying chairs that creaked with every movement. The flickering candlelight cast dancing shadows on our faces as we settled into our seats. The sounds of clinking mugs and animated conversations enveloped us, creating a comforting symphony that felt like a familiar embrace.

"How would you two like to join us on an important mission?"

"You know we don't have the ability to plane shift." Hyperion took a puff of his cigarette, his eyes shimmering with fascination.

"We have a way around that." I could sense his eager anticipation, his mind already envisioning the possibilities that lay ahead. "This is going to be dangerous, and we need people at our side that I can trust."

Rivka, always perceptive, nodded in silent agreement, and a sense of determination filled the air. As I looked toward the future, I couldn't help but marvel at the vastness of the countless worlds before me. The road of destiny stretched on, winding and uncertain, but I knew that within its twists and turns lay endless possibilities and untold adventures.

I looked forward to all of them, knowing I'd have Echo and our friends by my side. Our humble company would form the order of the Pale Horsemen, and in the face of uncertainty, we would protect, heal, and seek justice as long as we could.

For in the Sunless Crossing, nothing is set in stone.

THE END

BOOK CLUB QUESTIONS

1. How did the author's description of the Sunless Crossing and its various locations contribute to the overall atmosphere and immersion of the story?

2. The theme of fate versus free will is subtly woven into the narrative. How did this theme manifest in the choices and actions of the characters?

3. The theme of self-discovery and embracing one's true nature is explored through various characters. How did the characters' journeys of self-discovery resonate with you? Did any particular character's journey stand out?

4. Friendship and loyalty play significant roles in the story. How did the dynamics between Echo, Finn, Hale, Rivka, and Hyperion evolve and impact their journey? Which character stood out to you the most and why?

5. How did the author incorporate magic into the narrative, and did it enhance the overall storytelling experience for you?

6. The Sunless Crossing is a world where different realms and afterlives converge. How did the concept of multiple afterlives and the role of the Godless Monarchy impact the story? Did it raise any thought-provoking questions about the nature of life and death?

7. The narrative explores the consequences of forbidden knowledge and the pursuit of ultimate power. Discuss the ethical implications raised by the mad alchemist's book and the philosopher's stone. How did the characters' interactions with these artifacts reflect their moral compasses?

8. The climax and resolution of the story bring together various threads and plotlines. Were you satisfied with how the story concluded? Were there any unresolved questions or plot points you wished were further explored?

9. How did the romantic relationships and dynamics in the story contribute to your overall reading experience? Did you find the romantic elements well-developed and believable?

10. Reflecting on the overall story, what elements or themes resonated with you the most? Were there any particular scenes, quotes, or moments that stood out or stayed with you after finishing the book?

AUTHOR BIO

Recently recognized for her involvement in the Black Ballad Tabletop RPG campaign, this polyamorous, demisexual kitchen-witch just relocated to Reno Nevada with her high school sweetheart. She's mother to a brilliant theater nerd and two dogs, but she holds many other titles. Eccentric auntie, amateur artist, and bestselling ghostwriter to name a few. She's made a career out of helping others bring books to their readers. Now she's a rising star in the comic world, cowriting an Epic Fantasy series with the iconic artist Jonothan Luna. She hopes to spend the rest of her life telling stories in all mediums possible and encouraging budding writers to do the same.

More books from
4 Horsemen Publications

Fantasy

D. Lambert
To Walk into the Sands
Rydan
Celebrant
Northlander
Esparan
King
Traitor
His Last Name

D.A. Spruzen
The Turkish Connection
The Witch of Tut

Danielle Orsino
Locked Out of Heaven
Thine Eyes of Mercy
From the Ashes
Kingdom Come
Fire, Ice, Acid, & Heart
A Fae is Done

J.M. Paquette
Klauden's Ring
Solyn's Body
The Inbetween
Hannah's Heart

Lou Kemp
The Violins Played Before Junstan
Music Shall Untune the Sky
The Raven and the Pig
The Pirate Danced and the
Automat Died
The Wyvern, the Pirate, and
the Madman

Megan Mackie
Silverblood Scion

R.J. Young
Challenges of Tawa
Witch of the Whirlwind

Sydney Wilder
Daughter of Serpents

Valerie Willis
Cedric: The Demonic Knight
Romasanta: Father of Werewolves
The Oracle: Keeper of the
Gaea's Gate
Artemis: Eye of Gaea
King Incubus: A New Reign

Kyle Sorrell
Munderworld
Potarium

Discover more at
4HorsemenPublications.com

Milton Keynes UK
Ingram Content Group UK Ltd.
UKHW011219280324
440101UK00005B/466